FULL
FATHOM
FIVE

John Stewart Carter

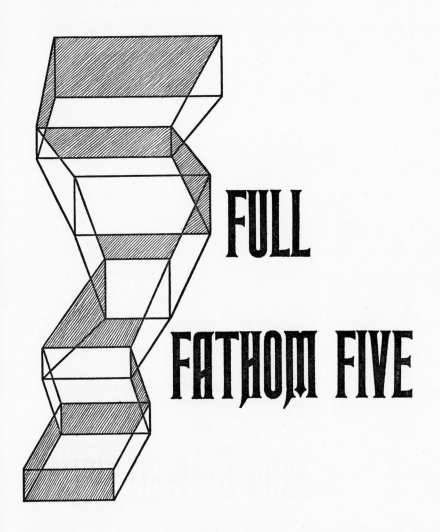

FULL

FATHOM FIVE

HOUGHTON MIFFLIN COMPANY BOSTON : 1965
THE RIVERSIDE PRESS CAMBRIDGE

In the memory of my father
Albert Howard Carter

*A Houghton Mifflin Literary
Fellowship Award Novel*

So tongueless shades cry out to us —
from misted mirror above a knob
      marked "Waste" —
to ride again the dolphin's back
through no enameled sea
but crowded deep in far-refracting
             glass
they ask the anguish of our choice.

from MR. DE PAOLIS AND THE SHADES

CONTENTS

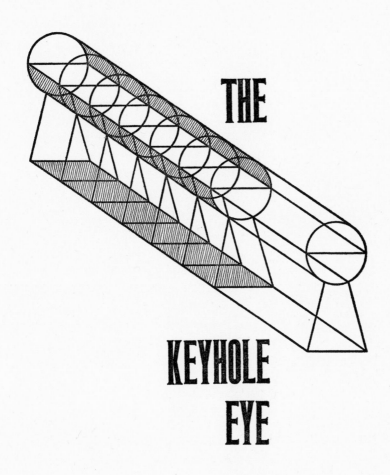

THE

KEYHOLE
EYE

THE KEYHOLE EYE

My uncle tom was the last of my grandfather's ten sons
and was fourteen years old the year I was born. He left
Princeton halfway through his freshman year to join the
A.E.F. and was briefly a flier in France. I remember, or begin remembering him best around 1920 when I would see
him at my grandmother's. He looked like Wallace Reid —
if you remember. I don't remember, but I know I thought so
at the time. Later I equated him with one of Scott Fitzgerald's rich boys, and for years I scarcely thought of him at
all. What has just happened is why I am writing this.

He was always nice to me in an offhand way and called
me "kid," which was racy of him because we were not supposed to use the word and were always being told that a
kid was a goat, which of course it was not. I suppose I was a
nuisance, but he never acted as if I were, and I used to hang
around his bedroom at my grandmother's, much preferring it
to my own. I know he was the first adult male I ever saw walking around naked, and the sight fascinated me mightily —
whatever the amateur psychiatrists will make of it. Also he
muttered to himself and used very bad words like "bastard"
and "bitch," and even worse. He never said these things outside of his own room, and it was wonderful for me at six to

hear them. He would let me get into his bed and watch him dress to go out, and I would keep very quiet — all eyes, all ears — until finally he'd snap up his silk hat, fit his silver flask into his pocket, and lean over the bed to punch me in the belly.

"You think I'll get it tonight, kid?" I had no idea what "it" was; I don't think I was even curious; the whole thing was a ritual as set as that in Proust.

My answer was, "Sure thing, Tom," and his, as he closed the door, "Keep your pecker up, kid." This left me limp with delicious, giggly laughter. I knew what a pecker was, but that a grownup should use any other than our nursery word to *me* was almost beyond hope. I never had to ask him or beg or anything; he just always left the light on in his bathroom and the door enough ajar so that I saw it but not so far as to be too light or to catch the bulb in his dresser mirror. I didn't have to ask to stay in his bed either. He just left me there, and when he got home, he'd carry me in his wonderful dance-stinky shirtsleeve arms across the lounge, down the three steps into the east wing to my own room and my own bed, all shivery cool after so much warmth. Most of the time I wouldn't wake up at all, although I always tried to so I would know about being carried, feeling so bundled and sweaty in his arms and all the whiskey and cigarette smoke deliciously sour on his breathing breath, the enormous dark house around us.

Eleven bedrooms gave off the central upstairs hall at my grandmother's. The hall itself — it was called "Palm Court" on the blueprints — was nearly square and was lighted by a series of skylights. We called it the lounge, and it was furnished as a living room; in fact it was the main living room of the house for the children who were visiting. My grandfather's idea was that each of his ten children should be able to come and stay, and each of the rooms had a name: Tom's room, Fred's room, and so on. All but Tom were married and had families of their own at the time I am writing of, and each of them had houses in town, as did we, but in the summer and at Christmas we would come to the big house on the lake where our parents occupied our father's old room, and their children, along with nursemaids, the east wing. I don't think all ten were ever there at once, but five or six with their families at a time were not unusual; so the house was run really like a very luxurious men's club.

Take the flask. If Tom wanted his flask filled, he left it on the dresser, and the footman who did his room filled it in the second floor pantry. There were few housemaids at Grandmama's, and most of the enormous amount of physical work such a place entailed was done by men. My brother has the household books, and in 1932 when my grandmother died, there were twelve indoor servants. The west wing was more elegant than the east, and that's where house guests other than the family were put. It had an indoor swimming pool — very Pompeian — in the basement, and there is an entry in the books of eighteen hundred dollars for "swimming pool towels," in case any social historian is looking; and in case anyone wants a *sic transit gloria mundi* note, the last time I saw one of them, a sort of Pompeian brown with black pillars across the border — they must have been specially woven — it was being used by a great-great grandson to polish his car.

On each side of the doorway leading down the three steps from the lounge to the east wing was a large console with a big pagoda'd mirror over it. If I was just pretending to be asleep when Tom carried me back, I would try to see us in the mirror. The lounge itself was light enough because of the skylights, which in summer were open to the moon and stars. I don't know whether Tom knew about my habit of peeking or whether he always looked himself, but one night he stopped before the mirror, and his eyes came together with mine and we looked full upon ourselves — upon ourselves, wide eyed, and each other.

After a minute he said, "You're a faker, kid. Why the hell can't you walk to your own goddamned room?" I just kept looking at him and us and he at me. His arms tightened around me and pushed me to his chest where I could no longer see. He put his lips into my hair. I could feel its fineness catch on the scratchiness of his whiskering face.

He put me down then, and we walked, our hands fingered together, down the three steps to my room. We looked at each other once more, no mirror between, after I had climbed into bed. He gave my belly its punch and said, "We're the two loneliest goddamned bastards in the whole beautiful world." Even today when I see moonlight through an open window in a darkened room, it is partly the moonlight of that night when weak with love and happiness I went to sleep.

I don't think he carried me much more after that. I was getting bigger. But he didn't stop right away, and if I was really asleep, he still carried me for a long time because in the morning I'd wake up in my own bed. When I wasn't really asleep, he'd know, but he'd walk me by hand, and as we'd pass the mirror he'd say, "Hi there, kids" in a conspiratorial whisper and wave, but that's the only reference either of us ever made to the night.

When I was twelve, Tom married Jay Henry, who was a girl we had always known; indeed I am married to her cousin now. It was a big society wedding, and all the cousins read every line in the papers for weeks beforehand. We were much less sophisticated then. There were dances and dinners, and people came from all over. Lady Moira Burton, the daughter of an earl, was the bridesmaid the papers gave the most linage to even before she arrived, and we were all amazed when she turned out to be nineteen and brought her own lady's maid. We had expected something at least forty. She always said "Thank you, deeply," and so do I and all my cousins to this day.

Of course the family was very much involved with the wedding which took place in the church we all went to. We didn't really go, but if we had gone, that's where we would have gone when we were at my grandmother's. The reception was at the Henrys', a mile or so down the road. The night before the wedding, my grandmother gave a big dinner dance with the tables on the terraces, marquees in the garden, and my grandmother herself in a completely beaded dress, long gloves, and her diamond tiara. We have moving pictures of the wedding the next day, and we used to look at them on Christmas after dinner. They were very funny with Jay in a dress that cleared her knees, a court train, and yards of Brussels lace, Tom very young and handsome waving at everybody as he got out of his shiny Packard Twin-Six wedding present, and everyone moving in the jerky way movies had then. My Uncle Harry took the pictures, and I suppose they are still around someplace.

But the night before is what I remember without any moving pictures. It was the first grown-up party I was allowed. I was the youngest of the eight older cousins assigned a table on the terrace, and it was the first time — the last time — I saw my grandmother's really *en fête*. My younger brothers

and cousins of course never saw it like that, and some of
them cannot remember the house; all of them must, I suppose,
have some of the furniture, dishes, silver, or pictures. I didn't
dance or anything. I just sat and looked. I didn't even talk
much to my cousins, who were trying so hard to be old that
I was disgusted. I was too young — in knickerbockers I
called plus-fours — even to try to be old, to talk about Lady
Moira, the dresses, the cars, the two orchestras, the boot-
leggers who had delivered the booze — that was the word we
used — that afternoon in a hearse. Tom himself came in
for a good deal of talk.

"I wonder what poor little Miss Payne is thinking tonight."
This was my much older cousin, Edith. A great frump of a
girl of whom it was said — in her hearing, I shouldn't wonder because the family was that way — that it was to be
hoped that she would be married for her money because no
one would marry her for any other reason. She was, however,
a stinker of the first water, and even now I can't feel sorry for
her. "Poor-little-Miss-Payne" — you can see the way we
were brought up.

"HeartBROKEN. GNASHing pearly TEETH. SIMPLY DEVas-
tated." This was Corinne, who talked like this all the time.
John Held, Jr., was her idol, and she had her own subscrip-
tion to the old *Life*.

"Who's Miss Payne?" Pete, who had told us earlier that he
had cut himself shaving. He was always saying, "A man has
to," too. "A man has to have at least a dozen bow ties" —
that sort of thing.

"Boys never know anything." Slobby Edith again. Tom
Charlestoned by us with Jay looking happy and waved. "She
was the blonde Uncle Doctor had one summer for their kids"
— that was us — "and they had to get rid of her on account

of Tom." I guess we all still looked blank because Corinne said, all in caps, "TOM'S FATAL CHARM."

"Don't you remember, Pete? All that WEEPING and getting SHOVED out of ROOMS, and GRANNY utterly FRANTIC? Some SOPHOMORE from Mass. AGGIE." Edith began talking like Corinne, but she'd get the accents all wrong. "And her father worked at the BANK which made it so emBARrassing for poor dear GRANNY and all of us because THAT's how she got the JOB. A PIECE of imPERtinence is what GRANNY SAID."

"Aw nuts. I'm sure you were just terribly, terribly embarrassed," — my cousin Georgie's voice cracked. Nobody could ever stand Edith — "Like heck." And then he said the cruelest thing he could have said. I don't think he knew it was cruel, but somehow he always said the cruelest thing without knowing it even though I, who was younger, knew it was cruel and, if it had been anyone but oafy Edith, would have felt sorry.

"Who else ever called Grandmama" — we all used the French accentuation but found our contemporaries' "*grand-mères*" highly affected — "Granny, for Pete's sake. You make me sick." And he pretended to puke into his finger bowl. Corinne, too, must have seen Edith cower, because she said,

"There's no HOPE from THESE SAVAGES, Edie. Let's see what we can find ELSEwhere," and the two of them left, shaking what we called their rumps.

I left, too, and walked down to the lake. Up above me on the bluff the party went on, and the waves lapped the shore at my feet. I sailed some stones out into the water, saying Tom's and my dirty words, and looked at the sky where there were more stars than I had ever seen. I made up a phrase, then and there, which is one of the first phrases I ever made up. I've always remembered it, and I must have used it in almost every story I wrote in school and in college: "The sky was vaporous with stars." To a twelve-year-old, it was a marvelous phrase, and there was the wonder under the wonderful sky of having thought it up. It had nothing to do with the ache in my heart at all or with what was happening. There was no one to use it to in my world; I didn't write poetry yet; I just thought it, and it made up somehow for the sorrow at beat under my thin breastbone.

Edie was probably right. There had been a Miss Payne, but we called her Miss Charlotte. She had taken care of us one summer and had disappeared suddenly in August. She was a wonderful reader and very pretty with naturally curly — she told us — blond hair. She let us play with her curls as she read, slipping them out with our fingers and watching them bounce back into place. I remember one such scene. It must have been raining out and late in the afternoon because Miss Charlotte is reading to us in the lounge and there is lamplight on her head. She is sitting on the floor and the book is on the needlepoint seat — unicorns, flowers, vines, Persian huntsmen with bows and arrows — of the huge couch. I am lying on the couch, my knees over one of its arms, my head at the very edge of the book from which she is reading. There are children — cousins, brothers, neighbors — all over the couch, some on the floor beside her, but I am looking up at her freckly skin, her golden hair and blue eyes, and she reaches over and pats me. Is it "Rapunzel, Rapunzel" she reads? At any rate, when it is over she puts her head down and spreads her hair as a fan over the unicorns, flowers, vines, and me. The children rush to gather it in their hands, to pull it — "It's all right. She lets you. Pull as hard as you can. You can't hurt her" — but I just lie there still, the hair on my face, and reach out with my tongue to pull a few strands to my mouth to taste. I have just tasted it now as I write, and strangely it is far more real to me, more immediate, than the last sight I had of her, although this too, had its elements of fairytale romance. I was in Istanbul, and on one of the narrow, crowded streets, the embassy limousine, complete with the ambassador's flag, pulled up beside me in a traffic jam. Miss Charlotte, now fifty, still bravely blond, sat beside her husband, Whitney Cobb, the ambassador. They must have been on their way to a dinner, for the light had all but faded from the sky yet rose through the hilly clefts of the street from the Bosporus whose waters shimmered still at the open end beneath us of the steep road.

I had met Miss Charlotte in her new role a few days before, and it was she who identified herself to me, coming across the garden to do so.

"Mr. Scott? They told me that's who you were. I was Miss Charlotte to you when you were six. I hope you will remember?" I don't think she did this through any sense of triumph; there was too much ease in her manner. Her eyes were clear and blue, and there in the sunshine and oleanders, I saw the same questioning affection of smile and gaze. The change in the light between the full afternoon of the garden and the twilight prolonged by memorial waters in the jammed, ancient street may have something to do with what I saw. Again her eyes met mine full. There was a little smile such as she might have given Tom — but never me — when I was six. Then I saw her glance towards her husband. She might have originally intended to call his attention to me, but he was looking out the other side of the car, and she thought better of it because, still with the same smile, she raised her hand — the downy hairs of her arm now covered with whitest ambassadorial kid — to her lips and blew me the kiss.

The purpose of all such girls — there was a new one every summer — was to keep us out of the grownups' way. I don't suppose we really knew this or would have minded if we had. It was just the way we were brought up. We slept in the east wing. We were dressed and taken down to the beach. Now that I remembered it, Tom did play with us a lot that summer, and it might have been that summer that I found a hairpin in his bed, but if he was tolerant of me, I was tolerant of him.

"What would you have a hairpin in your bed for, Tom?" He didn't start that I could remember, but I do remember his answer even though I didn't think it the least bit strange, and I can still feel the slither of the hairpin across my tongue and lips — for I had put it to my curious mouth when I picked it from the bedclothes — as Tom leaned down to me to retrieve it.

"Well, you're not the only caller I have, kid," was what he said. I suppose the measure of affection I had for him is that he never underrated me. He knew he didn't have to say "Don't tell on me, kid," or make up an elaborate explanation. That was all he said, and even though I didn't know the answer, I would never have thought of mentioning it to anyone else.

Couples began to drift down from the party then, and I heard one high-pitched, fashionable voice exclaim, "What wonderful, wonderful stars," as if Grandmama had provided them along with the champagne, and I hugged my "vaporous with stars" even closer to my breast. I heard someone else say, "Oh, it's just one of the kids. There are literally millions; you don't dare imagine," so when I had a chance, I got up the bluff steps, skirted the party, and went up the billiard-room stairs to my room. I got undressed in the dark and it was very pretty. All the lanterns swaying in the garden, the lighted marquees, and the stars in the sky. The orchestra was playing "I'm Forever Blowing Bubbles" real soft with brushes on the drums, and you could hear the feet shuffling as you sometimes can if you only listen.

I didn't have any definite feeling. There was no sense of loss that I was losing Tom or anything like that. If I had to say, I would have said that I was trembly-sad because the night was so beautiful and my vaporous stars so far away. But I didn't have to say. I just had to do what I did, and I did it so naturally that there was no thought behind it at all. Although I hadn't done it in at least a couple of years, although I hadn't missed doing it, or thought about it, I just walked up the three steps, across the lounge to Tom's room and climbed into his bed. Outside the party went on, and I could hear the orchestra, the laughter, the glasses tined.

I may have been asleep a little time or a long time; I don't remember; but I heard the door open and saw the shaft of light in the dresser mirror. Then I heard a girl say, "I thought you said this was Tom's room."

"It is. Shut up."

"But what's he got there?"

"Will you shut up? How do I know what he's got there. Just somebody's there, that's all." Then the door closed, and I could hear the girl's thin, drunken voice remonstrating, but I didn't know what they were saying and just drifted back to sleep.

It was broad daylight — ten o'clock or so — when I woke again, still in Tom's bed. Tom was looking at me, clear as the day, in the reflection which shimmered, hung in the air, somewhere between the dresser mirror in which he was tying his tie and me, whose eyes had been drawn from the sprawl of the bed to meet his looking back.

" 'Bout time you got up kid, huh? Today's the wedding day." My gaze went past the reflection into the mirror, and he looked very happy there. I smiled and stretched, drawing my eyes back into myself. "You sure look comfortable."

"I am," I said through my yawn.

"You know what I did?"

I shook my head and found him again in the mirror. "You looked so comfortable, so damned asleep when I came in — rough night, kid, rough night —" I lost his eyes then when he began to fuss with his cuff links, "that I just went to your bed, and that's where I slept."

Inside of me warm, wet, sudden tears began. I can still feel them flood my heart, so I know and knew what they were. But of course I didn't cry them then or now. They just exist in me and always have. I hope I have them in some poems someplace. I hope I have them here. Anyway we never looked at each other, ever again.

Another incident in connection with the wedding I suppose is significant enough for me to tell, although I — and I am the one who is writing this — really don't know, nearing fifty, just how it is important. Jay and Tom were married in the afternoon, so I suppose it was ten or so that night when they got ready to leave the Henrys'. All the cousins had been running around like mad at the reception, although the younger ones had been taken off sometime earlier. I was out on the side lawn with the older ones, but they had given up acting older. The girls had kicked off their high heels, and the boys had thrown their blue flannel blazers in a heap on one of the stone benches. All of us had grass stains on our white trousers because we had played real kid games like stoop tag and even statues, trying to whirl up the girls' skirts, trying to bump into what we called their "boobs." At the end we were all stretched out on the side lawn looking at the stars and trying to catch fireflies without moving anything except our arms and hands. Somehow, without anyone mentioning it, we all knew the rules and would have cried "cheat" had anyone sat up. On the other side of the house, the jazz band was still playing, and beneath us we could hear the lake. We had had a good time all week, but now we were exhausted with excitement the way kids get and just lay there. After a while our grandmother appeared on the side porch and called out.

"Edith, Edith, round up those children. Your Uncle Tom and Aunt Jay are going to be leaving soon, and you'll want to be there." She peered over the railing to see how many of us were there, still in her gold lamé mother-of-the-groom's dress, her brown velvet hat still firmly on her head. Only her gloves were gone, and I could see the great diamonds on her fingers — blue fire in the August night. Georgie tried to say, "Last one to the porch is a stinkpot," but it didn't work. The girls had to put on their pumps — that was the word — and the boys had to pick up their coats. Our grandmother just stood there looking out over the lake, her hands gripping the porch railing. I was the last one to straggle up into the light, and I was the one she caught.

"What a mess you are!" This wasn't unkindly. "Come, let me fix your tie. And button your belly button." The big diamonds fiddled with my collar button and pulled my tie up.

"You don't have to choke me."

"I'm not going to have you looking like that. And the grass stains. But come on." Then she did something that was strange for her; she took my hand and kept it even when I tried to get away to join the others. "I'm not letting you out of my sight, young man."

Now this is what I don't know even though it is my story and I am writing it. It is what I *can't* know unless I pretend I'm Henry James, which I can't do. Did she realize or sense the state of my unconscious excitement and want to protect me from myself, or did she want me for her own protection? All day long people had been saying, "Oh Barbara, your very last baby," and related things to her, and she'd been smiling and social, and she was as old as I was young. There is so much that you don't know about people. What aches are at work at any given time, what frustrations rage hectic in the blood to ravage so the moment-open heart. She had married my grandfather at eighteen. He was twenty years older than she, the daughter of an Akron judge, and the son of one of the real robber barons. Her wedding present had been the tiara she had worn last night. I sit here now and try to imagine one of my own daughters — and they certainly have had a more sophisticated upbringing than the belle of Akron at eighteen — transported to such a world, rearing ten boys, and then standing, nearly sixty, to watch the last leave. It will not work at all. So many truths, facts, operate at the same time that it is impossible to know even your own blood, and unless the intuition intuits the impossible whole, the separating of it, the ordering, must distort forever the part with which it is dealing.

I say again I do not know why she held me by the hand. Anything I can reconstruct, I can at the same time tumble down. I was annoyed then at being restricted and dragged her around to the scrunchy drive where the ushers were handing out rice and all the guests were standing and waiting for Tom and Jay to appear. When they did come and stopped to kiss Grandmama, I got free so that in their dash to the car I was after them like a skinny dervish — arms and legs flying every which way, frantically tossing rice more on myself than on them and screaming in my high soprano voice: "Keep your pecker up, Tom." I don't even know that anyone heard me, but my grandmother got me iron by the shoulder with one hand, there was a cruel flash of diamonds, and I was hit hard across the mouth with those great rings. My inner lip was cut against my teeth. I could taste the salt blood. Thirty-five years later I can put my tongue to the very place my mouth was cut and make physical again what I suppose was a psychic scar. The tyranny, the horror of cruelty, plunged to my heart. But was it cruel? Was I indeed hysterical? The woman had brought up ten boys and diamonds grew from the bones of her fingers. I certainly couldn't be allowed to make a spectacle of myself. At all costs I would want to keep my emotion private, and wasn't she helping me to do just that? All this reasoning comes now. At the time, or if I were to tell the story to a psychiatrist, the diamonds would become symbolic, and she a woman viciously loath to give up her son.

Tom and Jay went to England for two years, Tom to run the London branch, so I didn't see them, and I don't even now know what happened. At any rate Jay went to Reno when they returned, and I saw little of Tom that summer. In the fall he returned to London. When I went away to college, he sent me a check for $2000 and one of the three or four notes I have had from him in my life:

Hi Kid,
They tell me your real bright. I am not real bright and never was. But I will tell you something about the family. You can always have any money you want, but somebodies always going to want to know what you do with it. Here is a lot of money just put it into some *other*

bank and when you need something used it if you don't
want to tell anybody.

Keep your pecker up,

Tom

Somebody had always even spelled for Tom, and if the letter
had been dictated of course it wouldn't have appeared as it
did; but he had written it himself, and I kept it, quite unable,
typing it out now, to add the necessary *sic*'s. He was thirty
when he wrote it, and I was sixteen.

Two years later he came home for a while when my grandmother died, but we all stayed in town, and he stayed at
Fred's. I was only back a few days and returned to Cambridge as soon as I could. The brothers were fantastically
busy. It was the bottom of the depression, and they set
about salvaging what they could. We were still very rich people, but when it was all over the brothers no longer owned the
bank lock, stock, and barrel as they had, and none of them
could have afforded to keep up the house even had they
wanted to. Actually it stood empty until 1942 when, as a
tax deduction, it was rented to the Navy for a dollar a year.
My cousins as they married took a few acres here and there
and built houses, and finally the house was torn down and
the whole place subdivided into what the ads called (honestly!) "Junior Estates." A kind of Levittown for the rich
was the way Corinne described it.

Tom went back to London afterwards and was briefly married to an English movie star, whom he himself divorced in
a real English divorce case with "m'luds" and correspondents
and full coverage in the international press. At the time of
the abdication, he was mentioned once or twice, and Edith
had a picture of him in the *Tatler* where he was correctly
identified and Mrs. Simpson was "and friend." If that's not

fame, I don't know what it is. The *sic transit gloria mundi* boys will be happy to know that my daughters didn't even know who Mrs. Simpson was when I mentioned her the other day.

I saw Tom maybe a dozen times in as many years. I had gone through college and got a check, and got a doctor's degree and got a check, and he bought and gave away a hundred copies of my first book — I suppose to people who could have had no idea at all what it was about. He came to my wedding and there was some of the old warmth, but I was too excited to pay much attention. Two months later I was in the Navy, and so was Tom, a retread at forty-two. He was in Washington for most of the war, and I was in and out and saw him often. I was the best man when he married Mrs. Paget Armstrong — Nan.

Mrs. Paget Armstrong was not at all what she sounded. She taught French at the University of Maryland and was a quiet, restful, enormously well-read, and deeply sophisticated woman. She was five or six years older than Tom — at least she had a married daughter — and two people more utterly unprepared for, although not at all unsuited to, each other, it is hard to imagine. They moved into her apartment in Bethesda amid the department-store furniture that was all that was left of her marriage to a Spokane dentist and which had not been improved by its move across the continent.

Tom was perfectly happy and she was too. I liked going there very much, although the food was lukewarm and ill prepared and I had to sleep on what she called a "davenport." Even the bath towels — *vide supra* — were sleazy. She herself simply radiated sympathy, and it was touching to see how proud Tom was of me when the two of us talked books

and poetry. Little by little I noticed the furniture being replaced, and the "davenport" became a "sofa," and I
thought to myself, Aha, the little woman is learning.

They had been married a little more than a year when late
in December I called her up. She told me that Tom wasn't
there, but said she really wanted to see me and would I
please come. I had a hard time getting all the way out there,
so it was later than she thought it would be when I got there
and she had already had a couple of drinks. She was wearing a most beautiful navy wool dress — she had had nothing
like it that I had ever seen — with a diamond clip at the
neck and my grandmother's big ring on her engagement
finger.

"What a wonderful dress," I said as I kissed her cheek.
She looked pleased an instant and said, "Molyneux." As I
followed her into the living room she went on, "*Molly Ner*
is what you people say, you know." Never, never act to the
rich as if they were richer than you. It floods them with
shame. I guess she felt this go through my mind because
right away she said, "I'm sorry. But Tom's overdue a week."

"Hush-hush?" My own heart stopped a minute, too.

"Very. I don't know which way to turn or who to talk to."

"Well, talk to me."

"I've been meaning to for a long time, you know."

"The Molly Ner set doesn't go in for talking?"

"Something like that. But even so I don't suppose you generally say to a nephew —" She stopped and you could see an
agony hit her full in the face, and her hand went to her breast
as if to ward off a blow. You could tell, too, that it was the
sort of thing that recurred, that had been recurring for quite
a while. "Why did I marry him? Why did I ever marry
him? I could have just slept with him, just slept" — she

drew the word out and made it seem simple and beautiful and restful — "with him." She had the trick of repetition even under ordinary circumstances and now it was exaggerated. "He's an economic primitive. He doesn't read. He can't spell." There were tears in her eyes and you could see that she had just about reached the end of her rope. "He doesn't know anything. Anything at all. Nothing. He's been every goddamned place in the world. He knows every important person in the world. But he's, he's" — she shook her head at the incomprehensibility of it — "innocent." She looked to me for help.

"Is that bad?"

"For me, yes." She twisted the ring in. "When you can't be innocent yourself, yes. I don't even remember when I didn't know. For me there's always a feather of guilt." She looked to see if I understood and was satisfied because she went on. "Put me on the witness stand, accuse me of the most monstrous act, and always, always there'd be the moment's hesitation before I could deny it. In that moment I'll remember and I'll think, Yes, I could have done it because I know it has been done by people just as good as me, and I can imagine that I might have done it. I'd feel that it was only accidental — there but for the grace of God go I — that I haven't done it. The feather of guilt."

"There be much matter in this madness." I tried to laugh her out of it, but you could see that she was hurt at my failure to follow her, but I didn't want her to try any harder to make it clear, so I just said, "You mean you could have married him for his money?"

"Oh you Molly Ners, you Molly Ners. What in Christ's name do you think money is? What's so goddamned special about your money? Of course I could have married him for it and it wouldn't have been any trouble at all. He was married for it twice, wasn't he? That flat-chested Molly Ner bitch. That fantastic bosooooomed Frigidaire. No, no. What haunts me is that I'm really worse than they. I married him for his simple loving kindness." Her eyes drooped closed with a vast weariness, and when she opened them again they were full of love. "You see how that could be worse? Do you know the French word *accueillir*? It means *to receive*, but as a host receives a guest. This is the way Tom loves. He opens himself up completely. He's all there for the taking. But, like a guest, you have to take." Her eyes were so earnest, so pleading, that I took her hand and held it. "You see, he's afraid of embarrassing you by offering you more than you want, more than you are ready for, and yet his own hunger is so deep, his own heart is so transparent that you can't help wondering — the feather of guilt, and God I love him — if there's enough of you to receive all that he has to give." She took her hand from mine, turned the diamond around and looked at it. "I can't say this sort of thing to him, or at least I haven't yet, so I say it to you. He wouldn't be able to follow. It's not the sort of thing he thinks about; it's not the sort of thing he has to think about. That gorgeous, blooming innocence. But it's sure not a very practical way of loving."

She got up then, smoothed her dress over her hips and said, "I'm glad I said it. To you. To myself. To Bethesda, Maryland. But I don't know if I can stand much more of this kindness, this *gentillesse*, this christawful consideration." I smiled what I suppose was ruefully because she said, "The two with-rue-my-heart-is-laden boys."

"Oh, come off it. It is funny. You're all torn up because you haven't heard from him when you expected, so you complain about his kindness and consideration. Really, now."

She did smile then, but said, "Seriously you don't know what it is. If he'd just *say*. But no. It's all by the most god-awful indirection. How the hell did I know this place was a horror? I didn't know you could pay three hundred and fifty dollars for a wool dress. Yet you come in and your face lights up when you see it in the half dark. As far as I know — really, honestly, truly — it doesn't look any different from forty-nine ninety-five. Why didn't he just buy a house in Georgetown? I — I might feel uncomfortable. Nothing about his being strangled here. D'ya know what he did?" The frantic light came back in her eyes. "I'll tell you. For six months he kept a room at the Shoreham — everybody in Washington is screaming for rooms — to keep his thirty uniforms, his hundred shirts, his forty pairs of shoes in. Because he didn't like to say that there wasn't room for them here. He didn't like to say." She nodded the words out syllable by syllable. "I'm dizzy, just dizzy. I said to him, but they're all alike, aren't they, and he said he supposed so, so he just gave them all away. Just like that. It never occurred to him that I might suppose a room at the Shoreham meant a mistress, you know?"

I was laughing and said, "He isn't acquainted with the subject of French literature."

"It's impossible. Oh, I've seen you in Henry James and Fitzgerald and Proust and all over the place — and you've seen yourselves, but it doesn't do any good. I'm not prepared for you. You're not prepared for yourselves."

I've often had occasion to remember that "you're not prepared for yourselves," and I've wondered just when she said it to him, for from what happened I am sure she must have. Critics, speaking of Gatsby, always point out his romanticiz-

ing the rich; what they don't know is that the rich themselves romanticize the poor. It never occurs to Daisy that she
is loved because her "voice is money," and her weeping over
Gatsby's shirts — at his thinking that they can make any
difference — is as marvelously revealing in its way as Nick's
last sight of Daisy eating chicken. Take the ring. Nan wore
it as a status symbol — although the phrase had not then
been invented. It was the only way she could wear it.
Twelve-carat diamonds did not grow from her bones. To
Tom, who must have given his movie star an even larger
one, it was his mother's ring. To me — well, I've told you
about that.

Tom did get back, did survive the war, and it was Nan
who died cruelly of cancer toward the end of the forties. She
was in the hospital for nearly a year, and although he
never told her, toward the end Tom had a room on the floor
above to be near her. I saw her two weeks before she died,
and in her own phrase, she "received me like a guest." She
asked me to be good to Tom, to watch over him as he had
watched over her, but then went on, "But how can you?
How can anyone? There always will be the moment when,
like Sartre's man looking through the keyhole into the empty
room, he will see the eye of a stranger looking back. It happened to me a long, long time ago. I don't think it has happened to you yet, but it will, and I guess it will be all right."
A spasm of pain came over her then, but she was so intent on
finishing that she let it clutch her without closing her eyes.
"What will happen to Tom when he plasters his goddamned,
clear-blue boy's eye to that goddamned keyhole" — you
could see the pain run like a river of fire through her — "I
can't even think. Let Sartre think for me. It's his phrase —
'the burning presence' of the 'stare of Another.' Never to have

known shame. Jesus, I envy the rich." I went into the hall
to hurry the nurse.

Nan was buried in the family plot. I asked Tom if she had
ever seen it and was sorry that she hadn't. It would have
amused her greatly because it was dedicated to the proposi-
tion that even in death we were different. It was in the oldest
city cemetery, one of a half-dozen or so national-Catholic,
Protestant, and Jewish strung along what at one time had
been the end of the streetcar line. The street widened out,
and when I was little and went there with my grandmother,
there was generally a holiday air about the place. Streetcars
clanged; huge Polish, German, and Bohemian families would
wander around clutching flags, diaper bags, trowels, and
watering cans. You'd see widows in black pricing monuments in the empty lots, shawled women looking at grave
plants in the enormous greenhouse, and kids eating popcorn,
hot dogs from the whistling wagons. In the summer there
was an American Legion carnival with a Ferris wheel. None
of these delights were for us. The limousine would have to
slow almost to a stop, and we on the jump seats often had
to take the thumbed noses — "Pay no attention, children.
Act as if you didn't see them" — directed towards us by kids
our very own age. Inside the cemetery gates there was none
of the egalitarian nonsense of today's "Memorial Parks"
where all the markers are the same and everyone has to buy
"perpetual care." If you were poor, the stone was poor, the
grave sunk, and the grasses grew up around you. If you
were rich, you crossed over a little river that our father
called the Styx on a rattly bridge, and looking back you
could see the welter of domino stones where, crowded more
closely even than they had been in life, lay the many
dead.

On our side of the river, little hills rose, covered with a chaos of tombs, vaults, angels, columns, Greek porticoes, stone catafalques. The merchant princes, the robber barons, sometimes had whole hills to themselves, and one of them had been flattened off for us. There is a picture of ours in the book the family had written about itself, and they used to sell a postcard of it at the cemetery gates — a blue sky, white clouds, and geraniums, aromatic with July, in the flower boxes. Corinne bought a pack of them once and used to send them to us with "Wish you were here" scrawled across the back. The robber baron himself lay under an enormous obelisk of polished black marble, his name cut deep in letters as tall as a man. Around him in an ever widening circle lay the graves of his sons, my grandfather, granduncles, and their sons and son's sons. Each grave had its heavy slab of matching marble, and if such a thing can be said to have taste, I suppose the architect's conception can be admired. The obelisk stood as the center of an enormous sundial or clock face, and four flights of three steps each — at twelve, three, six, and nine — led up to it. The other hours were marked by either black marble benches or flower boxes, and it was because of the filling of these as one set of flowers died that we usually drove out with my grandmother and her gardener.

Well, the streetcar's gone long since; the monument makers have fled; the greenhouses stood empty for a while and were pelted with stones before they were torn down to make room for a Shopping Plaza, as if the dead could eat, wear shoes, or attend one-cent sales at the drugstore. Very few people are buried there now, mostly people like us who had graves to spare, but even so, when I was there for Fred's funeral, the narrow, winding gravel roads were all marked "One Way" — which greatly delighted Corinne who said, as we rattled over the bridge on the way there, "Remember the Ferris wheel we never could ride?" I rode it much in dreams, though, in fancy; and Corinne must have, too, there in the shadow of the obelisk. Years later I was to write "The Time the Ferris Wheels all Stopped," and Corinne, handing it back to me remembered.

"The day of Fred's funeral? Of all the people who read it, you and I will be the only ones who know that."

"Oh Corinne, I don't think even I knew it when I wrote. I didn't know it until just now when you spoke. And now my heart's all runny, and I love you for knowing." I didn't look to Corinne when I said this. My eyes instead were reading my own words as if I had never seen them before.

"It's silly to suppose, isn't it, that there is — or ever can be — any other Ferris wheel for us?"

Early this year I ran into Tom in the reading room of the Public Library. I had gone in to look up some things in connection with an article I was trying to do, and there he was, surrounded by encyclopedias, a big blue college notebook in front of him. He was nearly sixty; his older brothers had died, and even his grandnieces and nephews were getting married. He only appeared on such occasions, and the members of the family had commented with asperity that if you wanted to talk to Tom, you'd have to call him at the bank because he was never home and half the time your message wasn't delivered. He had even disappeared from the society columns, as indeed had the rest of us, and the only place you were likely to see his name was on the letterheads of charity solicitations.

"Well, look at the elder statesman," was what I said when I saw him, and he really looked caught out.

"I'm sure glad it's you," he laughed, but I felt sorry I had said what I did. A twinge of class consciousness, of course, because we were brought up to act as if there were nothing strange in the behavior, however outrageous, of anyone we knew or were related to. "Come on, I'll buy you lunch." He spoke to the librarian as we left about leaving his stuff out, and she said, "Surely, Mr. Thomas."

He was attending night classes in the downtown branch of the University, and he told me with pride that he was a senior. He hadn't said anything to them about Princeton; indeed, having become committed to education, he was ashamed, much as a Seventh-Day Adventist might be ashamed of an Episcopalian past. The detail which cost him the greatest effort to confess, however, was his use of the name Richard Thomas, but I quite understood the reservation. He was a trustee of the University; his own name was immediately recognizable. I didn't learn that day, but I did shortly afterward when I began to see a good deal of him, that Tom was living with a girl he had met in one of his classes and that she had no idea that he was anything other than an older student rather better off than usual. He had taken an apartment for her and her two children — one Negro, one blond as light — in a high-rise insurance company project and spent two or three nights a week there. Her name was Mrs. Temple — Jo.

She was very beautiful, with long, brown-red dancer's hair, and she moved like a queen. I often had dinner with them, and she went to no end of trouble with paperback French cookbooks and that sort of thing if she felt like it; otherwise we'd just have something sent in; she was witty, well read in a curious sort of way, and never said anything at all about her former life. One of the neighbors sat with her kids while she was in class, and Jo did the same for the girl during the day. It was all very free, casual, messy, high-brow. Tom was not the least self-conscious about it, and I suppose I would never have seen this kind of life if it hadn't been for him. I was fascinated. The idea of Tom's writing a paper on the effect of the restricted vocabulary in Racine and Hemingway was staggering. Yet the paper was very good, and the three of us talked it over, late into the coffee night for many weeks. We'd argue and walk up and down as if it were the most important literary discovery since the beginning of time. But, if Jo and I were excited about it, it was Tom's idea, Tom's paper, Tom's passion. He really knew what he was doing and brought to the job the kind of sensitivity that the late- or self-educated seldom have, but which no teacher can ever teach.

One night Jo was going to read Cleopatra in a Shakespeare class they were both taking, and Tom and I picked her up. She was wearing a thin silk dress, cut away to show her magnificent shoulders, and you could tell that she was wearing nothing but a slip underneath — not at all the sort of thing she ordinarily would have worn to class. She must have had quite a reputation around the college because there wasn't room in the classroom for all the visitors, and the instructor, a Mr. Newberry, laughed and said, "I see that word has got around that Mrs. Temple is to read tonight. I'll have to find us a bigger room." We all moved down the hall then to a chemistry demonstration room.

I suppose those who have never seen one have little notion of what a night course is like at any university, however eminent. On the one hand it is a shabby, heartbroken operation: the university intends to make money out of it; the only big boys who teach are those who want to spend the summer in Europe; the students intend to get credit. Yet if

the teacher is any good — and Newberry was good — there
is a cohesion, an interest, a completely democratic camara-
derie never attainable in day classes where the division into
cliques — both intellectual and social — is evident from
the very beginning.

I had intended to watch Tom as Jo read, but this was impossible. The students read their parts from behind a long,
waist-high sink desk normally used for chemistry demon-
strations, the symbols for which still smeared the chalky
blackboards. Yet in that bare, dirty room in a reconstructed
office building, under fluorescent lights, no one had eyes for
anyone or anything but Jo. It was a reading, you understand; they hadn't learned the parts; they didn't act them;
there was no business. They would read a scene; Newberry
would comment, and they might take up at his cue hundreds
of lines later on. Jo didn't even look up very often, and I am
perfectly positive that she used only four gestures in the two
hours we were there. Her voice was eloquent, varied, and
wonderfully colored, but each of the gestures I will remember until the day I die.

When she first stood up — Enobarbus was speaking and
she was obviously reading ahead — her hands went to her
hair and took out, one at a time, the three or four hairpins that
held it loosely up. Each she put to her mouth, never taking
her eyes from the text until the hair had spilled, coil by lustrous coil, over her shoulders, clouding her breast. Her hand
went to her lips then, and I could feel the tiny slick of her
tongue collecting the pins, which she laid between the pages
of her book at — oh God — the spine. There was a little
shake of her head and the hair streamed back as her breasts
rose and the marvelously supple voice began the cadenced
lines. If there had been anything conscious about it, had it

for a moment seemed calculated, it would have been the most naked striptease. But it was pure, unobserved "Woman Reading" — a woman who knew in her blood that what she was to read had to be read with her hair down.

I wouldn't be so sure about my recollection, I would distrust it as overobserved, overwritten, except that in the last scene just before she got to "Give me my robe, put on my crown," her bare arm arched, gathered the richness of that brown-red hair with its shadows, and the flower fingers pinned it again to her queenly head. Before this, in the scene with the messenger, her voice all whips and scorns, she had put out her hand, instinctively without looking up, toward the huge blond oaf who was doubling the minor parts. As she came to the words, "My bluest veins to kiss," she looked him straight in his goggling eyes, and turned her hand palm upward, baring the underside of her wrist and its bluest veins. At the tenderness of the coquetry, the boy blushed crimson, even as Shakespeare must have intended, and the ceiling lifted with the roar of delight from the class.

The last gesture she used was less overt, but I am just as sure it was noticed because I could hear the comments as we left the classroom. When it came to the asp, Jo — at once Jo and Cleopatra, Jo becoming Cleopatra despite the fluorescent lights, the demonstration sink, Jo with Cleopatra in her bluest veins — put her hand involuntarily to her breast. Her fingers trembled at the silk as if exploring the horror of hurt in

> With thy sharp teeth this knot intrinsicate
> Of life at once untie. Poor venomous fool,
> Be angry and dispatch.

Her voice was utterable tears, but when she spoke

Oh, coulds't thou speak,
That I might hear thee call great Caesar ass
Unpolicied

it whiplashed into such scorn as I have never heard in the
human voice, and her hand pressed flesh to its limit.

The power of her reading was such that the others were
swept along with her. Antony was Antony and every man
there read the lines with him where we are told he enters on
a monument, not only "I am dying, Egypt, dying" and the
great bravura passages, but even single lines and phrases. I
know because when Antony said "Eros, ho! The shirt of Nes-
sus is upon me," sixty-year-old Tom's hand became a vise on
my suit-coat arm.

After it was all over, a bunch of people including Newberry went up to Jo and thanked her, and I suppose *exalted*
is the word to express the look in her eyes. I, of course, was
irretrievably and forever in love with her.

Tom and I sat back when the others were making over her.
He was deep in thought and said nothing. I did say, "That
sure was something," but he just grunted and looked very
old. We walked out with the rest of the cast and Newberry
— Jo had invited them back to the apartment — and they
were all laughing excitedly, Jo very flirtatious, triumphant,
and young, swinging her hips joyously, tossing her red-
brown head. The halls were empty by that time, and a jani-
tor was standing by the elevator, waiting to turn off the
lights. Of course it was Tom who said, "Come on. Let's get
going. This poor guy wants to get home," but I don't think
anyone heard him above the jabber. While we waited for
the elevator, the not-at-all pallid Mr. Newberry made a sort
of pass at Jo. I don't think he had an idea in the world that
Tom was her lover. (I write *lover* now, but when I phrased it

to myself then, it was "Tom was the man who paid the rent," and an admonitory shiver went through me that should have warned me of the horror in store.) Jo avoided Newberry with a little dance step — I suppose he was thirty-two or -three — and came toward me, slipping her hands under my coat — cupped palms, moving fingers — across the small of my back, my spine.

"Here's the man who's Antony's age, you Dollabellas, you Enobarbuses, you Caesars." It was so outrageous that everyone hooted except Tom and me.

In the elevator going down, I was pressed close to her, and I know she knew my excitement because she murmured to me, "Not every soldier's pole has fallen," in the confusion of getting out.

The party at Jo's was very beery, young, and stupid. Lots of gossip about teachers and classes that greatly intrigued Newberry, who would be sorry the next day, and lots of wandering in and out of the bedrooms, the kitchen, and even into the public corridor. All I did was watch my chance, and it seemed to come when Tom went into their bedroom, saying he was going to make a phone call. I knew that Jo had been watching, too, because she was on her feet right away, pulling me into the front hall. The urgency of our kiss was so complete that when I looked at her there was horror in her eyes, and she could only return my gaze for a moment before she pressed my head to her breast and whispered to herself more than to me, "My bluest veins, my very bluest veins."

I don't think we were gone more than a few minutes; at any rate Tom came back after we had reappeared and were already sitting on the floor.

He stood over us, looking down — paternal, avuncular,

what you will — and said, "I just talked to Mary" — Mary
is my wife — "on the phone and invited myself out for the
long weekend."

"Sure, Tom, fine. The girls will love it." I couldn't find his
eyes, and I don't think I would have known what to do
with them had I caught them because I was totally unprepared for what followed.

"They're picking me — us — up in twenty minutes. I told
them we'd meet them downstairs. They don't know the
name on the bell."

To say that my heart sank is less than true. Of course there
was that awful, bottomless sinking, but I was flooded with a
fire of shame as fierce as my desire had been. A stain, like one
of those oxblood birthmarks you sometimes see on faces,
spread through me as if to devour my bones. I could look
nowhere, least of all toward Jo. Tom mercifully walked away,
and in a few minutes Jo got up and went into the children's
bedroom. I don't know — I still don't know — if I was
meant to follow her, but the fact that she had chosen the
children's room stopped me — oh shit on Henry James —
for long enough to realize that my knees would never have
supported me. I just sat there dazed, and I supposed I would
be thought drunk. In a little while Jo came back through
the door to their room — there was a bath connecting it to
the children's. She had our coats in her hand and said, "The
Bobbsey Twins are on their way."

Everyone got up — God damn them — the way the young
do for the old, and Jo helped us on with our coats. She
pecked us both at the door, but didn't come to the elevator
with us. I wondered if it would be Enobarbus or Newberry.
On the way down Tom said, "When I said *they* were coming
for us, I just meant Taylor. I phoned and told him to

bring a car and pack me a bag." His voice was perfectly normal, but mine broke over the "Sure," which was all I could get out. I wanted to say with Jo's scorn, "I'd call great Caesar pretty goddamned policied."

I was on fire with rage at what had been done to me. My tongue had shot between my lip and teeth as if to ward off the diamond blow. I was still, as Nan had said, "unprepared for myself."

Taylor came then with the big bank-president limousine, and it was clear that Tom intended to have him drive us the sixty toll-road miles to my house in the country. Great Caesar was afraid to be alone with me, was he? As if he had read my mind, Tom leaned forward and closed the glass partition, and another wave of humiliation filled me. In the morning, I thought, this is what I'll wake up to. And every morning it will be there, uneasy at my heart at first and then known in the blood. The walk to the bathroom, the very shiver as I pee, polluted. My hands trembled with *horror carnis* at the thought of touching myself in the shower, the look in the eyes looking back at me as I shaved. Tom. Tom had done this to me. Tom. As if I were a little boy who had disgraced himself at a birthday party. And I had allowed it. Had been powerless. The Bobbsey Twins. The Bobbsey Twins. Sissy. Sissy. Shitty sissy.

The paroxysm that seized me was completely real. My teeth chattered; my feet would not hold still, and I was in the grip of a wholly involuntary memory: the memory of sitting on a black marble bench, cold as the death that surrounded me, my six-year-old thighs, in their thin De Pinna flannel shorts, rigid with ache. It was the day before my mumps began. I had driven out with my grandmother in just such a limousine, glassed in in April, to see about planting the boxes with hyacinths. It was a weekday, so we had not had to run the gantlet at the gates. The Ferris wheel had stopped. There was a poor little funeral — two cars and the hearse — at one point before we crossed the rattly bridge, but we scrunched past it. The obelisk was very black against the dead gray sky, but the branches of the scarcely greening trees moved, reflected in the elegiac marble. I thought of my grandfather, whom I never knew, dying blind. Of the girl sixteen who had cut her throat. Of the little boy who a hundred years ago had wandered into a Canadian wheatfield and died in the August sun, his hair blonder than the wheat which hid him until he was dead. He was a favorite of mine, and the phrases were my grandmother's as she told the story to impress on us how we must never wander away. She moved now with the gardener, as if the two of them were hands on that enormous clock, from box to box, and I climbed on one of the benches. She called out, "You'd better get in the car, honey; you'll get cold," but I just sat there in terrible sadness watching not the trees nor the monument but the movement of the trees deep in its blackness.

My grandmother and the gardener had passed to the other side of the obelisk and were out of my sight when suddenly a black cloud of purple martins on their way north hovered above the monument, supposing in its depths a pool. There were literally thousands of them, layered, chirping, their formation abandoned as, purpled black from brown, wheeling, pecking, they swooped down to the marble waters of our graves. I could hear my grandmother's "Oh! Oh!" and the gardener ran out of the shadows, swinging his rake and waving his trowel. The deceived birds rose with a cry but, in the rising and wheeling round the obelisk, swooped over me on the bench. Their wings beat lice-feathered against my face; their claws caught in my hair; their dirt befouled my jacket; they thudded against my hunched breast and back in their wild determination to escape. When they were gone I was frozen with terror that burst within me, and I wet my pants.

My grandmother came running and took me in her arms, but I was far gone in the deep compulsive tremor which had lasted forty years to be relieved now with such exactness that I thought it was really urine which trickled through the hairs of my trousered leg and not the memory of a six-year-old shame. I had to put out my hand to know it was not.

After it was over, Tom pressed the button that lowered the window on my side, and I leaned back, limp with quiet exhaustion.

"If it's too cold, say so, kid."

"Kid? I'm forty-six years old."

"Kid." I drank in the real air that blew the graveyard air away and felt calmer. My hand lay on the seat between us, and after a while Tom put his hand over it and pressed it.

"Kid, kid, I had to do it."

"Sure."

He withdrew his hand and for a long time said nothing. The revulsions of my original *horror carnis* set up decreasing echoes as we lapped the night in toll-road miles until finally, as we stopped at one of the gates in the blue-green, unreal light and Taylor flung the coins in the basket, I gave a great sigh, and it was as finished as it was ever going to be.

For a while then I thought Tom was going to say, "Please don't see Jo again," or "If I ask you, will you promise not to go by the flat again," or "I'm warning you, don't go back." My mind phrased and rephrased the possible sentences, made up answers in a dizzy succession — evading, consenting, refusing — until the whole jewel-box cab of the limousine seemed ready to explode. I suppose I was never so far away from him as I was in those moments, for when he did speak, it was to say, "Did Nan ever tell you that about the man looking into an empty room, a room he knew was empty, through a keyhole?"

"And being amazed that an eye was looking back? Yes. A couple of weeks before she died. I've read it since, of course."

"So have I. You don't know who it is looking back. Whether it is the eye of God or your own eye or Shakespeare's eye." He cleared his throat. "You know that's why I went to night school? I never knew any of the things you and she were talking about. She once even told me that from something you said she was pretty sure you were in love with Charlotte Payne. At six? I just laughed. I sure unlaughed it tonight. I guess that's what comes from knowing things."

The old tenderness flooded me, washing clear like sweet water against a bitter clay bank. Poor Tom's a-cold. Did he still think that learning, even understanding had anything to do with desire or happiness — Nan's *innocence* again?

"She said she didn't know what would happen when you did look through the keyhole and saw the eye looking back. The burning presence."

"Well, now it's happened," he said. "It was your eye looking back."

TO
A
TENOR
DYING
OLD

TO A TENOR DYING OLD

A FEW YEARS ago I began to see a picture in my mind's eye, and for a long time it puzzled me because I could not tell where it came from. I might have seen such a picture in a gallery somewhere. It may even be a relatively well-known painting, for I see it in oils, as it were, and very distinctly. But I could not have seen either the actual occurrence shown or any of the details. What I see, I could not have remembered, even though it hovers uneasily on the fluttered edges of remembrance and is more real than much I have seen, much I have remembered.

It is a big impressionist picture. A careful one. It shows the vaulting height of the Galleria in Milan. Bars of bright, wintery sunshine drift from the open wings and end, illuminating the canvas to the point where the shop windows begin along the sides. These windows — of antique stores, picture galleries, goldsmiths — are done with jeweled strokes of high color and are lit by the shop lights themselves within rather than by the filtered sun from above.

The Galleria is crowded with loosely indicated shoppers — some in a hurry, some strolling — all done with a sense of flow, of movement. Although the figures are smudged in blue-murked grays, it is clear that they are dressed in the fashion of 1913 or so — a fashion I must remember from the frontispieces in E. Phillips Oppenheim, summer-cottage books. Long draped dresses, big plumed hats — that sort of thing. The men are in long-skirted overcoats and wear either caps or tall silk hats which catch the light from time to time and help define the smeared, reflected colors that dot — pointillist, although that is not the technique — the blurred darkness of the central flow.

The odd thing, the haunting peculiarity of this, is that I am perfectly aware that one of these scarcely suggested figures is that of Edward Sciarrha as a young man. His face, if I could see it, is beaming, so full with happiness and well-being that the flesh of his later years is made probable, and what was to become a pouter-pigeon chest is already fore-shadowed. But here those tremendous, sustaining lungs seem filled with pride and joy and triumph. The cheeks, the visage which I and the rest of the world were afterward to know as saturnine, if not actually sallow, are suffused with an almost russet, Tuscan, even Venetian glow, for his skin was always transparently fair and his eyes blue — though his hair and the shadow of his beard were black. Here his hair clings in moist, jet, very Italianate curls as a thick cap to his head. I never knew him when he was not balding, and he always had to wear a wig on the stage. It is odd, too, that of all that crowd he is the only one who is hatless. In 1913 it is almost impossible that he, a singer, should be so, but bareheaded he is. He is wearing my grandfather's black broadcloth, sable-collared coat.

I learned a great deal from Edward Sciarrha during the course of my life, and the appearance of this picture sud-denly a few years ago was a source of wonder. It would come upon me as I walked the dog late at night, as I lay in bed waiting to go to sleep. I even went out of my way once when we were driving from Locarno to Venice to stop off at Milan, where all we did was to walk up and down the arcade for twenty minutes or so.

"Well," said my wife, "that's the silliest yet," and when I said something about wanting our daughters to see it since they never had, they chimed in with: "Really, Daddy, we could see it sometime when we were coming to Milan. What's so special?"

What was so special of course was the compulsion I felt. It was as if I were being pulled back in time to the point where the involuntary memory would take over and where something that had happened would happen again with all its original emotion. This time, somehow or other, I expected the emotion, the passion, would be understood. Yet it could not be like that. I could not have been there in 1913. Or in 1923. I was never in Milan until December 1928, thirty-odd years ago.

I was there then with my mother and father, my next younger brother, Gordon, and my cousin Corinne. We had come to Europe in September because my father was giving a series of lectures at Guy's Hospital in London. My brother and I were at school in Paris — I was fifteen and he nineteen months younger — and my mother and Corinne, who was six years older and had graduated from Smith, stayed with us there, my father returning to London when he had a lecture to give. Corinne was with us that year, for those who like the *autre temps, autre moeurs* bit, because, in supposedly roaring 1928, it would have been considered impossible for her to come to Europe by herself, even though she had the excuse of wanting to study the piano.

Corinne was with us often during the twenties and today

explains our relationship with, "We spent the twenties together, you know." Her mother left my Uncle Frank when
Corinne was about ten. I was too young to have heard anything about their divorce and at the time had only one
strong recollection of my Aunt Louise. She had been in
California and was on her way to Europe. It was arranged
for Corinne, who was then twelve, to stay with us. Actually,
she never returned to her mother after that. Anyway, I can
remember inquiring of my mother when we knew they were
coming whether I should call Louise "ex-Aunt Louise" —
probably from having seen "ex-wife" and "ex-husband" in
the newspapers. I was told that plain *Louise* would be
just fine and to try not to stare.

"Don't be so *interested,* darling," my mother used to say.
But of course I always was and still am. I must really have
stared, because I can still see Louise and Corinne when they
came in from the train, Corinne with the long sausage curls
of the time, a beaver hat, probably even braces. Louise was
in black, a dress so tight that Gordie and I decided she had
to take it ALL off to go to the toilet. She could scarcely walk.
She teetered in, and a long panel swayed at the side. That
night my brother and I put both legs into one side of our
pajama bottoms, letting the empty leg fall as the panel. We
buttoned the pajama tops on each other backwards, and then
each took a down quilt in mock of her exaggerated furs and
bunched it around his skinny neck. With hands on hips we
waddled, waggled, wiggled, giggled back and forth.

"'Oh Doc, you smell so wonderful, so completely *ether.*
Just like old times,'" Gordie quoted.

"All bloody bandages and pus," I contributed.

"'You are NOT to do a THING for us, you understand.
Corinne and I have had to look out for ourselves, you

know, and just the tiniest bit of coffee, and a morsel of toast in the dining room. NO TRAYS.'"

"It was *morçeau* — that's French — of toast, you stupe."

"It was not. It was morsel —"

Then I think we probably beat each other up out of pure joy, because that's what we usually ended up doing when we got anything as good as this to work on.

The next day I heard my mother on the phone to her sister: "Frank's bracelets in the afternoon. How she got down off the Pullman, I'll never know. Dumping the child like that for God knows how long and then that about trays. I should have them keep the dining-room breakfast going until eleven o'clock. As if trays weren't easier. Well, she got a tray, you may rest assured. JUST as she expected. But why mention it? Of course it is terribly hard on big Gordon. He's so fond of Frank. We all are, I know. But Gordon was as white as a sheet. He was the best man at their wedding. Remember? Such simpering dresses, the bridesmaids. Well, Gordon and he went on that hunting trip together. Then, oh I must tell you. Without a word of warning she turns on poor Gordie. He's so proud of his new trousers because they have a buttoned fly? Yes, I know. Sweet, really. So I let him wear them yesterday because they were coming. Well, she turns on him and says how he's grown. Then her hand to her mouth and great rolling of great eyes, she says, 'And the dear, he's got a fly.' Corinne is sitting right there so I say '*Pas devant.*' Naturally. Oh, I know, I know. You don't have to tell me. It's the only place she ever does look."

I can probably reproduce any telephone conversation my mother ever had — domestic wisdom, a kind of acid wit which was not at all good, clean fun, and a dazzling irrelevance, an externalized Joycean monologue. We heard—

often — "and the dear, he's got a fly" because it delighted
our father, too. I put it in a telephone conversation because
that's where I'm sure it belongs. I have no idea where this
next belongs. It's isolated. But I know it is there. Sometime
in that day and a half while she was at our house Louise
must have said, "You and Doc are so much better equipped
than I. Your household is so much better sustained . . ." It
is out of character for the Louise the family talked about, so
it isn't likely I would imagine it. I don't suppose my mother
heard the pleading in it. I certainly couldn't have then, and
it is only now that it drifts back — the strangeness, the exactness of the words. It was Louise who knew "how to handle
men," but it was my mother who went on living in her own
houses while Louise went from hotel to hotel until she died.
It was Louise my mother cast in the role of *femme fatale*,
but it was my mother who had a rich, good-looking husband
— who was independently famous even aside from his name
— for all of his days.

Edward had written us in Paris that he was opening the
season at La Scala with Mazzini in *Tosca*. It was his biggest break — the biggest he or anyone else could get. We
had known him in America for more than fifteen years and
he had already sung at the Met, in Chicago, and all over
South America. But this was the opening of La Scala and was
equivalent to saying that he was the foremost lyric tenor in
the world. We had planned to go to Athens for Christmas
anyway — to get warm, my mother said — so my brother
and I left school early, we closed up the apartment, and arrived in Milan the day of the performance. Both Corinne
and my mother had new Paris evening dresses — *frocks* was
the word then — and my mother even let Corinne wear
some of her jewelry so she wouldn't look too *jeune fille*.

One of the reasons Corinne was with us was that she had abruptly decided that she would not, could not, marry Bob Patterson who had been her best beau — that still was the word in 1928 — ever since she came out.

"You dance with your eyes closed and that means that nobody — nobody — can cut in, Corinne?" I asked her because she was my final authority on the great world. Even better than F. — I still gave him his "F." — Scott Fitzgerald, because there you had to look for the answers, and Corinne you could just ask. Fitzgerald was all right for things like how horrible it was to wear a made-up bow tie with a dinner jacket, but I never saw a made-up dress tie until I came under the democratizing influence of Leverett House, so I had to ask around to find out what it was.

"It sure does, Enoch Arden. You like the arms you're in." Corinne had the advantage too of being slightly shopworn in my eyes. After all, she had been out for three years and had graduated from college. But she was what I called *svelte* and even in Paris college boys called for her and took her out dancing with onion soup in Les Halles and all. But she called them "college boys" — which is what I yearned to be — as if it were a term of reproach. She was on edge a great deal of the time that year, and once I came home to find her with a cocktail shaker — cocktails were still shaken and no one had heard of "bruising" gin — livid with rage at some youth.

"Give me those tickets," she said to him.

"What the hell. If you don't want to go, just say so. But why do I have to give you the tickets?"

"Just give them to me, that's all."

He handed them over, and she walked across the room to me, amazed in the doorway.

"Now here, Il Penseroso, is one for you." She walked back across the room and said to him, "And here, L'Allegro, is yours. The two of you can go to the Folies Bergère and drool. I won't be there. Corinna's *been* a-Maying long enough. Chicken-licken can teach Duckie-daddles how to be a college boy. Oh, get out! The two of you. Go — salivate."

I never did know my unexpected benefactor's name because he never came to occupy the seat next to me, and it stood empty until the intermission.

How shall I tell about the Folies Bergère of an American in Paris at fifteen? At fifty, it still seems to me one of the great national monuments, the equal of Mont-St.-Michel and Chartres; at fifteen, I had not even known it could exist. The year before, I had been to the Star and Garter in Chicago, but this had just resulted in a sniggering match with my cousin Georgie. On this trip, I had been to the Rue St. Denis one night, not as client but as tourist. It was still in 1928 lit by gaslights, but the strolling, stylized, bedizened whores, and the great mass of black, shadowy shadows of men moving like ghostly phalanxes from the lost armies of Gomorrah between the soot-soaked gray of the Paris houses frightened me. I had gone to bed with a clammy unease from which mushroomed nightmare terrors of fungus growths that withered sticky-wet even as they limply failed of bloom.

I came upon the Folies at the precise moment when I needed them most, for here before me stretched golden women, their breasts proud-eyed, their muscled softness polished by a dazzling light, their bellybuttons — oh — beseeching tongues, their thighs wanting hands and lips. I sat in dazed ecstasy, reeling not, I think, with immediate desire but with thankfulness that they just existed. Even the bronzed and gilded men in the grouped statues seemed gods, not hairy waifs, for their legs were smoothed and they were shaved under the arms. Gone were the locker-room stench of sweated gym shoes, the stink of yellowing, twisted jockstraps, the somehow even sexier mat of cotton stiff with brownish stain upon the feet of white, misshapen socks. These were men worthy of the flesh with which they postured.

The first half of the show always ended — it still does — with an "international number." The girls come down to the lights, lean over the frantic orchestra, shake their darling rumps, dangle their lovely breasts, and sing in French, English, German. In 1928 it was a song about millionaires and ended with their asking time and time again of the bald-headed rows, "Êtes-vous, are you, bist du, Millionai — re?" There was a bump on the final "e." The last stanza ended with their leaning back, arching forward their "G"-string clouded cunts — a word I had until then not even dared to use to myself — shaking their hands and bodies:

"Êtes-vous, bist du, are you, Millionai — re?"

I rose in my seats, for I had two, threw my hands over my head in a jittered echo of their waving, and cried, complete with bump, "Oui. Moi je suis millionai — re."

Now I know perfectly well that I did this in precisely the same spirit as a fifteen-year-old might rise at a revival meeting when implored to come forward and be saved. Goddamn it, it was a spiritual ecstasy. Maybe you didn't know, oh Henry Adams, but it really is Mont-St.-Michel and Chartres.

Let me prove it. After the intermission I had company in my extra seat. A girl in rose taffeta picked me up in the lobby and asked if she could have the seat beside me since she had paid only the promenade admission. Of course I said "Yes," but I was so enchanted by the continuing vision of what I had seen that it didn't occur to me that I was being picked up at all, that my confession of riches had been heard, that I was supposed to notice — although of course I did notice — the pressure of her breast as she took my arm when we went back to our seats. I never made the connection between the rose taffeta at my side and the golden nudes before me. Not even when she let her hand fall to what must have been my plainly tented lap. It wasn't her hand I wanted. I didn't even notice it, honestly, really, until I got home and looked with unflexed wonder on my own spread and glistening fingers. In the theatre, it wasn't release but communion with the gods that I sought. The ecstasy had come to me at last, and it was not at all more than flesh could bear. It seemed to me what flesh was made for.

In the finale, the girls descended — they still do — from the roof. This summer it was called "The Descent of Venus"; in 1928, they were the "Happy Balloonists." A kind of revolving platform is let slowly down directly over the audience. The girls are smiling, chalk-white with only powder over their nakedness, and in 1928 each held a dove aloft by a blue, blue ribbon which fluttered across their breasts. The mirrored balls turn shooting darts of glitter, the house lights come on full, the blare of brasses in the orchestra is orgastic, and the revolving girls are drawn up again to the gilded sky. In 1928, Rose Taffeta had fled.

At the holiness of my fifteen-year-old vision? Maybe. Maybe because she was French and knew. Maybe just because she had to get back to the promenade.

I told Corinne about it the next day, as well as I could, but the metaphysical vocabulary of fifteen is limited. What got across, though, was that, while I loved the girls, I had been able to fall in love with myself. I had been able to know myself as a lover. I would never again, I thought, fail of bloom. With this knowledge I could wait.

"That's nice, Porphyro," Corinne said. "But there are lots of things nicer about being a man — even a college boy. And hairiness, you goof, is one."

Edward had sent great baskets of flowers to my mother and Corinne at the hotel — "How *wop!*" Corinne said — but we didn't see him until we saw him on the stage, and he didn't see us until the first-act curtain calls when I waved. (I'm a great waver, you can tell.) He was in magnificent voice, and as I said about him in a poem I tried to write when he died, "He spun tenderness to song for me." It was another face of love I was seeing here — learning about — and the thunder of applause as he finished his last-act aria about the light of stars was deeper, more passionately resonant, than any at the Folies. I don't mean to say that I made the observation in those words at the time, but I certainly felt it in my heart, which crowded to my throat. Poor Tosca — who lives for art and love in a world dominated by church and politics and ruled by a man who says he has to have an unwilling woman!

Edward gave a large dinner for us and the principals after the performance. It was in one of those incredibly lush, red-and-gold Italian restaurants with mountains of highly decorated food and great sheaves of wired flowers. It was closed to the public — actually, it was the main dining room of the hotel where we were staying — by the time we got there, and a kind of Aladdin's cave had been created with marble serving tables and gilt screens upholstered in watered, scarlet silk. These circled the large round table at which we ate, which was placed directly underneath the first of three enormous ormolu and luster chandeliers, diminishing in splendor down the mute, heavy magnificence that throbbed darkly behind us. These were not lighted, but rustled with the prolonged flames of the candles reflected from the dinner table.

Edward and the rest of the cast were wild with excitement, glistening with happiness because they knew that they had been superlatively good.

"You were good, good. Very good. Say that 'Tutta Roma' again. And so beautiful." This was Edward embracing Tosca.

"Tutta Roma" — that wonderful, rolling triumph that had chilled the audience to panic.

"Oh, how good to be good." Edward sat attentive at the head of the table and kept the conversation in English for us as well as he could. But even so there was much Italian, much flirting, bare shoulders, wine and more wine. I was all eyes, of course. It was like the first act of *Traviata,* and the surprising thing was that my mother and Corinne seemed perfectly at home. Corinne so *svelte,* her hair with its plastered, jet-black curls nodding this way and that like a garden flower, my mother full-blown but soft and beautiful, gay, flirtatious as I suppose I had never seen her. When I was fifteen, she was thirty-seven, but I don't remember — and my brothers don't either — ever having thought of her as a sexual object at all. She and my father went out a great deal, and she always came in to kiss us goodnight, heavy with perfume, glittering with diamonds in the dark, rustling with silk. I can remember her loosening the skinny arms I had thrown around her neck and murmuring, "Oh, darling, my hair. You really musn't," but I still cannot even summon up a sense of rejection. Sex, for me, was Swedish maids, cotton slips with drawstrings, stained, cotton corsets flapping on the line on washday. It's all in a poem called "Dinner Party." When our mother kissed us goodnight, she ceased to exist. She certainly did not occupy our imaginations as did the odorous lives of the unmarried maids who slept above us on the third floor and who also kissed us goodnight — but with wet-mouthed abandon — and stroked our hair and sang us lonesome, tuneless songs in a strange tongue.

I suppose it was that night in Milan, beneath the enormous bunches of polished glass grapes lustrous with shadows, that I caught up with her. At any rate, to see my own mother smiling so sweetly, so poignantly — for that was her style — at the man who played Scarpia was a revelation. It may be obscurely significant that my mother's behavior I excused, but that I thought my father an old goat because of his interest, which he did nothing to conceal, in Tosca's fantastic — by American standards — décolletage. My mother and father were the same age, and Tosca herself could not have been much younger and certainly did everything in the world to provoke him. I was to learn years later from Edward that her lover at the time was a much younger man, a Roman count.

"Alfredo and Violetta, you understand? Except that she was a great artist and she gave him all her money and he was nothing nor ever would be. She did die, you know, in Rome. So Roman, so prodigal, so sumptuous she was. It was TB, too. But there was no letter scene, no arrival. Just death."

You will see as this goes along that Edward always described people, situations, attitudes in terms of their operatic counterparts, as if the real world were in the preposterous librettos and the unreal world was where he lived. His own wife-for-a-time's name was Sophie — the Sophie of *Rosen-kavalier* — and he came to grief trying to figure her out in Strauss's and von Hofmannsthal's terms rather than in terms of Chicago back-of-the-Yards where she had her being. *Alt Wien* rather than the hog butcher of the world.

The party was a great success, and Edward was consistently kind even to my brother and me, throwing us questions, trying to get us into the occasion. Of course, our dinner was very late indeed — even by Italian standards — but when our mother suggested that my brother and I be excused to go upstairs to bed, Edward jumped in with, "No. No one is excused, madame. Tonight I am making a speech. In America maybe you do not make a speech, but in Italy I do."

Everybody clapped and laughed, and Corinne put up her white, white arms and little hands and called "Silenzio."

Edward rose. "Thank you, signorina. Thank you, my friends." It was already clear that this was really to be a speech because you could see him take the kind of breath under his white waistcoat that he would take to sing. "At times like this you think long thoughts, and for many days I have had these thoughts, and I have made up in advance what I am going to say because these people I love so much are here." He named us all, and there were little firecrackers of applause after each of us half rose in his chair to bow.

"The trouble is, I am a great liar, and the newspapers are even greater liars. In *Who's Who* I do not put any date for my birth. I do not even know it myself anymore, but these weeks I have had to think, who is that Cavaradossi who is to open La Scala? Claudia, do not think, Maestro, do not think I do not know you — more than I — open La Scala, but you, Maestro, for many years, you, my Claudia, for three years have done this. Tonight is first for me. There may not be a second. If there is, I promise no more speeches."

Everyone laughed, but he was so obviously, so sweetly in earnest that we weren't embarrassed for him, or restive at having to listen.

"Tonight it will be the truth — except maybe for some little lies I cannot help because they make things more interesting for you and for me, too." There was one of those breaths as if the next phrase were long and intricate.

"I was born, the Cavaradossi was born in Tuscany, the village so small that even if you have been there you will not remember. There is not even a statue in the village square. Just a well, and dust when it is dry and mud when it is wet. There are sometimes a few sheep, a few goats, a few pigs, two or three geese and some hens. That's all. My father was cobbler in this village. *Ich bin nicht Lohengrin genannt.* Or at least he was until one night a robber even poorer than we took his tools. And then he was nothing. From being meat only Sundays, there was now never meat, and my father went away. I think he must have worked very hard away because he was in Genoa and sent word that he was going to America where an uncle of his was. He would send us the money when he could. He must have been a kind man, because my mother was a plain woman, and what is a boy of six? I was twelve before there was enough money, and there were new boys he could have had in America by softer women. My mother, I think, was rock. Not marble. The brown, clayey rock of Tuscan hills, crumbly on the edges but with veins of dirty gray hardness. Azucena, except she is Sicilian by temperament, and there is some excuse."

The Sicilians all laughed. You could tell he was trying to be very exact, very just. That this wasn't part of the speech

he had prepared. That it had just come upon him with bit-
terness. Suddenly, in the gilt magnificence of this room.

"She made us wait a year. I read the letter to her. She
could not read and she made us wait a year. A year before
she could bear to use the money for our passage. And when
we got to New Orleans there was a letter from the uncle.
And I read that too, standing in the Customs House. My
father" — he spread his hands palms outward in the most
Italianate of gestures, the thing you see in pale, primitive
frescoes of badly drawn saints — "was dead."

The Italians were weeping. It was the kind of sorrow they
liked. The "Piangi, piangi" of their operas. I could only feel
the uneasiness of fifteen mixed with an immense longing to
be taken in my own redheaded father's arms which now I
could scarcely remember, it had been so long. Corinne looked
up at him in undisguised wonder. He let his hands fall to
his sides. I don't suppose I ever was able to tell when Edward
spoke or sang how much of it was *timing,* how much of it
was instinctive. He never held his audience a moment too
long. He relinquished them — I'm sure that's the word —
always. They were there then when he wanted them again.

"I tell you this not for tears, but so that you, dear Maestro,
will know that your Cavaradossi was a revolutionary by the
time he was eight. That he is not now makes not so much
difference. And you, Marcella, so beautiful a shepherd boy.
I listen to every note as you sing backstage even though I
know you are already *en grande tenue* to come to this
party. I listen because I try to remember something kindly.
My voice must be kind when I write my letter by the light of
Roman stars. Of course such songs I sang in Tuscan hills and
just so beautifully too, because always I could sing. But
let me tell you something strange. I never remembered at

all. I did not see in my mind's eye or in my thoughts or anywhere, ever, the wild flowers of spring until I came back to Italy and saw them for the first time in the paintings in the Bargello." He looked up then as if to ask us if any of us had had the same experience.

"Does this make sense? I lived in those fields, sang there. I had never seen the flowers at all. Oh, bougainvillaea, crape myrtle — these I saw, you have to see. But the tiny flowers — daisies, wild tulips, primroses, violets, asphodel that sprinkle like stars the Botticelli lawns — these were there all that time, but I never saw them until I saw them on a palace wall. I saw them tonight when you sang your shepherd's song, Marcella, and I thank you."

Everybody began to clap, but he silenced them.

"We will have some more wine" — he motioned the waiters and they moved almost like a ballet with the dark green bottle heads in their white napkins pouring the pale, fizzy wine in that red-and-gold room with the crystal grapes heavy above. Fitzgerald says somewhere that the rich enjoy life young. I don't know. Maybe it was like Edward with the field flowers. I was certainly conscious of the room that night, of Edward's charm, and I was young to *enjoy* it. I even feel guilty that, having been given what Nick Caraway's father would call the "advantages," I can't do better by them. But I don't think I was conscious of *enjoyment* before that. I had other things — *vide supra* — to bother me. But, from that night on, I began to see what had happened to me in a different way. Oh, the change wasn't all at once. It took a long time happening and is still happening in a way, but it was because Edward saw my world as beautiful that I was able to see it so, too. Of all my enormous family, I don't suppose a half-dozen of us have the trick, and, since this has a great deal to do with the way this story is written, I mention it here. To get back to Fitzgerald, it didn't begin by my enjoying. I was just there at first, but later I had much to remember, much to *enjoy*.

I had sat in opera boxes from the time I was very little. I have the old Ricordi librettos with crayon markings on them, for my grandmother always took all available grandchildren to Saturday matinées because the family as a whole had the box for every performance. We were "Odd Thursdays," and every time I went, I would look us up in the program. Since my grandfather's death, the opera had been what she would have called her "big outside interest"; not only was she one of the principal guarantors, there were always opera people practicing about the house in town where she let them use the old-fashioned, third-floor ballroom with its gilded concert-grand Steinway. We were seldom at the house in town; she more often came to our houses. But we were often in the country, and that's where Edward became our friend.

"Hit me a B-flat real loud," he would call to anyone near the piano from any place in the house or along the terrace. He had relative, not perfect, pitch. You could give him a C, and he'd begin, beautiful golden notes floating over those beautiful gardens as effortlessly as the curtains, pennons at the long windows, floated up in the sun-bright breeze from the springtime lake. Those windows were not French, but enormous sash windows reaching from the floor toward the heights of the ceilings. It took two men to raise them. After a phrase or two, he'd know and come rushing in: "Villain, villain. I'd choke myself up there. Please, please, bébé, no tricks. I can feel it coming in my lungs."

We thought this very funny, and said so, but he pushed us

from the piano bench and began playing for himself very
badly — real loud, as singers generally do so that they will
be sure of the notes. Corinne came in then — let's say she
was fourteen — and said, "I'll play for you, Edward."

What he sang was, I know, "Il mio tesoro," and it was as
ornately perfect as it was ever going to be. I said, "Oh, Edward, that was wonderful."

"Yes, it was. You know Caruso cannot hear himself sing?
But I can, I think, and it is a great pleasure to me. Particularly when you are so pleased." He was always like that to
us, even when we were little, but then he said something
strange. At least I was unable to make the connection. "I'd
rather sing Almaviva or the Don than Don Ottavio."

I know now that this was said to Corinne, but I didn't
then, even though she blushed and said, "But they're baritones, basses even."

"Of course they're baritones, basses even," he answered.

The rest of Edward's speech was about his life in America.
His father had been killed in a construction accident, so
there were a few thousand dollars of insurance from the company, which made them rich in the eyes of the uncle and
the neighbors in the Italian-American section of the West
Side of Chicago. He had gone to the public schools, learned
English.

"Dago, wop, I was. But that was not bad at all. I was not
hungry, and I could walk to the grand hotels on Michigan
Avenue and sit there clean and warm and the scent of
women's furs and perfume. I could not sing because my
voice had monstrous cracks in it, but in my heart I think I
sang. I know no Giotto, no Botticelli had to tell me later that
marble pillars, ostrich plumes, overcoats with sable collars,

the trickle of water in an alabaster fountain were beautiful. I just looked and looked, and when the time came, I knew many things I might not otherwise have known."

There was a general sense of loneliness about what he said, and he did it very well. He'd seen Caruso once in the lobby of the Auditorium Hotel and had spoken to him in Italian. Caruso himself had been young and "only had an astra-khan, not a sable collar," but he had felt, he said, "the difference which was my difference too."

He began to sing again in his last year of high school, having discovered for himself a kind of baritone falsetto with which he could negotiate "Where e'er you walk" and "Una furtiva lagrima." With these he had brought down the largely Italian house at his graduation.

"It was terrible and anguish-sweet, and I knew it was terrible, but I also knew it was so much better than they who liked it would ever know."

His high school music teacher had got him a scholarship with the music critic on one of the papers who taught at the Chicago Musical College. He seemed to remember none of these people with affection, but the scholarship led to various church jobs, funerals, weddings, and solo parts in oratorios. He actually earned his living by singing very early, when you consider the tenor voice, and left his mother's when she married again "oh late in an always too late life. A cruel man, not a kind one."

Somewhere along the way he had met Alta Swanson, who was ten years older than he and a Swedish mezzo with, he said, an intense musical understanding. Later he was to tell me much about her, but that night in Milan it was only that she taught him more about phrasing, more about character than anyone else. It was she, too, who had got him into the

quartet of the church my grandmother attended after my
grandfather died. Of Grandmama, he said, "Sables, black
velvet, pearls that had once been the Empress Eugénie's.
She was the Marschallin come to life."

"A little old even for the Marschallin, don't you think, Edward?" my father called out. I tried to do the arithmetic
in my head. She was probably forty-five, the second wife
of my grandfather, who was twenty years older and had married her when she was eighteen — a circumstance we were
brought up to consider romantic.

Edward laughed, and from what he told me later said less
than he had planned, but he did go on.

"I was buying her a pair of gloves for Christmas once, and
the girl who waited on me was so young, so blond, so downy
soft that I said 'I'll take these, Sophia,' and that turned out
really to be her name, so she was amazed. Oh, there was no
silver rose, and her father was a Polish stockyards worker, not
a rich merchant, but I was used to providing the appurtenances for myself. I married her."

I don't remember how he glossed the next. The fact was,
I knew, that he spent little time at Sophie's and that
they never even had a flat of their own. Most of the time he
was at my grandmother's in the country; we even called his
room in the west wing "Edward's room." The speech was
arranged to do honor to us and how kind we had been to
him, so he didn't have to mention that the marriage had lasted
less than twelve months and that he had left for Europe for
his final years of study even before his son was born. The
silver rose tarnished quickly.

"I was never Rodolfo, thanks to these people, but I was
always afraid of becoming Rodolfo so that I knew him,
hungry and cold. *Che gèlida manina.*"

The party broke up after that. It was dawn when we walked across the lobby to the elevators, but I was still as alive as I had been at the beginning. And I heard him say, as he helped Corinne into the white broadtail evening coat with its sparkling white fox collar that Grandmama had given her for graduation, "The butterfly returns to its cocoon."

I also heard and remember my father's, "This only is the witchcraft I have us'd?"

"I want you to watch your bill. I'm willing to bet that dinner's on it," was what my mother said. But my father, even if he had noticed it, would never in the world have told her. While perfectly capable of being enchanted behind the velvet curtains of the dining room, my mother saw things by the light of dawn in what she was always calling "their proper perspective."

The trouble with the "proper perspective" is that you never have all the pertinent facts, and I didn't have all the facts about Edward until after he was dead. My father would have said — did say, really — that the only pertinent fact was that Edward was a man of talent. I too became an artist, a writer, and three years after the dinner in Milan Edward made an important distinction for me. He was in Boston with a post-season *Lohengrin* and took me to dinner — for which he did pay — at Locke-Ober's. I had by this time seen a made-up dress tie, but I was still technically a virgin, still content to wait.

He asked after Corinne, and I told him that she still saw a lot of Bob Patterson.

"People say, you know, that he married Marge Lawson on the rebound. I think they'll get divorced, and Corinne will marry him. Before she died even, Grandmama gave Corinne the gardener's cottage. She's added a wing, and there she is. Corinne seldom comes into town. Everybody's very poor, of course." This was 1932.

"Do not tell me, bébé, that Corinne is poor. In a cold-water flat with one toilet for the whole floor, Corinne is not poor. Starving to death, Corinne is not poor. She is never poor because it is not something she can imagine. What you cannot imagine, you cannot be."

"Well, you know what I mean, *poor*."

"You want to be a writer, you say. Let me tell you something. This is different from me. I am a performing artist. If you are good, you will be a creative artist. It is not the same thing. Not the same thing at all. You are not obliged to become someone someone else has created."

"Shakespeare played the ghost in *Hamlet*."

"Ah, you take my point. The ghost, not Hamlet. Hamlet is for someone else, for the world, even. He is given away. I think it is like having a child. Flesh and blood — genes, is it? — you give him. But the lungs, the lungs must be filled with someone else's breath. After he is created, even Hamlet is no longer Shakespeare's."

"But Corinne knows about being poor. I do, too."

"About other people being poor. Not about yourselves. You can create me a poor boy in the Tuscan hills, on the West Side of Chicago. But you cannot create yourselves poor. You cannot be poor. I sing Lohengrin. My father was not Parsifal. I do not believe in Parsifal. I am not holy in any way. I have never been holy. Holiness is not my métier. But I am a performer, and as long as someone imagines Lohengrin for me it is all right. I sing, Magda sings. In the action we become. We follow someone else's notes, and it is for us heavenly music. We are what we perform.

"Let me tell you. In bed even, always I perform. I am conscious of the cat curled up on the chair, the eyes in the photograph if there is no cat. The crash of cymbals at the height is not within me, but without — as if other people had burst into opera house applause. You are a great noticer, bébé, and you see my cat on the chair, the eyes in the photograph. But you note them only. It never occurs to you that they see you."

Of course, when anyone talks to you like that, you remember it all your days, and you always wonder why. There is no use trying to figure it out. There is no use, even in a story, trying to make it credible. It just sometimes happens. It simply is there and, if you are going to write at all, you have to write it. I suppose that it was the attempt to make it credible to myself that led me to say to Bob Bonney, who was studying in my room when I got back to Leverett House, "I had dinner with Edward Sciarrha at Locke-Ober's."

"For Chrissake. How the hell do you know him so well you have dinner with him?"

"He once was my grandmother's lover."

"Wow!"

I practiced a great deal on Bob. Sometimes I told him lies of great circumstance, which he usually believed. Sometimes I told him unadorned truths, which he found incredible. I hadn't at all turned into the Charles Macomb Flandrau college boy of my dreams of a few years back, and the truth is that I had no pattern at all for what I did become — half-truthful lies, half-lying truths. Coming home one night I had related so minutely to Bob my supposed seduction by a Boston second-year girl, who had merely let me feel her up a very little on the front steps, that his "Wows!" took on the awe of "Oh rare for Anthony!" In honesty I should add that the odorously imagined scene became, without change, my own bedtime and completely satisfactory fantasy for the months that remained of my virginity, and that I have even had occasion to use it since. My own actual seduction I later gave — in Edward's sense — to one of my characters, and though I know it is all true on the page as I read it — I can, like Dickens and Christopher Isherwood, even weep — it no longer belongs to me in the sense that the unpublished, nonexistent, second-year girl does.

When I said that Edward had been my grandmother's lover, I had no idea that it was true. It was an uneasy intuition made swiftly conscious — but not necessarily true — by the necessity of explaining to myself the intimacy, the honesty, the seriousness of Edward's tone. It was this far more, I am sure, than the touching, grandiose homage he had meant to pay us in Milan when my father — whom I never before this moment had ever suspected of any overt social sense — stopped the reference to the Marschallin. One of the troubles with writing this is that the clues to what I finally uncovered occurred — and should therefore be recorded — at a time which I remembered only after their significance became apparent. As Edward saw it, Grandmama *was* the Marschallin; it was he who had to become Octavian.

I don't want to make a big production about my true lie to Bob that night. I don't think I thought about it at all after I uttered it. It came back only at the time of my own wedding, when I suggested that I could ask Edward to sing.

"I don't think so, darling," my mother said judiciously. "It's so much like asking for the return of past favors, don't you think?" It was said with the aplomb of Madame de Sévigné, but I understood my mother by this time better than she thought, and it only took a moment to remember that he had not sung at my grandmother's funeral or at any of my cousins' weddings. He hadn't, literally, been in any of our houses for twenty years. I let the matter drop. He sent a score of *Tosca* inscribed to him by Puccini in a magnificent Rivière slipcase — I looked up the spelling of Cavaradossi in it when I came to use it here — but he didn't come to the wedding.

Edward's voice lasted through the thirties. The last time I heard him was as Don Ottavio in *Giovanni*. He was fat — almost a haystack in the black cape — but the notes of "Il mio tesoro" floated in the same way as they had the day Corinne had played for him at Grandmama's. Of course, I couldn't remember to compare. The youth must have gone, surely, but the big windows at my grandmother's that gave so largely on the sunny gardens and the blue lake opened once more, their curtains blown pennons in a springtime breeze.

The war came right after that. Edward was caught in Rio and sang there for a few years, but toward the end, he told me later, "I'd look up and see those people in the galleries and know that many of them had done without lunch. I just wasn't that good any more, bébé, and there wasn't any chance at all that I'd get any better. Oh, I would have liked to sing 'An die musik' as a last encore at Town Hall, but I just climbed into my swan and rode off into the wings. It was the end of the season, and I never went back. *In fernem Land.*"

At the end of the war, he didn't come back to the States, but for a time he was in Lima as artistic director of the opera there, and from time to time he'd meet his old friends — "All on the way down, bébé, all on the way down — it was too sad." After that he lived in Mexico City, which is where I saw a lot of him.

One day shortly after Nan, my Uncle Tom's wife, died, Tom called me and asked me if I'd go down there for him.

"Edward Sciarrha's there, and I don't want to give him the idea we're checking on him, but I'm curious. It isn't money. He has $8685 in his checking account here" — you could tell Tom had had the records brought to him and was looking at them — "and he hasn't drawn on it in over a year. Then he has $37,000 in bank stock. The dividends are deposited on order. He must have some other stuff, but, even if he hasn't, it isn't money. I could understand if he were in Italy or California . . ." His voice trailed away.

"Why don't you go down yourself, Tom? You ought to get away."

"No, he'd smell a rat. You take the kids and all. You can say you're down there writing."

"But what am I supposed to do?"

"Come off it, kid." He laughed and I laughed too, but he went on: "You're supposed to find out something. I don't know what, just something. I got to thinking he might be sick, alone, just lonely. You could find that out and anything else." He must have swallowed a couple of times, because his voice shifted from its speculative melancholy into the defensive good nature required for "Snoop, kid, snoop. I talked to your dad, and he didn't see any reason why not, and don't you tell me you wouldn't like to know."

The picture of the Galleria had already begun to haunt me for no discoverable reason, although neither Papa nor Tom knew about it, so I suppose I was less honest than Tom — snotty, even — when all I said was, "Well, I'd love to go to Mexico, of course. Sure, we'll all go. Thanks a lot."

Tom was always quick at picking up things. It is hard to explain, but, even though we were talking over the telephone, it was as if he put his arm around me when he said, "You don't have to tell me, you know. It's not knowing like that that I care about. Just so one of us knows, and if anything can be done it's done."

As it turned out, we didn't all go. Measles. I went by myself and saw a cake in a shop evidently for someone recovering from surgery. A spun-sugar operating table with a spun-sugar patient, complete with red abdominal gash. A couple of spun-sugar, bearded doctors, and nurses in sugar nun's habits. A pail full of scarlet sugar slops had been artistically knocked over, and there were spun-sugar, blue-bottle flies glutting themselves on the offal. I ordered the cake sent to Edward with my card and ordered another set of the figures for my younger daughter, who has a fine taste in these matters.

Edward called the hotel in ecstasies and sent his Chevrolet with a villainous driver for me the next afternoon. The driver spoke no English and assumed that I was speaking Italian, because he agreed violently with everything I said — "Sì, sì, signore."

"How long have you been with Mr. Sciarrha? How far is it to his house?"

"Sì, sì, signore."

Mexico City has some of the most beautiful private houses in the world, and often they are set to take advantage of the spectacle of an enormous city spilled beneath the sumptuous rise toward the bluish heights. Edward's house was ordinary on an ordinary street. An apothecary's house, he called it. There was a small, lush, ill-kept garden where a cock strutted, and an upright majolica fish dribbled water from his chipped mouth to a small, shell-shaped pool. This

in turn overflowed in a trickle that merely damped a darker
vein in the hard-trod sand of the walk.

He heard us arrive and came out to meet me, kissing me,
Italian fashion, on both cheeks.

"Bébé, no longer bébé." His eyes were shining with pleasure, which is always endearing, and he patted me toward
the living room, the salon, which had been devoured by the
enormous black bulk of the Steinway. There was literally
only room for a hard, Spanish couch of powdery leather under the three high, flawed, leaded windows, and even that
had a pile of age-brittled music on one end, the overflow
from a large table that was stacked high, and under which
was a portable phonograph and a half-dozen books of recordings.

"We sit here now. Afterward there are more comfortable
places. But we must be formal for the sake of Conception."
Conception was evidently the barefooted Indian woman with
the condor beak who brought us a bottle of rum and three
glasses that, for lack of room any other place, she put on top
of the piano.

"S'il vous plaît, madame." Edward bowed to her in French
— a little French nod, not at all the Spanish bow — and
writing this now I feel again the ultimate loneliness that always somehow clung to the Edward I loved. He spoke English in Milan, French in Mexico, and sang Pinkerton in
Spanish in Rio. Later on I was to know he spoke German in
Pasadena. Always the language was different from the place,
as if he never was at home. Even the name Sciarrha is more
than vaguely Arabic, for the *ci* and the *rh* are incompatible
in Italian. I asked him about this once, and he said, "I'm the
original Displaced Person, bébé. Sciarra Colonna was the

man who hit the Pope in the face with an iron gauntlet, but that name's Roman and I am Tuscan. S-h-a-r-r-a-h would be the Arabic, I'm told by Giorgio de Santillana." He was quiet a moment then. There was the singer's breath and he went on, "But of course it all came — the preposterous spelling came — from a man I only saw once through twelve-year-old tears — the immigration clerk in the Customs House in New Orleans."

Edward's French nod that Mexican afternoon was curiously endearing to me and I think it was to Conception of the condor beak, too. It was as if he were giving her something she never would have had in this life except through the accident which brought them together. At any rate she bowed to him in Spanish and did not speak at all, but poured out three glasses, handed us each one, and then retired to the other side of the threshold where she bowed — again in Spanish — to me, raised her glass to her lips with ceremonial unction, and departed toward the kitchen.

"*Pique Dame,* I call her." Edward was laughing at my pantomimed bafflement. "She is from the third act of *Carmen* and looks with horror through the electric firelight as Carmen tells the cards. *La mort. La mort. Toujours la mort.* It is good to grow old with such a one around. Far better than Zerlina."

His mood was by no means elegiac. He was witty, urbane, his wit sharpened by the excitement of the occasion. He opened himself up, as he always had to me, and there was no constraint, no groping for suitable topics of conversation. We talked on and on. That first day it was mostly vital statistics. The deaths among my uncles, their wives, my cousins. Pete and Harrison had been killed in the war, as had Bob Patterson, whom Corinne had married after all. He wanted to know about Corinne, and I told him that she still lived in the country, showed no interest in remarrying, and had gone rather to fat.

"The sleek Corinne?"

"Yep. *Gemütlich,* I think, would be the word. She even cooks when you go out. Marvelous dinners, course after course, flour on her hands."

"The brittle ankles, the tiny feet, the glitter of those perfect calves?"

"Skirts are long now. Her eyes are still beautiful. I suppose I notice them most when she plays the piano for you — for one — after dinner."

"How is that?"

"Very good. Real authority, you know."

He seemed surprised and said, "That, I never heard."

"No, I suppose not. She's only had it for a little while." The two of us went on like that. I was rather piecing together these people I knew so well and had had little reason to think of or to try to bring up to date. "They never had any children, but she's fond of Bob's son by Marge Lawson. He'll get all of the Patterson money, of course."

"Maybe that's why she's fond of him. Because he doesn't need her." He looked at me shrewdly, and a whole set of relationships began to shift and re-form in my mind, as if what Edward provided were a kind of moral kaleidoscope which, when it was tapped, sent prismatic chaos scurrying into nonprogressive, geometric form.

The visit was so successful that I left the hotel the next day and went to stay at Edward's. He insisted on giving me his room because it had a large table in it for me to work on. The villainous driver carried the bags up and Edward said, "I've left everything just the way it was. At this late date

there seemed no point." He waved me in, and I saw immediately what he meant. There was a Boldini drawing of my
grandmother in a black net evening dress seated, very *femme
du monde* — as she herself would have said — on the foot
of a Louis Quinze chaise. She has her diamond star and a
black aigrette in her sooty hair and is leaning forward, fingering her pearls. The length of the chaise, which is on a slant,
is exaggerated, and its back is scooped out to repeat the
curve of her body. What you have is a pair of arched wings
fluttering into flight. She herself is seen as an exquisitely elegant bird, white-throated, with acquisitive eyes. I had never
seen her anywhere nearly so young as that, or in that way at
all. I mentioned the eyes to Edward, and he said, "*Appraising* would be kinder, perhaps. A kinder word. They're
your eyes really, you know, whatever you do to disguise it.
It is best to be kind."

"They're in the Paul Helleu that Tom has, and in the Sargent we gave to the university." I could not take my eyes
from hers, and you could tell that Edward too was looking at
the picture for the first time in a long while, but he drew
himself together and stroked the signature and its date,
"Venezia, 1913."

"The winter before you were born, bébé. The first year I
was with her." He moved toward the door, but he wasn't
afraid of my eyes, nor I, strangely, of his. "Octavian to the
Marschallin. Will that make it all right?" His smile pleaded.
His hands turned outward in the Italian gesture I had seen
that night in Milan, and it occurred to me that the only possible answer was the kiss on both cheeks. I had even stepped
forward when the room was invaded, the sky was rent, with
the clamor of tuneless bells from the nearby church steeple.
Bong! Clang! Cling! Bang! The house shuddered under

the demon assault of iron clapper-tongues lashed into furious discord by the whirred, wheeled descent of the turning bells. There was nothing to do but to stand there, scourged by the obscene whips of sound gone mad. Edward was used to it, may even have expected it. At any rate, he was able to laugh as the assault diminished, and to absolve me from the awkward kiss on the cheeks with, "That's the veritable voice of God, bébé. It calls me to a kind of prayer, too, for now I have a student." He patted me on the side of my arm. "Come down when you like. Neither Pique Dame nor Spoletta knows about such things, so you will have to unpack for yourself." He closed the door behind him.

I did unpack, hazy in my mind, my feeling unfocused by the flaying of the bells, the moral kaleidoscope lashed from my hands at the moment its radiance might have assumed the proportions of bloom. I was incapable of either surprise at what Edward had said or relief because he had confirmed what I had suspected for a long time. Usually, I think the detail of revelation rather than the revelation itself has the power to move, to give the turn of the screw, and I suppose Henry James knew this, but the brutality of the bells was an outside force, was completely accidental. It had nothing to do with Edward or me or my elegant grandmother. In the interest of art, in the interest of achieving the well-made tale, shouldn't I exclude it? Temperamentally, I can't. The blows were real; they happened. The insane clangor of their derision made it possible for me to look with both my eyes instead of squinting through one at bits of glass arranged in specious order at the end of a confining tube.

I was made aware of this change of view almost immediately, for I think the dissonances still clung to the room when I first saw on the dresser the incredible array of gold-backed brushes, gold-topped boxes, bottles, picture frames, clock. Everything was gold, and each piece was decorated with raised, scaled, twined, even copulating snakes twisted into the initials "E.S." Suddenly, I saw even more distinctly than the brushes, bottles, boxes of the dresser top the grandmother of the Boldini, the woman I never knew. There she was at a Venetian goldsmith's, in re-embroidered lace, the pigeons of St. Mark's rising in fluttered chaos from the dazzling marble of the square. I stood there for a moment, dizzy with vision, but I didn't see Edward at all until I picked up one of the hairbrushes and saw the soft gold dented, the bristles sapped by time, and the "E" and the "S" worn smooth with use.

I lay down after that and slept a warm sleep, a soft sleep without dreams in the waning Mexican afternoon. Waking too was pleasant — as if knowing fingers were folding back one by one the layers of silky sleep to free me for a known happiness. What really happened was that I became conscious of Edward's pupil singing "Allerseelen." It would hover in the air a moment, then fade, return. A phrase would be repeated, the piano might insist, reiterating strictly a note that had been blurred, but none of this was unpleasant as practicing usually is. Instead, it was as if the song itself were opening up at the same time, in the same way as I was regaining consciousness. It was getting dark, but, as I twisted with enormous comfort to yawn upon the bed, my grandmother's eyes caught mine and I smiled to her as I might have when I was a little boy, and we shared some delicious secret.

When I went into the upstairs hall, Edward was standing with his student below and called up to me.

"Come down, bébé. José is going, and I would like you to meet him."

José was a spectacularly handsome boy in a flamingo silk sport shirt. He shifted his music roll in order to shake hands with me, but he cast down his eyes and perceptibly drew his body back in an exaggerated bow.

"I am trying to tell him that in Austria *Mai* is really May. *Im Prater blühn wieder die Bäume,* and not at all like Mexico, so he must sing once with the bloom on and young, 'Wie einst im Mai.' He has the voice but he does not know about *Mai.* And already it is with him *Mai.*" The boy looked up then, and I saw his great, lost, tragic eyes.

"The man who begins the song is old, and it is All Saints' Day — November — but he is capable of remembrance." Edward lifted his hands in an operatic gesture, as if they held all the Austrian springtimes and he was afraid of the apple blossoms spilling over. He let them fall then slowly, and, even though he did not sing, he made love to the phrase, "Wie einst im Mai."

When the boy left he said, "He is queer, that boy. You got that? And it is very sad. Mostly I do not think it is sad, but this time I do. So beautiful himself, such a beautiful voice. Real talent. Real understanding. But he is afraid, and he says he is going to become a monk. His father is a rich man and does not want this, naturally. A priest, maybe. At least they have to say so because they are devout. But a monk is nothing. So silly. So stupid. I cannot say to him 'The opera houses of the world are full of accommodations. It is nothing so terrible. You will be happy or at least as happy as anyone else ever is.'" He was silent a moment as if considering the effect of such a statement on the boy. "No, I cannot say it. It is all wrong that I cannot. He would wither before my eyes. So cruel, so deep the shame. Already his eyes are haunted. He cannot even in May imagine May. Oh, bébé, there is so much shit in this world. So much shit. Maybe it is better a monk, a nothing."

Pique Dame came in then with the rum, and he looked at her startled. "In the garden, *s'il vous plaît*," and we went out there and sat under a patch of sky still too light for stars.

We talked for a long time that night and in the nights that followed. I was supposed to write during the day, but apart from taking notes, I could get nothing finished onto paper. The notes I'd shuffle around aimlessly while I listened to Edward's pupils downstairs. Faust, Rodolfo, Cavaradossi, Pinkerton, Rhadames, Tonio, the Almavivas. It was like the Victor ads in the Christmas magazines of my boyhood. The whole company was spread in an arc across the top of the double, glossy page. Melba was at the lower left, larger than the others, with a pocketbook on a chain around her waist, as Marguerite. Caruso in what I thought were Boy Scout boots as Rhadames; Scotti as Scarpia, elegant with lace cuffs; De Luca — was it? — with mustaches as God knows what. Only John McCormack was in evening dress. I was too young to have heard or to remember having heard any of them in the flesh. In fact, I haven't any idea who De Luca was, but I remember the name and the mustaches. I hope somebody else does too. I heard them all on records, of course, but mostly I remember looking at them spread before me as I lay, belly down, legs in air, on the Persian carpets that flowered softly for my youth.

Well, this was like that. The pupils were like the people in the ad. I listened and listened, just as I had stared and stared, but they had nothing to do with what I had to write, and the only relationship between the notes that I scribbled and the understanding that I had somehow to arrive at was narrative and not, from my point of view, important. Here is one.

"Went to bullfight with E. Neither of us interested. Could possibly do something about color, circular crowd, blood and sand but *moment of truth* pure crap. Maybe poem."

Here's another.

"Struck by fact that E. has NEVER called Gm. *mistress*. He is always her lover. I am *bébé* because they spoke French together so that he could learn it. I was much around then. Never *tutoyer* between them. Never *Barbara* even. Always *Madame*. Two forces operating in conversation. Regard for me then and now, and love for each other. Try to describe *eloquent hesitancy* in E.'s eyes as he tells me story."

And a third.

"E. remembered dinner in Milan down to last detail. On Papa's silencing him on the Marschallin bit, 'How swift you people are! How sure! The *grand seigneur* as well as the surgeon wielded that knife. It was over before it could be said. I could not say it then. I have kept silent over twenty years.'"

I knew I had to put these notes in order. "It is your métier, bébé," Edward kept saying. "Without this you cannot really write. It is your subject matter. You cannot help that, but I told you once it is not enough for you to *be*, you must imagine what you are."

The narrative facts are simple enough. Most of them I have already given, have come to terms with. When he was nineteen, Edward had been seduced by Alta Swanson, who had indeed later sung Octavian. He had led a strange and violent life with her, for, as he said, "She knew everything there was to know about music, and a good deal about love, but nothing whatever about life." It was she who taught him how to work, how to study, how to hear a phrase. She was quite merciless, and made him practice at half-voice until his own should be stronger. She was professional in the best possible sense, and determined, in the worst possible sense, to keep him for herself. She would make him lie on the floor and then sit on his diaphragm. "Surely the god-damnedest exercise you can imagine" — and tears of laughter would stream down his cheeks — "with both of us naked. Half the time I was dizzy with fulfillment, and sitting next to her in the quartet on Sundays — that beautiful voice, my own beautiful voice, the sunlight through the stained glass, the great bouquets of expensive memorial flowers — I was very happy."

They had lived together for over two years when a series of violent quarrels began: "But I knew my *Bohème*, and they were to be expected." One night he had awakened to find her over him with the butcher knife — "It was castration I feared, not death" — and she had begun to cry "Kill me. Kill me. Murder me. Murder me," in the extremities of her pleasures. This was not *Lucia*. She was quite mad by the time Edward arranged for her to be taken to a sanitarium. My grandmother paid for her there for over a year, and then the doctor told them that she had no idea of her surroundings and that she might be better off in a state hospital. People are always telling the rich things like this, and they are happy to believe them. The poor, however, are customarily bled of their last sou.

Edward and Grandmama went out to see her there at Christmas, when she was performing in a program. She sang the Gluck "Divinités du Styx" without accompaniment to the thunderous applause of madmen.

"The voice was still prodigious, the phrasing exact, the plea for pity heartbreaking. And all contained in perfect classic form. Not a shade too much. Not a shade too little. The ornamentation exact. It was that day that I knew about the independent life of a work of art, for how could Gluck have ever foreseen, even for a moment, that moment? A madwoman in a madhouse to a mad audience singing that aria with such exquisite precision?" He stopped a moment and knew my quietness.

"Well," he said, "I have had that scene for many years to haunt me. Your grandmother had it too, for soon after we were lovers. Now it is yours. See what you can do with it."

Edward will never see this now, and I don't know if he knew then, but, in his saying "Your grandmother had it too, for soon after we were lovers," he told me a great deal more about their relationship than he would have had he provided me with the most circumstantial account of their lovemaking.

They had been very circumspect and very careful, and there had been, he thought, no talk because the house was usually full of chaperons in the form of children, grandchildren, and other visitors. Even though it was well known that a room was kept for him, it was in the west wing, far removed from Grandmama's, and when they went to Europe they went on different boats. My grandmother had returned from Italy shortly before my birth, but Edward had stayed in London, where he had a contract for minor tenor parts at Covent Garden. He described his first meeting with my grandmother on his return almost a year later. She had not come into the hall to greet him, even though he was expected. Indeed, he had been announced as if at a party at the drawing-room door. It was a November day of icy rain, and Grandmama had me in her arms. She was wearing what was then called a tea gown of sulphur velvet, and my mother, who had evidently just come in, was standing by the fire, still in what would have been called a *tailleur*, hat, gloves, furs.

"It's so nasty, why don't you stay all night and hear Edward's news," my grandmother had said.

"No, no. I just thought you'd like the baby while I was at Maud's lunch. But now I must fly!" Edward did my mother very well. "Oh, it was interminable, bébé. I did not know where I stood at all. I wasn't used to this endless talk as I became later. That dead-white skin, that blue-black hair, that sulphur-yellow dress with *point de Venise* across the breasts. But you in her arms so that she could not press my hand, could give no sign, could not even look into my eyes until your mother was gone. Then it was all right. I knew. But you know, bébé, we could not even eat by the fire that one night? The dining room. Two men handing dishes."

During the first war, Edward had been a sergeant — "The Singing Sergeant, bébé. No college degree. Clearly not a gentleman. But I sang 'Keep the home fires burning,' 'There's a long, long trail awinding,' 'We'll be waiting when you come back home' to Liberty Bond rallies, and God could I wallop them with 'Mother Machree,' the last phrase in my most expensive voice. Not a dry eye in the house."

The affair had dwindled during the war — "A balding sergeant is no longer Octavian" — but in 1920 they had spent the spring and early summer in Venice again and had been "softly happy." After that there had been nothing, even though he continued to stay at my grandmother's house whenever he was in town. Later, Corinne was to tell me what I suppose I could have figured out for myself, that "Grandmama traded him in on Charlotte Payne." Grandmama could not have foreseen the Charlotte Payne Cobb I last saw in the treeless, watered twilight of the steep street in Istanbul, nor could she have reconstructed the set of circumstances by which Miss Charlotte became the third wife of an ambassador. These were simple enough. Her husband of nearly twenty years had been killed in the early days of the war, and the forty-ish war widow had got a job at the War Production Board. There she was much thrown with Whitney Cobb, and she — even as Grandmama herself, the belle of Akron — had married a man many years her senior. I can't think that Charlotte's rise would have much impressed her, for Grandmama was used to the ironies of the great world, and I can hear her saying once, in another connection, "After all Ambassadors are essentially *political people*." To Grandmama, Charlotte was only "little Miss Charlotte," and little Miss Charlotte was clearly "unsuitable" in 1920, and so she had stepped in and "put a stop to it." My older cousins knew all about it, but I was only six at the time and didn't hear the story until later. Corinne's theory was that Grandmama, having taken a "firm line" with Tom, took an equally firm line with herself. Neither Edward nor I knew of this complication at the time we spoke, and Edward's explanation was that he had become too well known and that the grandchildren were older.

"But we just did not love each other anymore. It was sad to me, but now it seems that even while I loved her I did not really know it was she I loved. I know now that everybody, always, creates the image he loves, but I don't know that I knew it then. If I tell you this you will not hold it against me? Many times when I have had other women, it has been *Madame* in my arms? I do not know. I cannot say it. With Sophie this was most true, and I thought, 'She is peasant. I am *snob.*' So *snob* that she was dough, and I could not, except with other visions — Alta, your grandmother. Oh bébé, you will have to create me. I am an old man, and I do not know. I hope to know. I think I am honest with myself. And I am glad you came because you make me be so, and I can listen to the words I speak just as I could listen to myself sing."

The day I left, Edward played me some records of himself at his prime. I had never heard these because they had been done in Buenos Aires. He and Borghese sang the duets from *Bohème* in Spanish to the thinned, wheezing orchestra of those thin old recordings. But the voices were full, passionate, sure, and the accommodation that each made to the timbre of the other was in itself an evocation of love. (In the old Garbo *Camille* there is an example of this sympathy made visual when Garbo and Robert Taylor walk toward the bed and Garbo corrects her step to fall in with his.) Puccini could not have written what they achieved into his score. There is no system of musical notation or guide word to scrawl across the page to encompass such performance. It was something they did on their own out of their own hearts, out of their own lives, for the people they played.

I watched the thin tears of age gather in Edward's eyes and spill to his fleshy cheeks crisscrossed with minute veins. His ageless hand with its still swart hairs moved, beating time, in and out, in and out of a shaft of sun that dazzled with light the drifting dust of the Mexican afternoon. Then it fell upon the piles of scores, their spines long since torn naked and splayed so that you could count their gatherings, the very strings of their bindings now raveled until caught in brittle, still faintly opalescent daubs of long-dried glue.

Critics speak of the moment of revelation or understanding as if all of a sudden everything became clear, as if the dramatic incident — Isabel Archer coming upon Madame Merle — could exist without what had gone before. As if the catalytic moment alone, however underwritten, however underplayed, were in itself sufficient. I can tell you with Edward that nothing like that happened. There was no one "moment of truth." He puzzled me, stayed in my mind until he died, and even though there were important incidents in his life that he did not tell me about, at the moment when I learned of them there was no sudden realization that here at last was the key. He had told me to "create" him, and you might argue that I was free — indeed duty bound — to invent the dramatic incident that would show him in his entirety, as he really was. But the moment I do this the relationship we had will vanish.

I could "discover," for example, that he was in truth my father and that my supposed mother had agreed to the deception with her mother-in-law. Believe me, there is nothing in the character of either woman which would have made this impossible, and the dates, as I look back, would take little or no juggling. Whenever I am tempted to write the scenes involved, oh Edith Wharton, I run into myself. My relationships to my own father and to my Uncle Tom, the men of my family I was closest to, were entirely different from my feeling for Edward. They were a part of me. The feeling of consanguinity was there and was very strong. I knew, really knew, my father and Tom as men. Either one of them could have been me at the Folies Bergère, and I never looked at them or thought of them as figures on the glossy pages of the Victor ad. When their pictures did appear in the society columns of the newspapers, there was never any *wonder* on my part. I knew who they were, how they lived, under what black marble they would molder when they were dead. I loved them, even though I was sometimes oppressed by that love, which was not something apart from myself but as intimate as the stirring within my own heart.

And this is strange. Strange because Edward's continued, probing concern with the artistic process was, in truth, central to my own life and of far more immediate importance to my existence, in the philosophic sense of the term, than the often vague but constant identity I felt for the men of my own family — sons, certainly, of Edward's *Madame*, but fathered by the blind Titan of another myth. Corinne has tried to tell me that I never really knew Edward, that by the time I was six or seven he was no longer "lover-in-residence" but merely a voice in the house. "After all," she pointed out, "the twenties were only your boyhood. The thirties were your youth, and apart from seeing him on the stage, hearing him sing, you seldom saw him."

What I would like to think, what I am sure Edward would expect me to think, is that hearing him sing was the final intimacy, an intimacy stronger than that of blood, an intimacy still not explained even if I were in the interest of art to make him my veritable father. What existed between us was a creative sympathy, and we met each other outside of ourselves on an intensely imagined but never, I think, intuited plane. Any one of the incidents I have told you about could be used artistically, even in the good sense of that term, as if it were the catalytic agent which would bring Edward to life. But in the end there would be no Edward, no me. What Edward had said when he said, "But there was no letter scene. Just death." I know what I have to do, and it is nowhere so easy, so sure of success, as a dramatic incident would be. I have to modulate my voice as Edward did in the duets from *Bohème,* giving much of my own that his voice may become purer, but at the same time taking the timbre of his that both voices well sweet with unwept tears.

In the years that intervened between my visit to him in Mexico and his death, I don't suppose there was a day I did not think of Edward. Not sadly, as you would of a lost lover, but with wonder. He might cross my mind only for a moment, or something might remind me and I would puzzle for a long time. I know I never wrote anything without considering the effect it would have on him. What I was trying to do all this time was to reduce to poetic terms feelings of his about art and love, feelings of mine. Some of the poems had direct quotations from him, and I'm sure that the rather peculiar rhythm of his speech is responsible for what one reviewer called my "un-English line." Since I think, feel, speak, even see in terms of a loose, Jacobean line — you can scan whole pages of this — I was amused, but I saw its justice. Edward never appears in the poems as Edward. Only I can feel his presence, the pressure of his still "uncreated" being, and he himself never mentioned any of the poems I sent him. It may very well be that he had no idea that he appeared at all. He had "given" himself to me — as he used the word, as indeed I used it myself to myself and have used it here in speaking of my own seduction. Apparently, he had no further interest in the Edward who was becoming a character. I used him shamelessly as he used Puccini. I was in danger of losing my own identity even as a poet, for I would ascribe to myself as speaker of a poem a virtue and sensibility which were not mine but Edward's — yet, even so, even now, the result does not ring false in my ears. If Edward emerges from these pages, it will be because I have given him blood of my own store. In telling me to create him, he had said, "I can give you the lungs, bébé, but the flesh and blood must be your own."

The most successful of these poems were three longish pieces called "Conversation," "Mr. De Paolis and the Shades," and "Triptych." Even today they seem to me skillful in the blending of the two of us. Only because I am the author, the ultimate authority on my own Road to Xanadu, do I know when Edward speaks and when I answer. It's like the time when people wrote in from all over the world to the Victor company to settle arguments as to whether Caruso or Scotti sang the first phrase in "Solenne in Quest'-ora" from *La Forza del D.* I "gave" him some of my best lines, and "took" in return many of his. His low voice so overlapped my upper register, as it were, that it is impossible to tell the difference. Maybe it will help if I say that if in schizophrenia you have the division of a single personality, here you have the coalescence in one personality of the traits of two.

At any rate, "Triptych" uses the famous passage from Freud about man and the stars as its epigraph and has the figure of "Icarus lashed to Ixion's wheel." The phrase had been written for over a year before I, who wrote it, knew that it had really come from Edward's dependence on my family. Just how deep, how tragic this was I must now try to tell you. There was no "revelation," you must understand, for although I had no idea of the precise detail I had, as Edward said when we gave him C instead of B-flat, felt it coming in my lungs.

Corinne had me out for a few days one May when Mary,

my wife, and my daughters were visiting with her father.
"Come and sit under my leafing surgeon-tended trees," she
had said, and I had gone. When I arrived, she was in the
kitchen with the most fantastic chaos of dirty pots, smeared
bowls, beaters stiff with cream, broken eggshells, butter
papers, peapods, lobster claws, strawberry hulls, flour-
smudged wine bottles that I had ever seen.

"What beautiful, expensive garbage!"

She laughed and kissed me, giving me a chocolate finger
to lick.

"I throw a pound of butter out the window before I begin to get into the mood. Alma, I'm sorry" — this was to the
maid who had let me in and who would have to clean up the
mess — "but I do get carried away."

"Modom can do as she likes in her own kitchen."

"So I can." There was no ice, no steel in her voice. It
wasn't nasty; it wasn't good-natured. She even resisted the
inclination to say "So *Modom* can" as she walked out and up
the stairs with me to show me my room. "There's a dinner
jacket of Bob's in the closet. Try it on. If it fits, take it home."

It did fit, and I was glad to have it. I kept it on to show her
even though I had no tie, and when I came down I saw that
she had dressed, too.

"How elegant we are!" I said. 'Wouldn't Grandmama be
pleased?"

"The suit's fine. Turn around. I don't see how it could be
better."

"Much nicer than mine. Thanks."

She seemed really pleased and said she thought there'd be
a tie in the pocket of the jacket she kept for the man she had
sometimes to wait on the table. In the interest of Emerson's
all things hastening back to unity, I have to report that it was

a made-up tie, but I put it on anyway. You couldn't tell.

After dinner was when we really talked. When I first got back from Mexico, I told her about Edward, the gold brushes, the Boldini, and when I first began to be haunted by the picture, I had told her about that, too.

"I felt a little funny — a wisp of shame — at giving you Bob's jacket. Like Edward in Grandpapa's sable coat. It wasn't just a collar, by the way. The whole thing was lined."

"It crossed my mind, too, as I came down the stairs. It's a funny thing. Neither of us really knows she gave him the coat. It's just there in my picture. I never saw the coat, even. He was dead before I was born."

"Oh, you could have seen it in snapshots, newspaper pictures. But I didn't remember it until you saw it in your goddamned picture."

"The only thing I can think of is that I picked it up from the reference to Caruso in an astrakhan collar. But how the hell would I have remembered that detail unless the other detail was there to make it significant?"

"You know, don't you, Marcel, that the trivial persists when the significant is gone?" She put her hand to the flexible diamond-and-sapphire bow she was wearing. "Grandmama's been dead under a black marble slab since 1932. I've still got the pin, but I have no idea when it was given to her. What sentimental occasion? With what special fervor was Grandpapa thanked? You want to know about the suit? I ordered it for Bob when I thought he would be coming home and he hadn't had a new dinner jacket since college. Now it hides your hairy ass, not his."

"Not to worry, darling, not to worry."

"Oh, I don't worry. It doesn't even make me sad anymore. But, God, I patted it, rubbed my cheek along it, sniffed it, and when I gave all the other stuff away I just left it hanging there. It couldn't even smell of him because he never had it on. He never even saw it."

She talked on like that for a while, and I asked her in what I thought was an oblique manner how much she really loved Bob.

"Johnny-jump-up, Johnny-jump-up. No one would believe you. How would I know? How do you know what love is, especially at fifty? I wasn't frigid, as they say on the Women's Pages now, but when you think what was done to girls like me, the way we were brought up. There weren't books to read. There weren't even people to talk to. I used to wonder about myself, 'Am I really sexy?'" She laughed. "Remember you at the Folies? Well, I didn't get any kick out of it. None at all. I'm not really a looker, a noticer. I had no yen, as a yen, for Bob at all. There was my mother, of course. Look at where it landed her." She stopped, considered, and then went on, "And Grandmama."

"But you didn't know. You said you didn't know. That you thought none of them but Tom ever knew."

"Knowing? What the hell is *knowing*? Did it make any difference when you knew? Knew that THE act took place?"

"No. I suppose not."

"You're one of us, George Gordon, Lord Byron. There's not one of us who hasn't admitted the possibility, even the probability. But how loyal do you think our aunts by marriage were with their families? Your mother and her sisters? As long as nothing is said to those involved, such things can be arranged. It was just Edward who didn't really know the rules, so even the inlaws could be affronted, and we slammed all the doors in his face."

"I don't know how you can say that."

"Come off it. Come off it, Little Nell. We never let him establish his claim, his kinship."

"And that's what he wanted?"

"Certainly. Always. Even now."

"You don't think I love Edward?"

"You can't just gaze and gaze and gaze. You've got to be able to look with someone else's eyes. At least, that's what I've always gone on. When you do that, then I think you love."

The next day we walked up to the house. One of the reasons I'd come out was that it was to be torn down, and I wanted to go through it again. There, if anywhere, I should be able to find Proust's uneven flags. As we took the turn in the drive that brought it into view, Corinne said, "It's certainly not the House of Usher."

The day was bright with May, and the rosy gray limestone house looked as it always did to me, beautiful. Sturdy, contained, gleaming with hundreds of big windows. It was in the French style, balanced, formal, restrained. The main block of the house was flanked by the two wings which formed a forecourt. A balustrade ran around the flat roof, and there were great stone urns of stone fruit, six of them, on the long front. Over the ground-floor windows and the front door were swags of limestone flowers. From a distance, the house looked as lived in as it ever had, and the builder who had bought the property had even, after a fashion, kept up the lawns. The brass and wrought-iron gates that had closed in the court were gone. "Sold," Corinne told me. "You'd be amazed. The urns are sold. Almost everything had a buyer."

At the front door the brasswork was all gone, and we had to let ourselves in by removing a big padlock to which Corinne had the key. I remembered how I used to wonder just when I would be able to reach the big dolphin knocker, and I told Corinne how that was all I was able to think of the year we came back from Edinburgh.

"All the tugs, the bridges, the skyline, the Statue of Liberty, and that's what I thought of. Can I reach the dolphin now?"

"Could you?"

"No. I don't know that I remember that. I do know that all the doorknobs were so high. So much higher than at home."

The hall was cavernous before us. Emptier than merely empty. The fireplaces were just holes, and even the bronze stair railing had disappeared, so that the steps seemed to slant drunkenly to the outside. The big rooms ran along the lake front, the back of the house, and that's where we went first. These rooms too were stripped. Plaster dust, bits of lath, bent nails strewed the floor, but the rooms were still beautiful, just as a tree is when it has lost its leaves. You could see the essential proportions, the architecture, the magnificence of the conception that took into account not only the rooms themselves but the sweep of the three planted terraces that descended to the bluff above the shifting blue lake where today whitecaps rolled toward the shore and brought the eye back from that immensity to the lilacs drunk with sun, rumpled by the wind that tossed pale blue across lavender, purple, wax-perfect white. The two of us stood looking out for a while and then turned together to look up at the wall where the Sargent had hung. The claws of the toggles that had held it in place were still there, and the brocade of the panel which it had hidden was a brighter, harsher gold than the warm, pale yellow that was all I had ever known and that still clung, tattered, to the rest of the walls.

"Even if you'd had room for it, would you have wanted it?" I asked.

"No. It wasn't just the room in a room. It's room in a life. God knows we live in a cherry orchard as it is." I poked my finger into the damask and tore off a strip which I wound around my finger as a kid will wind a string or a rubber band tight so that the blood stops and the lines leave welts. It was difficult to arrange our voices as we walked through the empty rooms. Sometimes they came out too loud, and sometimes the emptiness reduced them to mumbled inconsequence, but I don't think that was the reason we gave up trying to say anything. The six years difference in our ages just meant that we had different things to remember and to not remember. The rooms along the sides of the ground floor were lower ceilinged and had always had more comfortable furniture than those at the back, but strangely we had not used them much. When I mentioned this to Corinne, she just said, "What are you twisting that damned cloth around your finger for? Look at your hands. They're a mess."

I looked down at them and saw that the damask was now just strings and that the dried paste had melted to a gritty stickiness.

"Freudian. Downright Freudian." She laughed, but there was still an edge to her voice.

We crossed the big hall then to the dining room, and from there went on to the pantries, kitchen, and servants' quarters, where the whole machinery of the house was laid bare. Although at home we spent a great deal of time in the kitchen, at Grandmama's we were only allowed in this part of the house when Grandmama herself was there. At home we

were never allowed to ring bells for servants, but at Grandmama's we were *supposed* to — "Your grandmother runs
her house the way she wants. I run mine the way I want,"
our mother said firmly. "If you want a glass of milk, go ask
them for it in the kitchen. And drink it there." As children,
of course, we would have liked to reverse the rules, to have
been able to ring at home, not to have had to ring at Grandmama's. Something of this must have been going through
Corinne's mind because, when we came to the back stairs
which we were never supposed to use, she said, conspira-
torially, "You think we dare?"

"I dare ya. Double dare."

"You know why it was done, don't you?" She stood with
her hand on the newel post, her eyes laughing at first, but
then a kind of haze came over them.

"Oh, there might be people coming up or down with trays,
their hands full?"

"That, I guess. But do you know what I was told, Karl
Marx? Do you know what I heard with my own ears? 'You
must always show the most exact consideration . . .'"

"For the servants."

"Oh no, Karl. That was *your* mother. Think again."

"Don't tell me it was the lower orders. That I can't believe."

"Come again, Karlie-boy. I think maybe it's worse." She
looked at me and saw I couldn't get it, so she turned and
stomped the syllables out, one to each step, as she went up
the stairs: "FOR THOSE WHO ARE DE-PEND-ENT ON YOU. CHEE-
RIST. JE-SUS H. CHEE-RIST. JE-SUS. H." — and then she ran out
of steps.

Upstairs, a kind of numbing loneliness set in, for there
every room was associated with a distinct person, but even

Tom's room was no emptier to me than Walter's, and my own room in the east wing was just another kid's room as we went methodically from one to another. I looked out from my window, kneeling on the now padless seat. The apple tree that had bloomed popcorn was gone, and the landscape was strange with new roofs where once there had been woods. I must have been there longer than I realized, because Corinne asked me from the doorway, "You've had enough?"

"Oh, sure."

"Should I have let you come alone?"

I looked into Corinne's honest, inquiring, kindly eyes, and my heart gave a tremendous thump. "I don't know why everybody's always so goddamned *nice* to me. You, Tom, Edward, my own father. As if I were the only sensitive plant around. You know, don't you, that I know what has happened to you here?"

"Do you? Do you really?"

"The enormous, fantastic machinery of a place like this. Moral, emotional machinery. Not just physical."

We were back in the big upstairs hall that we called the lounge, and the May sun was pouring in through the skylights, washing back the shadows into radiant emptiness. The memories held back by the unconscious will because they really could not be used then and there flooded as tears to my eyes.

"You, Horatio, are our only chance. Report our cause aright. We're the shades that beg Ulysses for the cup of blood."

I started perceptibly. I had already written but Corinne had not seen "Mr. De Paolis and the Shades," which begins:

Of all the blood Ulysses shed
with his broad sword to clot the parched
and during dust of storied plain
or flow in dilute crimson through
those far refracting sky-impacted seas
where thought like restless dolphin
darts with gleaming back to breed,
he could not spare a little cup
for those poor shades who cried aloud
to feel again—remembered pain?

Those shades are at me now for life
and I am no Ulysses who
could stand upon the bourne of world
to shake a brine-encrusted beard
in high rebellion at the graveless dead,
but am suppliant myself
whose one day's stubble with due rite
is sacrificially removed
before a porcelain altar
by priest in Jockey shorts.

What was even more remarkable was that — again after I had written the lines — I had come upon the idea in a letter of Proust's. Here in the sunlit emptiness was the idea again from one of my own "characters."

"We're the eyes of Edward's cat. The eyes in the photographs. We can see you better than you see us. Our eyes are wide, wide open. There's no aesthetic distance. We don't even blink. But we're mute." The house had come crushing down on us both.

I stared at her, this fifty-year-old cousin-sister of mine in a tweed suit, and wanted her. I felt strong and sure and young in the wanting, and I put my arms around her, but there she became old, and I was old, for coming toward us up the stairs were two women I had never seen. It wasn't necessary that they had seen the embrace. You couldn't tell. They hadn't known that we would be there, and our lips had scarcely touched before I was aware of them and had broken away.

"Oh, Mrs. Patterson, I'm Sharon Ober, you remember?" In the reverse snobbery of the day, she was in blue jeans, loafers, a sweater and an unfinished Add-a-pearl necklace.

"Mrs. Ober? Certainly." Corinne was sure of herself, but I saw the appraisal in her eyes.

"I would like"— Mrs. Ober indicated the other woman, who was in city clothes complete with heels and gloves — "to present my husband's sister, Brenda Burns."

I thought, Christ, the woman's going to curtsy, but Corinne stepped forward, offering her hand as she had always been taught to do at Grandmama's — "You girls are at home here. When you're here, it's your house, and you must shake hands with guests, just as I do." I could remember Edith standing at thirty when even a younger man came into the room.

"How do you do, Mrs. Burns? This is my cousin. He and I have been having a last look around." Corinne, I thought, isn't sure. She didn't give them my name — that was characteristic enough — but any kind of explanation was totally out of character. I looked to the women to see if it was noticed, but I think they were still flustered at having been caught where they had no business and amazed at Corinne's exactly modulated courtesy.

"This was Mrs. Patterson's home, Brenda. I bet they have some tales to tell." The archness of this was so out of date, so remembered, as it were, from women of her mother's gen-

eration that I knew it sprang from embarrassment —
whether at having been caught themselves or at having
caught us, it was impossible to tell. "Did you come out here?"

"No. My grandmother did give a tea dance for me that
year, and I was married in the drawing room downstairs."

"What a fun thing." Mrs. Ober was back in her own generation now. "Brenda and I have just been decorating those
rooms in our mind's eye. We bet each other you used those
darling rooms to the west and scarcely ever went into the big
rooms at all."

This would have been too much for Corinne even had we
been caught in THE act, so she said, "I think if you knew us
you would find us essentially formal people."

"Oh, you can't say that, surely. I never knew anyone her
age so completely *fun* as Edith." She must have felt Corinne
bridle because she retreated to "your cousin, I mean, for
her years." Mrs. Ober was lost, but Corinne was merciless.

"Mrs. Atwater is coming for dinner tonight. I'll give her
your compliment."

"What I meant was, a fun grandmother is something rare."

"You see, you didn't know ours." Corinne's smile was her
social smile, interested, attentive, polite, the head at a
scarcely perceptible slant. "Mrs. Ober, Mrs. Burns —" There
was a nod to each, and each was looked squarely in the eyes.
Then, I swear to God, Corinne gathered her short, rump-
sprung tweed skirt in her hand as if it were trailing, sulphur
velvet and stepped by them to sweep with remembered
grace down the suddenly recarpeted, rebalustered stairs.

The Corinne who became Grandmama on those stairs
was, of course, the same Corinne who not half an hour before
had stomped with such violence up the back, just as the Corinne who lived in the gardener's cottage and had no room

in her life for the Sargent was the same Corinne who over the course of the years had spent $100,000 doing the cottage over. She laughed when I mentioned this to her and said, "The trick now, Thorstein, is *inconspicuous consumption*," and of course I knew she was right.

The two of us stood at the turn of the drive which would take the house from sight and looked back. It was awash with a vast emptiness that seemed to flow from the distant windows that by some trick of light had caught the blue lake where the white, returning breakers moved.

"No, it's not the House of Usher, Edgar Allan. There's no crack, no fissure. It will take the bulldozers, the iron ball swinging on a chain."

I got a poem out of the ball swinging on the chain, but I didn't get the rest of Edward, or as much as I ever was going to get, until five years later. It was just such a day, blue as heaven, but late in June, and Corinne was with us. She had let her hair go completely gray, but she had looked very elegant the night before at the dance we gave for our daughters and which was the reason she had stayed over. We had been very late at the party, and although it was noon no one else was down but the two of us. Bob Patterson, who was indeed a nice boy, had got very drunk and had had to be put to bed. This worried Corinne; when I reminded her of how much really heavy drinking we'd done at twenty, she countered with, "Aren't you afraid for the girls?"

"Oh, God, yes. I stay awake and all that. But how else do you grow up?"

"Well, I was a bitch, and I just don't want Bob to end up Tom Buchanan."

"He won't. Remember, he had to get into Princeton. And

stay there. Things are different now. It's no longer *droit du seigneur.*"

"I was pretty goddamned bright myself. It's no guarantee."

"Not at the moment, no. But in the long run, probably. Anyway, you're not so bad."

"Okay, professor."

"Are you going to mention it to him?"

"Should I?"

"I think the Tom Buchanan bit might be pretty good, but then I believe in Gatsby and art."

"What chance has Art — upper case — got when he'll have three million dollars next year and the rest when he's thirty?"

"That's been the problem all along, hasn't it? The history of America."

"The history of America is the history of us?"

"Well, that's what we were taught, and it's easy enough for us to look back and see it, but they teach them something different now, I'm sure."

"But what chance has the teacher got, what chance has even art got against that much cold cash? Doesn't art always lose? Look at Edward, the dinner in Milan. The very top of his profession, thinking that what he gave us back was so much more than we had ever given him."

We had taken coffee out into the yard and were sitting on deck chairs there when my father drove up. His hair still glinted red in the sunlight as he walked toward us, but I noticed with a pang that he took the walk instead of coming, his arms swaying happy arcs of balance, across the sloping, rolling lawn. He waved, though, and we waved

back. I was just about to call to him to bring himself a chair
when I remembered and went to get him one myself from
the stack in the garage. From the distance I saw him lean
over and kiss Corinne, but by the time I got back he was sitting on my chair, leaning forward, his fingers pressed together.

"Tom's been on the phone, and Edward Sciarrha's dead in
Pasadena." I knew right away that he had already told Corinne, because they both looked at me as if there were some
understanding between the two of them.

"We were just this minute talking about him. What was
it?"

"Stroke, Tom said. Magda Feuer was with him." Magda
Feuer had always sung *Lohengrin* with him in this country,
and it was because of her that he had left Mexico City a few
years back and gone to live in Pasadena, where they rented
from my Uncle Harry's estate the beautiful, towered Italian
villa with its spectacular view of the thickly lighted canyons
and hills. "Fiesole, bébé. Montmartre. The third act of
Louise," Edward had said the year before when we were
there and were sitting on the huge, arcaded porch that was
the top of the tower. There was a big colony of singers and
musicians around, people you would have thought dead
years ago, and while we were there Edward and Magda had
had a big party for them after the performance of *Rosen-
kavalier* in the Shrine Auditorium the night the *Staatsoper*
had been reopened in Vienna. Magda, who had done the
coaching on the opera, had been asked to read the congratu-
latory telegram to the audience from the stage during the
little ceremony between the second and third acts. Edward
was worried that she might not be able to negotiate the long
walk from the wings to the center of the enormous stage; she

was badly crippled with arthritis, and in a short skirt her legs were now monstrous. There was some business with microphones and a movie "personality" who did the introduction, but the moment she appeared, far at the left, the stage was hers. You knew what was really meant by *personality*. This woman whose half-Jewish grandmother had kept her from Hitler's Reich for all of her greatest years read the telegram, which was gracefully phrased, in English, and then, although it had not been planned, spoke it quietly in German with the tears of the world in her voice and with all the vast forgiveness of her artist's heart. Even my daughters, to whom it meant little that Magda had first sung at Vienna under Mahler and to whom the rubbled horror of the war was only something on the Late Show, recognized it as purest poetry and to my great joy said so. To me it was more than "when the lights go on again all over the world," because I had seen the desolation of Germany twice — once with terror in my own eyes and again a few years later when Magda, before I knew her, had transformed the intense and beautifully realized but essentially nineteenth-century and personal lyricism of the *Winterreise* to general heartbreak with the last song, "Der Leiermann." She sang it with a numbed perfection beyond sadness, as if the flames of loving hopelessly had gutted it even of sorrow. Hideously, only form was left in a formless world to give, as the angry, the beat have not realized, the final turn of the screw: Edward and my grandmother hearing together Alta in the madhouse and his "your grandmother had it too, for soon after that we were lovers." I have a poem, "Antiphon," which I hope does this, but here I am going to give you the Müller poem that Schubert used. The song is about the poet, the composer, who sees the insane organ grinder, barefoot on the ice, poor, with an empty cup. No one hears him, no one sees him, and dogs dog his heels. Meanwhile, the hurdy-gurdy plays mechanically under his numbed fingers, and the old man is asked if he will use the organ for the songs the questioner has written from his heart. Well, in 1946 I looked out on the leveled desolation of Hamburg and some-how, somewhere, impossibly with spring, a barrel organ was playing "Der Lindenbaum." When Magda sang, I saw it, smelled it, felt it grit between my fingers, tasted the eddying dust. Ten lines, fifty bars of music *etwas langsam.* Here it is. Even if you can't read German, even if you don't remember the music, I think you ought to try it:

> Drüben hinterm dorfe steht ein Leiermann,
> Und mit starren Fingern dreht er, was er kann.
> Barfuss auf dem Eise wankt er hin und her,
> Und sein kleiner Teller bleibt ihm immer leer.
>
> Keiner mag ihn hören, keiner sieht ihn an,
> Und die Hunde knurren um den alten Mann.
> Und er lässt es gehen alles, wie es will,
> Dreht, und seine Leier steht ihm nimmer still.
>
> Wunderlicher Alter, soll ich mit dir gehn?
> Willst zu meinen Liedern deine Leier drehn?

This was a personal memory, of course, but, except for the young, every memory there must have flooded with the old griefs of those terrible years and at the same time been brought to peace by the gorgeous faith in Magda's spoken voice. The Jewish producer, who was sitting on the other side of Edward, lifted his Viennese wife's hand to his lips and kissed it. The cast lined up behind Magda were in tears of shining hope, and the movie personality with his "beloved Madame Feuers," unused to such thorough upstaging, had completely disappeared. Magda, laughing about it on our way home, said, "It wasn't fair. Even though it was Los Angeles, I was on my home grounds and he didn't know it. Apart from a dozen or so starlets, everyone knew much more precisely who I was than knew him."

After Magda had finished, there were the national anthems with us all standing, but, before the applause could break, Magda moved backward to the line of the cast and, ignoring the place the Marschallin and Octavian naturally made for her, slipped in on the far side of Baron Ochs, leaving the center of the stage picture for the actual performers. The courtesy of this was so exquisite, so exactly the sort of thing that would have sent my grandmother into ecstasies, that a tiny thrill of aesthetic pleasure crept up my spine. There was no humility in the action. The gesture was one of simple, comprehending justice, eloquent with the belief of seventy-odd and wise years that the rights of man were the high concern of art. The party Edward and Magda gave after the performance was a larger if less poignant indication of the same spirit, for even though Edward warned us that it would be "the fifth act of *Götterdämmerung*, bébé, your Victor ad in shrouds," the party was given out of the goodness of their hearts. The producer had invited them both to the party he was giving for the actual cast, but they had gathered together all the strays and would not hear to any of the young performers neglecting the movie producer in their favor. I heard Magda on the phone: "A mistaken kindness. Without you we will seem brilliant to ourselves. I intend to be Madame Verdurin become the Princess de Guermantes. Ar-

mand, like Charlus, can call the sonorous roll of the sonorous
dead, and no one will mind. Indeed, we will congratulate
each other on having remained alive."

Oh, it was good that Edward had Magda at the last, for
the Magdas of the musical world are few. Prima donnas in
their prime, however sumptuous their voices, are not generally women of intellect or even articulate musical understanding. What they do, they are more apt to do intuitively,
and when their voices are gone and they have become the
final wives of their final, businessmen husbands, even their
raffish ebullience disappears in what Edward called "the last
throes of refinement." There is nothing left of them except
the evening gowns of their concertizing days and the diamond brooch the box holders gave them upon their re-
tirement. In addition to the brooch, a one-time famous
Carmen was wearing her Yale '08 chairman-of-the-board husband's fraternity pin, and the possessor of one of the most
gorgeous voices I have ever heard, who once had to be for-
cibly restrained by a frantic stage manager from appearing
from the depths of the well in Respighi's *Sunken Bell* loaded
with the five dozen gardenias that her banana merchant
sweetie had sent her before the performance, spent all her
time showing me the gold charm-bracelet disks that clattered
with the names and birthdates of her husband's great-grandchildren. With Magda it was different, and even my older
daughter saw this, for she said, "Magda Feuer means Magda
Fire, doesn't it, Daddy?"

I said, "It sure does, honey." I was glad they had one another, and I was enormously touched when I noticed that
Edward and she spoke her soft Austrian German together. I
could remember how Edward had hated learning it when
we were kids and how he could send us into giggling fits so

fierce that we had to clutch ourselves to keep from wetting our pants by exaggerating the northern gutturals, gathering them in the back of his throat and spitting them out as if they were I-thought-it-was-an-oyster-but-I-guess-it's-snot.

I have told you all this partly because it raced through my mind when Papa said that Magda was with him when he died, and partly because it explains what I said next. The day we left, Edward and Magda came to the car in the drive, and after we were all packed and in, the engine already running, he looked at me quizzically, his head tilted to one side as if to avoid the sun that glanced from the tower. I saw his lungs fill with a singer's breath, the eyes become brighter, and then he put his head and shoulders through my window to leave a stubbled kiss on my cheek.

"Ah, Housman, that was stupid stuff, that dying while the laurel's green" were the last words I heard him speak, and I spoke them again to Papa, who was himself to die that year, and to Corinne, my fingertips against the left cheek his happy mouth had kissed that day. We sat there, the three of us, after I spoke, in quietness. The day was incomparably beautiful — "Oh what is so rare as a day in June," as Papa was always quoting — and the white, northern climbing roses and the blaze of red moved along my brick wall with little breezes that didn't touch us in the hollow where we sat with the bluish shadows of the dark chestnut rising above us, the still leafing maples limp with thin green tatters of springtime silk. Papa was the first to speak, and he cleared his throat as if apologizing for breaking the stillness, for intruding on our private memories of Edward.

"*In fernem Land.* I suppose it will be Forest Lawn, or Hills, or whatever. That place with the Wee Kirk o' the Heather and the replica of David."

"You know, there it's nude and disgusting, not naked and real like it is in Florence with people sprawled about it, reading newspapers, carrying briefcases," he had said years ago when he had first seen it, and now for some reason I heard the rest of it. "When I was a kid — the first time I was in Florence, it must have been — I remember my father boosting me up and putting my whole foot on his toenail. It wasn't any bigger, so I must have been very small. I remember looking up, too, to those" — he remembered Corinne and changed what he would have said to me — "that marble nakedness. I'm told that what I said was, 'He's very big even for a big boy.' I remember the guide showing us the blue vein in the marble at the back of his wrist, and looking at the blue vein in the back of my wrist for the rest of the day. Anything anatomical always fascinated me. I was thinking though of Edward in that place where even David looks vulgar. He came a long way. A long way from the Tuscan hills."

Corinne gave no indication of having heard what Papa said, but just lay back in the deck chair, her head tilted toward the sky. Her arms lay along the sides of the chair, and the thumb of her left hand kept turning around her wedding ring. When she did speak there was an odd timbre to her voice that at first I could not identify. It had nothing to do with what she said; indeed it was wildly inappropriate, because I soon placed it as the flat, toneless chipper of the society voice of the twenties. It was a voice she hadn't used for thirty years, and I'm sure she didn't use it consciously now. It was the voice of her mother that had somehow come back to her.

"The olives rot on the brown hills of California, too. Black purple. Black purple bruised. Disgusting rot. And they have to be shoveled up and carted away in bleeding bushel baskets. With my mother once — oh, I was ten — I ate one. A great believer in the empirical method, she. Not an olive at all. Nothing like. Soap and death. Greasy death."

Bertolt Brecht, you see, not *No, No Nanette*, but the twenties just the same. Zelda Fitzgerald in the sanitarium. The violation of love. My every nerve, every nerve of me — it would be better if I could use the Elizabethan "every my nerve" — was laid open and quick as if Papa with a scalpel had folded back the flesh and flooding wads of gauze dammed the blood. I had never heard Corinne talk like that. None of us ever talked like that at all. Had I constructed an interior monologue for her — and that's what this surely was, for she kept looking toward the sky, fiddling with the ring as if we weren't there — I could never have caught the rhythm, the syntax, the observation, the puritan horror. I started toward her, but my father stopped me with the peremptory gesture of authority that I remembered from his youth — the hand jerked out, the fingers spread at the end of the slanting forearm while the upper arm was held stiffly to the suddenly rigid body. When he spoke it was softly, his voice full of love.

"It's all right, Corinne. It's all right. I'd tell you if it weren't. You've known that, you've always known that, haven't you?" She rolled her head slowly back and forth against the fabric of the deck chair. "It's a long time ago. A long time."

Of course I thought they were talking about Grandmama, and yet I knew they couldn't be. Corinne and I had spoken of it so often that it couldn't be that. She let her head fall forward, and not looking at either of us said, "Tell him, Uncle Doc. We were just talking about being twenty. Tell the goddamned noticer." There was a tiny giggle. Pure ex-Aunt Louise. I looked to my father and knew before he spoke.

"What Corinne means is that Edward was once her lover. It was a very short time. But it was." My father's voice was deep with embarrassment.

"Tell him when. I want to get this over and I don't want any of his" — she snorted — "indirect questions. I just don't want to cope."

"It was that time in Milan."

"But how could —"

"It was about a month. Corinne was supposed to go to Louise at Cannes when we left for Greece the next day."

I remembered that this was right. "But we took her to the train." The whistle now shrilling to pierce my ear, I couldn't be mistaken. "The brown seal coat. The porters with straps shoving the bags through the carriage window. The steam rolling along the floor of the train shed to be turned back by the walls. All of us waving and you waving. Mother saying, 'I don't like letting her go off like that alone.'"

"You could remember that all right. I had a brown seal coat. The porters always had straps and shoved bags through the carriage windows. And steam has rolled along the floors of sheds ever since Monet, ever since Garbo in *Anna Karenina*." Corinne looked from me to Papa and went on. "You see. It's the detail he wants. The goddamned detail. Right this very minute, he's writing, you know. It's what I can't stand. It's one thing to come to terms with it myself, but to watch him struggle you'd have to have the eyes of Edward's cat." She turned back to me. "It wasn't like that. Your train left an hour before the one I was supposed to take. I never took it. Edward and I saw you off, snooper, and we went to the station hotel. For a description of that sylvan glade, see E. Hemingway, *A Farewell to Arms*. Talk about the shock of recognition when I read that two, three years later."

"Really?"

"Really." Corinne put the coffee cup on the lawn with elaborate care, but as she straightened up, her eyes caught mine which I had cast down — I suppose to hide the surmise I could feel burning there.

"There I was deflowered. You want the bloody sheets? I give them to you with all my heart. And valets, not chambermaids, made up those rooms, in case you want to know. There I stayed for three weeks. Telegrams to my mother signed 'Doc.'" She looked to him tenderly. For all his fascination with the anatomical, the sheets would have hurt him.

"That part of it, honey, I always forgave." He looked at her as if she were still twenty.

"I'd keep telling myself that it was romantic and" — she hesitated — "free, for that was the word then. But it wasn't much fun. I found out what I wanted to find out, but when I went to hear him sing it wasn't in my beautiful white coat and your mother's diamonds in a box, but in my brown seal way on the side of the orchestra. Even Christmas Day, we didn't dare one of the big restaurants, and God how I wanted you all and laughing. All my presents had been sent to Cannes for me, and all I had was the little gold cupid with tiny sapphire eyes that he was so proud of giving me and which I ought to have loved but didn't. Remind me, I ought to give it to one of your girls, if you don't mind the wages of sin. I don't think I ever had any thought that we'd keep it up, and if I'm going to be fair I have to say

that there was always 'the exact consideration for those who
—'" She couldn't speak the words, "were dependent on me,"
but indicated them with a wave of the hand in a gesture once
common with her but which I hadn't seen in years. Tenors
were tenors, no matter how distinguished, and Corinne
could not have learned in what was left of the long-ago December that the descendants of robber barons were inferior
by every rule of life and art except the one rule in which
they were bred. For the first time since my father had
brought the news, I felt sad for Edward. Not the Edward
who had died old, but the Edward in Milan where he must
have arrived at the "Maybe that's why she's fond of him.
Because he doesn't need her."

My father half rose as if to stop Corinne from going any
further, but she kept on. "No, Edward's dead now. He's got
the right to whatever life you can give him. That was good,
that Ah, Housman bit. That was me, of course, and his
remembering me." There was a sharp quiver of her hand,
but she went on. "Edward and Magda. The greatest
Marschallin of them all because she didn't have to bother
about being real."

She looked to my father, who said, "After the first, I never
minded. When the first war was over, it was just one of the
things I came back to. I never put it into words before, but
I'm pretty sure she loved Papa — my papa — while he was
alive, and she was good to him when he was blind. Afterward — well, if you're not young when you're young, I think
you've got a right to be young sometime. At least that's the
way I hope, I still keep hoping, it was." The two of us put
out our hands to him at the same time, and he pressed them
together between his own. "Mama never knew about Corinne.

Your mother doesn't know, either. No one knew except me and now you."

He was still holding our hands, leaning forward to do so, when Corinne said quietly, "He'll want to know how I got caught, Uncle Doc."

"Same way everybody gets caught." He snorted. It was the sort of thing he loved about life, but he spread his hands, letting ours fall, and lay back in the chair.

It was Corinne who spoke. "I was pregnant, and I knew it soon after we got back to Paris. I tried to get money out of you. You had sixty bucks of Christmas loot, but you were hoarding it to spend at the Folies."

My father began to laugh. "Never knew that. Wonder we didn't run into each other, bud."

"Don't begin that. I want to get this over with. No loose ends. No questions ever. Understand?"

"Sure, Corinne, sure."

"I did get Gordie's money, and I had a couple of hundred of my own. But it wasn't money. It never really was money. I just got scared and lonely, and I went to your dad. He wasn't even shocked."

"I was. I was shocked to hell. But what good would that do? I just thought, 'if she trusts me so much, I'd better be worth the trusting.'"

"Oh, Doc. You were always worth the trusting, and you didn't act shocked." Corinne was quiet a minute and Papa knew and I knew just how much she had said. But then she turned to me and went on: "He set it up for a friend of his in Metz. A doctor he had known during the war."

"But I always intended to do it myself. I just had to have a place. The next time I was supposed to go to London,

Corinne went with me, and we went to Metz instead. I must say, I haven't been back since. I'm sure no one there believed us and that they all thought me damned lucky." He was grunting these things out, keeping, I could see, a close watch on Corinne. "You sent me a postcard from there once. House Rimbaud lived in or something. Wondered if you knew, could have known, from Edward. Still have the card under the glass on top of the desk in my office. Never heard of Rimbaud in 1928–29 — '29 by then. Certainly no plaque on a house. Flower clock in the park."

"Edward never said anything." I thought they both should know, and, although I wished he had told me, I was proud of him in a way.

"You know, I think that was the trouble." Corinne was serious. "He tried so hard to be a gent." My heart gave a thump. I loved Corinne, and I didn't want her to say anything. I thought, I can keep her if she'll let me write the words for her, but, once she's spoken, it'll be too late. Somewhere in *Tender Is the Night*, Baby Warren says of Dick Diver something like this, "Let him do it. Why shouldn't he? That's what we educated him for." After that I put her permanently in the lowest circle of hell, and I knew — I suppose for the first time — what the lowest circle was for. Baby Warren's sin is a sin of the heart, not just a sin of manner, and I didn't want Corinne to be guilty because with her guilt I would myself be somehow involved. I didn't at all like the sound of "He tried so hard to be a gent." It had the glitter of high cruelty about it, and only when I put it against what she had said of Magda — "The greatest Marschallin of them all because she didn't have to bother about being real" — could I begin to forgive her. A great wave of sorrow came

over me then, and for the moment I lived the deep loneliness of the svelte Corinne in the station hotel.

She must have been looking at me or have sensed in some
way what was going through my mind, for again in her
twenties voice she said, "I never told you this — not, I think
from modesty or shame, but because I couldn't be sure.
Couldn't be sure you wouldn't turn it into some John
O'Hara or Tennessee Williams crap." She looked at me, the
appraising eyes. "Or old Hank James. Keep your damned
omniscience to yourself. What I've said, I've said, and that's
all right. What happened, happened. Okay. But none of
your odorously imagined scenes. I am what I am, and I
don't want to be created. I don't —"

"Here are the kids," my father interrupted, and waved
over his head to Bob, who had a girl by each hand and began to race down the slope to where we were. His legs were
longer than theirs and the giant strides he took were too
much for them, but they were laughing, jerked by one arm,
the free arm flying high behind them. The girls stumbled
just before they reached us, but he dragged them the rest of
the way and pulled them together in a heap in front of us,
saying, "Any ol' white slaves for say-ul. Any ol' white slaves
for say-ul?" He stood above them in laughter, his faded-
blue polo shirt — we had called them necking shirts — moving with his breath, the jersey band tight and high around
the surprising muscles of his upper arms. My eyes went to
his feet — he was barefoot and in madras bermudas — and I
thought of my father and David's toenail. The girls had ex-
tricated themselves from their tumble and stood beside him,
each with a negligent arm hooked to his shoulder in angular
grace, their hair so shiny, their eyes alive with light, their

perfectly cut lips moist and parted with the gladness of the day. They too were in bermudas, but with shirts of mine, the tails looped loose beneath their waists that Bob's enormous David's hands had risen to define. It was a handsome sight, a beautiful sight really in the sun of June, and it crossed my mind that it would be the new century nearly before they, like us, sat in deck chairs in the hollow to look upon the flesh of their now beautiful flesh, the bone of their deep-marrowed bone. A hundred years would separate them from Edward, who once burned a shepherd's fire against the chill of Tuscan dawns from twisted forks of olive wood. The flowers of spring that Edward had not seen when he had sung his boy-sweet song were gone forever now from all but palace walls, for the hills themselves were lighted day and night with the fantastic, gassy blooms of factory fires.

My father, I think, noticed how Bob's spread thumb caught the oxford cloth of Amy's shirt to outline her breast, because he said, "Isn't the old man going to get a kiss —" and both the girls slipped away to make over him with exaggerated embraces.

"Poor old Papa" — they called him *Papa,* which left only *Daddy* for me, and often I felt a pang about it — "doesn't he know we have this thing for older men!"

"Not old. Mature."

"Devastating maturity. So sexy."

"Positively Chinese, the veneration."

"So it's not good for us to have you encourage what we fight all the time."

I could see Papa becoming restive under the barrage, and I was thinking of some way to stop it, but they themselves were sensitive to how far they could go. Amy slipped to his feet and sat there, leaning against his knees. "Little" Corinne, my older daughter, came over to me and sprawled upon the grass, looking up to Bob who stood now, feet apart, hands on his hip bones. Was it Tom Buchanan's "cruel" body? Was there such a thing as a cruel body? That bodies became cruel, I knew. And that they were cruel to you, too, I also knew. Was there something beyond the arrogance of beautiful twenty there on the green lawn? Did the three million dollars next year and the rest when he was thirty inform his blood? He had become rich early, the only son of an only son who lay beneath the Coral Sea. It wasn't the mere appurtenances of money that he would have — we all had these — but the golden power itelf. His grandfather, old Mr. Patterson, had literally shriveled away, but hadn't that been because he had never realized the aesthetic possibilities of power? There was a little click in my head as I phrased this. I thought, "Aha, Edward's error has trapped me." There are no "aesthetic possibilities" to power. He had supposed there were, and outside, looking in, it seemed as if there should be. I couldn't be poor, he had told me, because I could not imagine myself poor and would always cling to the idea that there were aesthetic possibilities in poverty. Well, even on my Uncle Harry's tower porch of arcaded marble, he had never once felt the loneliness of possession. He didn't, as Corinne said of Magda, have to bother with being real. The reality was outside of himself. Look at the way he denied his son, who called himself George Shearer, as if the stubbed pen had never scratched the spluttered S-c-i-a-r-r-h-a in thick official ink on the immigration form in the basement light of the Customs House in New Orleans — as if the twelve-year-old tears had never been wept. "George Shearer Associates," the sign said on the real estate office in Los Angeles and on signboards — To Let, For Sale — all over

Southern California. Edward was perfectly capable of quoting "Mignonslied":

> Kennst du das Land? wo die Citronen blühn,
> In dunkeln Laub die Gold-Orangen glühn

to me on the dusk of the porch with the half-dozen orange trees of the garden rich beneath us, while not two miles away the bulldozers were uprooting a grove once fair with blossoms, heavy with scent, globed with fruit, glossy leaved. It would never have occurred to Edward to feel even an ironic responsibility for the billboard which said "SHANGRI-LA, A New SHEARER Development. Live Modern. Live Shearer." He had never felt within himself the scalding need to imagine his own son.

My own hand went then, compulsively I suppose, to my daughter's, my darling Corey's, hair, and I pulled the scalp together with my feeling fingers that remembered so well the soft spot and how they would touch it with a fuzzy sense of miracle just after she was born. In and out my fingers moved now, flexing, relaxing, pulling, releasing. She looked to me with thankfulness and said, "I'm utterly purring," but then her gaze went back to the bermuda'd David.

"There be none of Beauty's daughters," began within my mind, and the fingers reflexively took up the beat in much the same way as when we were children Corinne would play the soundless pianos of our skinny spines, demanding that we tell her — from the fingering, the trills, the thump of the bass — which of her pieces it was.

" 'Turkish March'?"

"Nope, dope."

"Beethoven? Mozart? At least that much?"

"That's Beethoven." There'd be a wild arpeggio running

up a back. A spate of triplets might be Mozart. "But it's
not the 'Turkish March.'"

The kneading, needing fingers hardly seemed a part of me
at all, but I was heavily conscious of a constriction in my
heart and another rhythm alive there, beating in my chest,
throbbing in my arm, beneath my wrist, quivering in the
moisting palm of my hand. I felt it clot with tiny pain in my
elbow as if protesting the physical return to the heart of the
rhythm the fingers had denied. In a minute, I'd know, but
I couldn't know yet. I let my fingers go limp in the sun-
warm tangles of hair.

"More, Daddy, more."

Slowly, with silky insistence, the fingers coiled and then
began "Sen-T-imen-T-al Jour-ney." Oh, neoned Navy town
in war when juke-box trio whined the song through beaver
board of sad motel with slimy shower floor! Not even
"motel," then, my elegant elder daughter. El Dixie Cabins
Bar and Grille. It was there your mother and I went hot to
your begetting. Our veins poured sweat in noisy heat of
Florida that mid-July beneath the dusty rattle of a land-
blown wind in parching palms. Terror-sweet those nights
when each might be the last of all the nights forever in a
world my bride made bright with arms, soft-curious hands,
eyes, smiles, and slumberous depths of newly wakened voice.

SenT-imenT-al Jour-ney. With the increase of tempo in
my fingers, the secondary syncopation disappeared, and I
was back at El Dixie the night the drunken tires shrieked in
skid on gravel. Neon expired with the dawn and on the
chance that the high winds among the palms might now be
blowing crouched along the ground toward the sea, I took
the long, naked step toward the window to raise the shade
and let the dewed air in. I stood there while it had its soft

way with me — the *triste* of "Dover Beach," I suppose —
but I was young and it wasn't very long. On my way to the
window, I had had to shrink back from the chair that held
my Navy white dress jacket on its low back, but, to return,
I rose on the ball of my left foot, raised my right thigh, and
swung my muscled leg in an arc over the back of the chair.
Whether it was this unremembered attitude of body, the
rippling play of fresh-found muscles, the freeing amplitude
of stretch in arc, or the fact that I was touched — stroked —
from beneath by the braided epaulet of the coat in the descent of my leg, I don't suppose matters. I was as far on my
way as if I had been continent a month by the time I reached
the still moist heaven of the bed.

It was then the tires shrieked, the gravel ground, and headlights swept the room and bed from darkness. There was a
wild, woman's, drunken whoop from the car.

"Ride her, caowboy."

I dared not move. My own nakedness was the only possible shield for the bride who lay beneath me.

"Honk the horn. Gyoddamn it I wiul honk it." He evidently kept her from it because she began a tattoo on the
echoing side of the car with a bottle. There was a brief
struggle and the bottle broke. For a second he got the headlights out, and before she could get them on again I, pendu-
lous, was able to get the sheet from the wad at our feet
to cover us. Even our heads we covered.

"Come on, Darlene. The show's over. We'll get our own
show on the road." The headlights were gone.

Both of the car doors lurched open, and she scooped up
some gravel and threw it at our screen before he got hold of
her. As he pulled her along her nails clawed the rusty wire

mesh, and she bawled in ghastly Southern, "Hah hoe the day-re-oh, the fahmer's in the dale."

My fingers were released from "Sentimental Journey," and Corey gave a contented shake of her head as I withdrew my hand. They had begun talking about Edward, and Papa was telling them, but I still had the last of the memory to deal with. Over the years the part I've told you so far became curiously tender and uniting to us. We'd laugh and grimace "Our Song" when the orchestra'd play "Sentimental Journey" at a dance, and once we had gone upstairs for a while in the middle of a children's party — say the girls were five and six and I had got home early to see it — so ironically sweet was the sight of "Farmer in the Dell." The part I tell you now I have never managed to mention, even to Mary. It is the last modesty between us, and it never really became a part of the shared memories of El Dixie. If I had mentioned it, I suppose it would have, or if she had picked it up I know I would have gone along. But neither of us ever did, and this in itself is significant. It only takes a moment to tell, although it has lasted all these years.

Twenty minutes, a half hour later we were lying there, the cracked shade pulled again, the heavy sheet thrown back. She had wept for a time with rage, and then it had been just weeping, but now she was quiet, although the sleep of exhaustion had not come. I had comforted her and become weak with love when I realized that in her letting me comfort her she had sought to comfort me, but I don't think either of us had made any attempt in our minds to think about what had happened. What had happened, had happened. That was all. I have never been even tempted to construct interior monologues for us. The fumes of Citronella, the Mark Cross honeymoon luggage, the sand-worn Congoleum rug, the Betty Grable decal along the edge of the dresser mirror — I have the period props for all this, but somehow they make no difference. They aren't a part of it. If they had been I would have planted them awhile back without knowing it really, and they would be here now. But all there was, all there is, is a voice and the words it spoke.

The voice was the voice of the man from the car who had dragged the screaming Southern bitch from our window. He had returned to the car for something, but on his way back to their cabin he stopped, a shadow on the shade, for the sudden sun had risen behind him with morning. In the moment he stood there, he spoke, spoke with such resonance that the high absurdity of the situation became something more than comic. For all our never having spoken of him, I know Mary heard him too. Her little, rich-girl's hand, cupped loose in mine, trembled in reverberation. We were lesser mortals than he if afterward all we could bear to remember aloud had to wear the mask of comedy, for "How hairy assed, the gold-braid lies" was what the voice said — clearly, distinctly, incredibly in the accents of verse. Slowly, silently, for all these years, we have let it lick away at our lollypop hearts.

It is not easy for me to write because writing, Edward taught me, meant turning myself out of house, home, skin. Having written, I tremble naked waiting for the reader to breathe — Edward's lungs, I need — my words for me. That mirror-up-to-nature business won't do, and, although I have experimented with nut-house mirrors wildly skewed, the most they achieve is a single point. Henry James's figure-in-the-carpet might serve, except that in examining the figure or any one of the figures, or even the happiest conjunction of one with another, the shimmer of life, continuing life that gives the carpet sheen, is gone. Narration, like history, cannot be imprisoned except conventionally within an arbitrary beginning, middle, and end. When it is, it is no longer felt, warmed by the curious heart's blood, but merely perceived by a single, Cyclops eye. I was thankful as I sat there that day in June that I heard Amy say when they were talking of Edward's death, "Rudolf Bing will send an orchid wreath. And Magda, I think, sad-foolish flower swan. White rosebuds. Greenish. Wired stiff."

It might have been I who spoke, but just as clear to me was the counterpoint of Edward's treble voice soaring in a Tuscany I knew was gone. A third voice entered then, the voice of the man in the car. It came back now under the chestnut blue with shadows — a bass, if I were telling the story to Edward, as indeed I am — the voice of the ghost of the Commendatore, the Statue come to dine with the unrepentant Don.

ENTER
ON
A
MONUMENT

ENTER ON A MONUMENT

I KNEW from the very beginning that it was a dream. An important dream, a dream that would recur, but a dream. In real life, life itself immediately dilutes its own fundamental reality, but in dreams this doesn't happen. Oh, the incident fades away, is dissolved in some nonnarrative sequence, but for all its dissolution, it is still there ready to be dreamed again as sharply, as poignantly as before, to recur with the exactness that drowsy children washed sweet with sleep insist upon when numbed by the ritual drone of a bedtime story. Leave out an adjective, call the "little prince" but "the prince," and some heightened awareness close within the closing flower will cause them to call out, "The *little* prince. You skipped." A dream can happen — at least it has with me — as an un-dream, too, because it becomes a permanent part of the consciousness undiluted by the necessity of answering the phone, of making arrangements for the funeral, choosing a necktie, controlling the shame-darkened voice, of going immediately forward to a lived future. In a dream such as the one I am going to tell about, the dreamer is freed from space and time, and the dream itself has no grammar, its verbs no tense.

In the dream I drive up in a cab to our house, my father's

house, where I lived until I was married. It is a big house, but it looks even bigger blazing with lights in the wintry dark. For some reason, I say, "In my Father's house there are many mansions," as I lean forward to pay the driver, who does not think this strange. When I look up, I see that it has begun to snow, the snow of the Christmas parties of my youth. Fitzgerald's St. Paul snow, not his Paris snow — large, wet, clinging flakes whose methodical geometry can be seen with the naked eye as they drift glistening through the bluish path the headlights make in front of us there in the December dark. A long tunnel of green canvas with a red carpet has been stretched from our front door to the curb that still has its carriage block with "Scott" cut into it as a tombstone. There is even a chauffeur posted there to open car doors. I recognize him as Joe Patera, which never was his last name, but as children we gave other people's servants the last name of the family they worked for, and while it would have astonished us to hear our own William called Bill Scott, so indeed he must have been to everyone except the people in our house. The Pateras called Joe "Joseph." The Scotts called William "William." But it is Joe who is opening car doors in the dream, and when he first appeared I hadn't seen or thought of him in many years. He was little — almost a dwarf — and he had a hunched back, the only hunchback I have ever seen from day to day over any period of time. I can see him now, a lemur, high on the open front seat of the Pateras' bottle-green and brass Pierce-Arrow limousine even though his final reality must be not only now but forever at the tombstone end of an awning, opening the doors (at this date Grandmama, Papa, Mother — all would have said "the doors of motors") of cars arriving for a party — a service I am sure he never performed for us.

The carriage block — it, like Joe, had disappeared by the time I was six or seven — is not too high for the taxi in which I arrive, and this disturbs me. My twenty-year-old limbs — for I am that age in the cab — carry within them the leggy memory of having to step up from the running boards of Marmons, Packards, even high Locomobiles. I am amazed to step level with the block and look back at the cab. Gold letters, cursive, curled on the black side, say "A. Zeller." At the very first there were Zeller cabs, then F.O.B. (Friar, Olsen, and Banholzer we were proud of knowing — "Guess what F.O.B. means! Just guess once! Please just guess") and finally plain Yellows and Checkers. But Checkers were never quite respectable, and if we were sent up to the Boulevard to hail one, we were always told, "Not a Checker." A. Zeller must have vanished before I was in first grade, but my legs remembered, my dream legs recalled that his running boards were level with our block. I don't suppose I could have been in a cab even a half-dozen times before that. Joe speaks to me and I speak to him.

"Big party tonight, Joe?"

"Miss Constance. She sure is a beautiful young lady."

Constance was my Uncle Fred's — my oldest uncle's — daughter and I never had any memory of her at all. There was just what people had said to go on. At sixteen she had gone out in the afternoon, had her hair done — odd in itself because in those days hairdressers came to the house — come home, and put on her first evening dress. She had arranged herself then on her mother's and father's bed and cut her throat. Ophelia was always Constance to me, although there was no hint of a love affair and no one ever assigned any reason for her action. Her story didn't enter into the consciousness of the dream, and so it doesn't seem strange that we are giving an elaborate party for a girl who, had she lived, would be almost old enough to be my mother. Remembering the dream, though, I can feel my feet cold on the carriage-block tombstone as I look toward the front-door end of the awning tunnel. Outside the snow is heavier now and is beginning to pack.

Long after the dream, the dream itself came back — rehappened in life, if you want to say it that way. My Uncle Fred and Aunt Maud outlived four of their five children, and at the end of the forties, Fred was buried on the day my cousin Corinne and I noticed for the first time that the winding roads of the cemetery had been marked with arrows "One Way." "More arrows for Sebastian," one of us said, for he was a character we had instinctively despised from the moment we came across him in an art book. It was late in May, a muggy afternoon, and there had been violent thunder showers all morning, so the undertakers had set up a large marquee across the graves and provided a green awning with a carpet from the road up the hill to the flattened top of the knoll where the robber baron's marble obelisk rises above the black slabs that memorialize his descendants. Pete, my cousin Pete, exploded high in the air and his bones even then were whitening shards in a Burmese jungle. Harrison lies beneath the icy waters of the Murmansk run, iron-locked forever behind a bolt compartment door. But they have their slabs, polished, deep-cut with their names, the stated limits of their little time.

I don't think I remembered the dream as we stood for the graveside service, for I remember smiling when the minister said, "In my Father's house there are many mansions," and my brother Gordie whispering, "It's a good thing. Fred's counting on that." My father must have heard Gordie because he said as we stood around afterward, "No, Fred certainly wasn't the ranch-type type. Or even split-level." We stood about afterward for a few minutes because at "ashes to ashes, dust to dust," the heavens opened and thunder rolled over us in great grinding rushes so loud that the minister's final words were lost and the last of the service was pantomimed in the dark like a flickering silent movie. When it was over, his robes billowing crazily about him, he walked across to my Aunt Maud, old, tiny, cowering in her remaining Benjie's huge black arm, and we all waited to see what she wanted to do — go toward the cars in the downpour or wait under the marquee. Slowly she turned, still with Benjie's arm about her, and they walked down the hemp carpet stretched beneath the awning tunnel. We were right behind them when they got to the car, and I saw her take off her furs and hand them to Benjie. My eyes met hers then, and their lost loneliness was so fierce, so overpowering that I had to look away. A great fork of lightning clawed the split sky, and a gust of wind sucked the rain under the awning that strained and flapped heavily against its guy ropes. Everyone — even Maud herself — looked back to make sure that the big bellowing marquee had withstood the onslaught. I saw the shoulders of her black silk suit were wet, and because I was still avoiding her eyes, I noticed that the diamond pin she wore on her lapel was bright with water. It was a snowflake.

We got into the cars just as they drove up after that. The weather made it impossible to sort ourselves into our married families, so my mother, father, Gordie, and my youngest brother, Lee, were together, leaving our wives and our cousin Corinne to follow in Uncle Tom's car, which was next in line. It was then I first knew that it was the dream I was living. The awning tunnel, the graveyard scene hadn't done it, but the sight of Maud's pin, which I had never even seen, had caused the dream to overflow into life, giving existence to its anticipations. I heard my mother say to my father, "Did you see what Maud was wearing?"

"I sure did."

"Odd. I haven't thought of it in all this time."

"I have. Not often, but I have. I've never seen her wear it though. I unpinned it from Connie's dress that night. The little green-apple breasts. And those things were called 'breastpins' then. I washed the blood from it under the tap in the bathroom."

"Funny your remembering that. Yes, they were. The sunburst you gave me. That's a breastpin." Even with her own family, Mama was conscious that this was a social situation so she went on about "breastpins" and dropped the reference to washing the blood from it under the bathroom tap.

The cemetery road was rolling — hilly even we would call it in the Midwest — and the headlights of the car behind us descended through the back window, dispelling for a moment the murked darkness. I saw my mother take my father's hand, and heard her say to us, not him, "We're talking about the pin Maud was wearing. So odd for a funeral, really; but you never know how long hurts last. Father, your grandfather, gave it to Connie for her sixteenth birthday, two days before she died. So odd of Maud to bring it out like that today. There was a lot of conversation about how inappropriate for a girl of sixteen" — my mother was talking against time, against the numby darkness of the limousine and my father's memory of his sixteen-year-old niece— "and I remember his saying, 'I probably won't be around to give it to her when she's eighteen, and I like it.' And this was odd, too, because of course he couldn't see it. But it's a lovely pin, I will say. Not big stones, but Cartier, so you can't see any of the setting at all. No prongs. Nothing. Smooth as silk. I suppose he could feel that, you know."

My mother could have kept on like this all the way home, but the car with Maud and Benjie had come to the Styx, which is what we called the little river that separated the east from the west side of the cemetery. Spring had brought the river high so that the tinny, rattly bridge that crossed the stream looked insubstantial above the rain-wet clayey waters. Maud's car stopped, and the lights of ours crowded up its back. At first we thought something was wrong with the bridge, but Benjie got out, a great crow in his too-tight morning coat and silk hat, slopping and flopping back to us.

"Uncle Doc! Uncle Doc! Something's happened to Mother! Come quick. She was crying and then she wasn't." Benjie was in his late forties, but he talked like a little boy. It was a choirboy's voice, too, for all his enormous bulk.

My father grabbed my mother's bag — she always had nitroglycerin ampoules — and was wading up the road to the car. Benjie had left the door open, so the light streamed out on the gray gravel to the brightened green grass beyond. Maud lay, terribly tiny, on the big seat, the snowflake glistening, still wet with rain, her glassy eyes still wet with tears. Papa got in beside her, although he must have known she was dead, and pulled down the jump seat to work on her. He broke the nitroglycerin under her nose, and Benjie and I drew our heads from the car in revulsion at the clinging, acrid sweetness of its smell. By that time Tom's chauffeur, Taylor, had been sent ahead to us, but he came up on the other side of the car, so it was Papa who spoke to him and

asked him and Arnold, Maud's chauffeur, to go up the line
and stop other people from getting out. All up the road you
could see the monstrous, lighted snake of cars curled among
the Doré vaults, Piranesi columns, Daumier tombstones of
the neighbor dead. Papa moved efficiently, methodically,
doing what had to be done, and then he turned to us.

"She's gone, Benjie. There's nothing I can do. There's
nothing anybody can do. I think we might just as well take
her to Ashenbrenner's just like this." Benjie looked stupid
and frightened, so Papa said, "Get in our car. I'll ride with
her. But it was easy, boy, and not sad. Not sad at all, you
know. Remember your dad." Fred had been in pain that
even massive doses of morphine could not control for over a
year.

Both Benjie and I were soaked, standing there, the rain
dripping from our stiff, ceremonial hats, the archaic padding
of our coats heavy with water. Papa twisted himself quickly
from the jump seat, which slowly folded up, and was beside
us. His fingers took Benjie's limp wrist to feel his pulse, and
he said again, "Go back in our car. You're not a boy anymore. No use taking chances." Benjie moved in a trance toward our headlights, not even grateful to Papa for the excuse he had handed him. I offered to go with Papa, but he
shook his head. "No. This is to be between Maudie and
me, I guess."

I helped him into the car and watched him as he slipped
his arm under Maud — Oh, the practice of that arm, when
you were sick, under your shoulders. So sure of itself. So
much better than any nurse's. The two of them sat there
like lovers, Maud's tiny head on his shoulder. For some
reason or other, he reached over and took off her hat even
before he closed her glaucous eyes with his thumb and mid-

dle finger. Even before, tenderly with his whole hand cupped, he closed her slackened jaw. I heard him say just as he would have to us as children after the setting of a bone, the lancing of a boil, "Well that wasn't so bad, was it, Maudie old girl? Much easier than lots. You needed something easy for a change." Arnold came back then, and I closed the door, leaving them in the dark. I had to walk around to the other side of the car to tell Arnold to take them to Piperson's. Papa had said "Ashenbrenner's" and that's what we all said, but it was Piperson's. Willie Ashenbrenner — Wilma — was a girl we all had known years ago, and when I was about nine she had married an undertaker named, to our delight, Tom Piperson. I have a long poem about it, "Historic America." It was a famous mésalliance, and I remember my grandmother's saying to my mother, "A woman has a right to her husband's position, but a husband never takes his wife's." I also remember the rest of the exchange.

"Oh Mama, I wish you wouldn't talk like that in front of the children. It gives them such wrong ideas."

"Well, it's better to have wrong ideas that are right, than right ideas that are wrong like silly Willie Ashenbrenner." In fairness to Grandmama, I know I should say that when it came to putting the screws on Willie — for put the screws on, they all sure did — she was less relentless than Mother. Anyway, when Willie inherited the Ashenbrenners' big house, instead of selling the land for an apartment house site as the rest of us were beginning to do, Tom Piperson had invented — really, I think so — the idea of a "Funeral Home," and had turned the house into the first I ever knew of. My father, of course, had a great deal more to do with undertakers than most people, yet even he — no matter how often he saw Tom Piperson, no matter how successful Tom became — still spoke of "Ashenbrenner's." I had noticed wryly at the funeral how smooth and perfect Tom Piperson's morning coat was — not at all like ours, which had been bought years ago when we were getting married and being ushers at weddings but now were stretched tight across our backs and cut into our armpits. My trousers even had buttons, not a zipper on the fly, and I couldn't button the top one at all. Undertakers, I suppose, continued to wear morning coats to funerals for a few years after this, but I haven't had one on since Fred's.

The car pulled away then, and I waded back toward ours on the slicked, unsure gravel of the road. It took a matter of two or three minutes, so our car became the head of the rolling dragon-snake stretched memorially behind us, linked with lights, that crawled winding until it reached the cemetery gates and dismembered itself — each part, like a worm, coming to new life as it swung into the larger traffic of the public road.

Grandpapa's fly had always been buttoned — and unbuttoned — never zippered, and fifty of us there that day — the four remaining of the ten sons, grandchildren, great-grandchildren — grown and zippered, never buttoned, for the great-grandchildren had no morning clothes — had proceeded from his loins. I give you joy of the worm, old goat. "Enter on a Monument." Buttoned. Oh so tender-buttoned during life, now perdurable in marble against a lightning-cloven sky. I looked back. Stark, proud, erect in thrust above long-moldered death. And Papa — zippered? buttoned? — with death already close beside him, speeding away ahead of us, the vast tenderness of his freckled arms! Unafraid, my papa. Used to death. Two syllables. Who the hell did I think I was? Walt Whitman? Acquainted with grief.

Heavy on the second beat and in the past tense like the *Messiah*. That great blubbering ox, my cousin Benjie, his eyes more sheened with wetty tears than his mother's with death. His heavy red hand under my mother's black kid clasp, bumpy with rings.

The Red and the Black, my mother always called us, and indeed it was spectacular how we all conformed to type. My grandfather had married twice. First his own Scott cousin, and upon her death, her niece — again his cousin — my grandmother. Four of the ten sons were Red, like my father, enormously freckled under the whitest of skins, and their eyes were heavy brown. The rest were Black. But the Black had the eyes of blonds, and this was very beautiful in people like Grandmama and Corinne. In the next generation, Benjie was Red and I was Black. I always wanted to be Red like Papa, and once when I wanted it so fiercely and I was little, he had said to me, "I can tell you this, if it's any comfort to you — and it shouldn't be — the Black are more largely hung." I was so little I didn't know what this meant, but I asked my Uncle Tom (Red, too) who was so much younger than Papa and never minded your not knowing things. He told me.

I soared with rage against Benjie now. No, he could not ride his mother dead to Ashenbrenner's, Silly Willie Ashenbrenner's. This fat segment of worm. Nearly fifty years old and still not alive enough by himself to rise from his wallow and lead the parade — hip! hip! hooray! — his arm about the woman who had borne him Red. I wasn't much of a one to talk, I knew. I had little enough feeling for the pangs of birth. The fruit-of-the-womb business never really moved me. It was just a place you'd once been like a house taken in Florida or Majorca for nine months. Had the robber baron understood the phallic magnificence of the obelisk? In the winding, falling, rising of the snake we had come to the spot where we could see it last, black in the rain. Probably not. In those days, no one would have, but had it marked me? Probably. Probably. I shook my head. Violently, I guess, for my brother Lee said, "What are you twitching for."

I was able to answer him — "I was just thinking of Papa" — and I began to remember that Papa himself would be incapable of my rage toward Benjie, would be able to say, "Benjie is Benjie. The Benjamin of an old man who was my brother."

When my grandmother died, Fred had taken over the house in town. It was the last of the houses the family owned there — the rest of us had moved to the suburbs, to apartments — but it had been Fred's mother's house much more than it had ever been Grandmama's, and he had bought it from the estate. Fred, too, remembered his own mother more than the others, although, in truth, Grandmama had reared — the word she would have used — all the boys. Grandmama had the house in the country. It had been built for her as a bride, but Fred and the older boys had been brought up in town. When they went to the country, they went to the farmhouse. Ironically, the farmhouse still stands and my cousin Edith lives a chintzy, Better Homes and Gardens sort of life in it, but the big country house — so much more of a city house than the house in town — is gone. The house in town is gone now, too, but it stood at the time of Fred's funeral, on enormously valuable land perpetually in the shadows by day, blazing with lights, reflected from the heavy buildings that surrounded it, by night. I haven't called it a town house because it never was that. It had

been built in what was once a suburb — a fifteen-minute
carriage ride from the bank. I know it would take a half an
hour in a taxi through traffic today. It stood in its own yard
and garden still, with a porte-cochère, a drive, a tennis court,
and big carriage houses long since converted into garages
across the back.

Grandmama and Fred after her had always kept the house
up, and as we drove in that day in the heavy rain, it looked
like the kind of awninged, flower-boxed rustic "cottage"
that people once built in Maine or along Long Island Sound.
"158" was what we called it because of its street address, but
Idlewild or The Elms would have been more appropriate.
When we were children, we used to stand behind the bridal-
wreath hedge that lined the iron spiked fence and watch
the rubberneck buses draw up in front while the guide mega-
phoned its — and our — splendors. I don't suppose any of
us ever imagined the women in from the farms, the school-
teachers from the little cities of the veritable, not metaphoric
plains, who sat on the rattan seats sticky with varnish, along
with their dressed-up children and captive males. We met
the women later in Ruth Suckow and Willa Cather, but no
one I think has ever done one of the meekened men, and he's
hard now to imagine. Then, we knew nothing whatever
about life on the other side of the iron spiked fence from
which an incomparably adenoidal voice bawled:

"Thirty-five rooms" — twenty-two by actual count — "the
Entire Third floor is a Ball Room with a Separate" — he
said, "Sep-A-rat," which is how I learned to spell the word —
Supper Room with a Complete Kitchen" There was a stove
in a kind of pantry connected with the downstairs kitchen
by a dumbwaiter. My father had marvelous tales of how
he and his brothers used to ride it until, for that reason, it

was taken out. In our day, it was just a scary hole you could look down but which was no good for spitting. Sunday afternoons were long when we were children, and in all houses — even Grandmama's — we used to spit down the clothes chutes at one another, the object being the eye. Ingmar Bergman could make quite a thing of it. As far as I know, no ball was ever given in the Sep-A-rat Ball Room after Grandmama Flora's time. Grandmama Flora was what we called our grandfather's first wife when we had occasion to refer to her; even her own children called her "Mama Flora" after they began to call Grandmama "Mama." As a matter of fact, the rubberneck barker must have had a hard time finding sufficient grandeurs, for there were no Carrara marble staircases; onyx bathtubs, or solid gold bathroom fixtures at "158" as there were at "300" where the Henrys lived. He had to settle for "The Three Stained Glass Panels on the Main Staircase are by the French Artist, Gus-Tave Dar-LONG and illustrate incidents in the life of 'The Lady of the Lake,' a famous poem, especially imported from Paris, France and installed here at the Cost of Twenty-Five Thousand Dollars. And those were pre-War dollars, folks." I will say this for Benjie, he could do the adenoidal barker better than anyone — and without even holding his nose.

When we pulled into "158" the day of the funeral, Maud, poor Maud, had been expecting us, and there were caterer's men all over the place. She would have been pleased at the stir that arose from the arriving cousins, nieces, nephews, in-laws. Benjie himself was flushed with importance as he stood at the head of the two steps that led up to the living room — long, low-ceilinged, bayed. No room in the house was level with another. I suppose this was considered picturesque,

but it made it easy for everyone to see Benjie and gave him a
chance to explain the circumstances surrounding his mother's
death. In reality, however, he was completely isolated
from what was actually happening. When they arrived, my
Uncles Harry — Harrison, the lawyer — and Tom — the
banker — went immediately to the little cupola study behind the library and began making phone calls and figuring
out the legal and financial aspects of the second death. My
mother and wife went into the kitchen to see about what
Maud had arranged and to talk to Fred's own servants
who had been at the cemetery themselves. Benjie was a kind
of island in all this, and although everyone sought him out,
they were more interested in seeing each other than Benjie,
who had lived in New York for twenty years and whose wife
hadn't come on for the funeral. Even I went to see about
setting up some sort of bar because, under the circumstances,
so many of the cousins had come back that the caterer's men
weren't able to handle them and at the same time turn a sit-
down supper for twenty-four — the tables were already set
up — into a buffet of funeral baked meats for what threat-
ened to be three times that number.

By the time my father arrived, the last party The Lady of
the Lake was to look down upon was in unexpected bloom.
The rain hadn't stopped, so all the lamps and lights were on,
glinting against the long-polished wood, and there were
enormous, heavy arrangements of flowers that Maud had
decided to keep rather than send on to the funeral. Everyone was relieved not to have to sympathize with broken
Maud, and all pretense that this was a house of mourning
had been dropped. Papa stood for a moment dazzled by the
life spread out through the downstairs rooms. Day by day for

a year he'd been coming here, talking to Maud for a few
minutes on his way up to Fred, maybe having a cup of coffee
with her on the way down.

"Maud was bad today. But she won't hear of the hospital,
and I don't think it has ever occurred to her that I could put
a stop to it all. At least she has never asked. She'd think it
was bad — wicked — you know, and when she feels like
that, you just can't." My mother was a great believer in
euthanasia and would say, "But it is Fred who has the pain.
Not Maud," but Papa would just shrug and say, "When pain's
gone on that long, it's a kind of life." A great believer in
life, my papa. Even the unexamined life. But I could feel
him bridle at the life that had suddenly spilled over the
long-numbed house, and he said to me, "Get Benjie and
bring him up to the Poop. I've got to talk to him."

The Poop — poop deck — was what they had always
called the room over the porte-cochère. It was all leaded
glass that through the years had stretched and buckled.
Palms were in each of the four corners. Before Grandmama
died the palms had grown in Chinese jardinières which I
never really looked at until after they had been left to the
Art Institute and were put on display there. Fred still had
the palms, but they were in hideous brass jugs he'd bought
once in Benares. The whole room was fitted with a tightly
tufted, upholstered velvet window seat that ran around
three sides. There was no other furniture except for a large
table in the center where there were usually magazines but
which today held an enormous bouquet of American Beauty
roses. We used to kneel on the window seat as children to
look down the drive. It was also a good room to play doctor
in because you could hear anyone coming on the stairs

before they could see you — an important consideration in a life as fully chaperoned as ours.

What Papa had to tell Benjie was that he had arranged graveside services for Maud at ten the next morning, that there would be no announcements until afterwards, and that Benjie should tell the cousinage that they didn't have to feel that they must come back for the new services. He also told Benjie that we would spend the night there to be on hand. Benjie seemed relieved, and with a new topic of conversation, went down renewed to the party.

Most of the bedrooms in the house had been closed for years, but after dinner my mother got three ready for us. Our wives went back to the country to be with our children, but that left my mother, my cousin Corinne, my two brothers, Papa, and me. Gordie and Lee took one room, Mother and Corinne another. Benjie had his own room, and that left the third room for Papa and me. In all that house there was not one room with twin beds, so for the first and only time in my life I slept with my father.

I suppose it was nearly eleven when we all finally went upstairs. We sat with Benjie for a while after the others left, but there wasn't very much to say, and we were really grateful that Harrison and Tom had so much for him to sign. It was understood that Tom should take over Fred's place in the bank — he had been doing the actual work for three years — and it would probably be necessary for Benjie to return to Chicago. He could easily use his father's place in the country to live in the year round, and there was no question but that "158" had outlived its usefulness even thirty years ago. Fred had never collected things as Grandmama and Grandfather had, so there was nothing of great value there except things in which he had only a life interest. I don't think Benjie himself had any affection for either the house or any of its furnishings. He was polite and invited us each to choose something before it was inventoried. Actually I took a Chinese porcelain vase that I once used in a poem — "Chinoiserie: Mr. De Paolis long after Gautier" — although I didn't explain the reason. Benjie himself, we knew all along, was going to be very rich, but what he would do with the money or even why he would want it, I don't think even he could have said. I'm sure he had no feeling for money as power; he had no children, no expensive tastes, and although he did not get along with his wife, they had been married almost twenty years, and he could have kept a dozen women in extravagant style at any time. But Benjie was not a wanter.

I spoke to Papa about this, and he said, "Well, he's a not-wanter then. You and I are such intense wanters that it's hard for us to know about other people. It isn't wanting what you have that counts. It's wanting something beyond. Always wanting. The Spartan boy with the fox at his vitals. Although I must say there wasn't anything particularly Spartan about the way you cabbaged-on to that vase."

I was really taken aback. Long ago I had learned Papa was apt to know my motives better than I, but I thought myself innocent in choosing the vase, so I said, "Is it very valuable? Was I really greedy?"

He looked at me slyly and shrugged. "Probably. Things beautiful and rare usually are — as you very well know."

"I'm sorry. You make me ashamed. I took it because it was in a poem of mine. I didn't think of its value."

He relented. "I recognized that. It's a good poem, too. At least I like it. But it's greedy. A greedy poem." I knew

what he meant in a way, and he knew that I knew. He didn't
as a rule comment on what I wrote. He'd hand me back a
poem and say, "I like that very much," or he'd tell me what
he knew about something in the poem to indicate that he
felt the force of the image. "There's nothing so white as trillium," he said when he read "Dawn Song." I had been
afraid to emphasize the whiteness of that trillium within the
poem for fear of smudging it; but oh, how I had wanted it
seen, and I glowed with pleasure when Papa spoke. But usually it was a long time later that he'd mention a poem, use it
as an illustration, and I'd know it had clung to his mind.
This was wonderful of him, really, for he knew more poetry
by heart than anyone I ever knew, and to hear myself used
as he'd use Keats or Shakespeare always made my heart sing.

"You spend a good many more hours in museums than
most people. You're knowledgeable, aren't you? Did you
ever see that vase before?"

"No. I suppose not. Not that *particular* vase." I heard
my own tone of voice on *particular*. It was my little-boy
voice. The voice of a little boy being serious and exact.

"That's why you asked for it, you see. You've already got
a poem out of it. The poem's unique" — Papa always used
words like *unique* exactly — "but that wasn't enough, you
wanter, you. You wanted, really wanted the tangible,
the valuable fact. 'The blow of flowering peach' — writing
that wouldn't do when you had a chance to have the vase,
which is far more fragile, in your greedy, even grubby,
hands."

"What about your bronze?" Papa had taken a small, ten-
inch bronze of an old man — presumably Ulysses but maybe
Prospero — lying on his side exhausted, naked, washed
to some final beach. At least there's a tiny conch shell at

his feet, and the base is swirled to suggest seaweed or waves. His beard, come to think of it, is matted, too, as if by salt water. It had always been kept — as a paperweight, really — on the desk in the study behind the library.

"Oh, I didn't say I wasn't greedy. That I wasn't a wanter. I just said you should know that you were. I studied for my State Boards in that room one July when everyone else was in the country and I was alone. I'd mark incisions on his belly, his back, and wipe them off with the sweaty fat of my thumb. I operated on him for everything in the calendar. His trunk, you know, is long for his legs. A prime hernia suspect. And when I wasn't operating on him, but just reading, after a while I'd find my pencil tapping, tapping on that minutely long foreskin. Many a reflective pencil I've broken between his bronze-green thighs. They had a firmness surprising in so old a man."

Papa's voice faded toward the end of this, but I didn't want to lose him to these memories, so I said, "Why didn't you ask for it before? Fred, Maud, Grandmama herself — anybody'd have given it to you. You could have just put it in your pocket and taken it."

Papa looked startled; his voice came back. "I never thought of it until tonight, and then I knew that's what I wanted. God knows I've explored enough prostates, removed enough kidneys to have forgotten the half-drowned man — the half-drowned man who kept me company when I was twenty." He laughed self-consciously. "The heat of that summer. The heats for that matter, too." Papa's voice faded again, but I didn't have to bring him back this time. He shook his head. You could actually see the effort of will it took to return from the still private past to me, his son. His tone was strangely defensive as he went on, "But tonight I wanted him. There's something tactile about all this. I think I have always wanted to touch." He looked down at his hands. White as milk, the tannish freckles blotching underneath. To see him wash them, even at home, was to see a sacrificial rite, a veritable ablution. He'd scrub each finger separately as if for surgery. The water'd be so hot that as children we couldn't believe it. And after his hands were scrubbed, he'd rinse them, and then fill up the bowl again, massaging the now pink hands with fresh soap. When we'd ask him "why," he'd say, "An act of prayer, boys, an act of prayer. Come on." And we'd give him up our little-fingered hands — Gordie from one side of the bowl, I from the other, reaching up because we were very little. He'd take them between his enormous, firm palms and rub them together, slippery with soap. Together, until you couldn't tell whose slithery fingers were whose. We'd giggle, Gordie and I, giggle with joy and adoration. There were so many stubby fingers there, crushed soft and loved and tickled. Yes, even little we were a tactile lot. Papa instead of going into the bank went into people's insides and cut away the rot and put them back together again. Gordie and I tried to get inside people's minds. We were always copping metaphoric feels. And the funny thing is you can either put it that way — as low, as vulgar as you like — or you can see yourself as God up there on the Michelangelo ceiling reaching out a yearning finger to mankind.

By this time Papa and I were in the big bedroom that once had been Grandmama's and in which we were to spend the night. Fred and Maud had never used the room, preferring its architectural twin, where Fred was to die, on the quieter side of the house. Most of the house was really in Grandmother Flora's taste, but my real grandmother had done this room over for herself, and it was grand, elegant in the French Manner while the other rooms were merely luxurious. There was an Aubusson carpet, a small Venetian chandelier of massed, pale-pink wild poppies flecked with gold, and a big caned and ribbon-carved bed of rubbed gilt on a low dais. The bed was hung with a thin blue-green silk, brocaded with loosely strewn poppies, and the curtains, sofas, and chairs were covered with the same stuff. "Sumptuous" was the word that came to mind when you first saw it, but it was really more than that when quietly the detail emerged. Critics, I know, have criticized Edith Wharton for what they call her Woman's Magazine habit of describing interiors, but in the days before interior decorators such rooms were a key to character, and Lily Bart looking down from the stairs at Bellemont — "The hall was arcaded, with a gallery supported on columns of pale yellow marble" — is quite a sight. Life, in the act of seeing, is seen. I like people to see where I am, too, and to know that I see as I saw that night. The wheat-colored carpet, the dark pearwood paneling, the pink poppies and the faded blue-green silk — these, anyone could see, and they were immediately beautiful. After you'd been there awhile, though, you became conscious of the eye that had been aware of the relationship between the color of the silk and the marble facing around the fireplace, so different in texture from that of the cloth. The marble was verd antique and in its green, mottled depths you could see — if only you would look — the shimmer of a long-dead, miraculous blue, and you could trace in its dimness the finest random threads of scarlet. The andirons were brass peacocks, and that's what Lee asked for, although I knew his wife would hate them.

All the doors in the room — to the dressing room, the

bathroom, the closets — even the door into the hall matched the lustrous paneling of the walls so exactly that when they were all closed there was no visual way out.

"I can't stand this," Papa said. "I never could." He opened the double panels to the dressing room and turned on the light there. The dressing room was all mirrors, reflecting in themselves back and forth, back and forth. It's a funny thing; I had these mirrors when I wrote "Kitchen Klenzer —" which is about reflections of reflections — but I didn't use them. The cook looking into the polished pan, the pan repeating the aproned cook were easier to deal with than the cut-glass dazzle of that cave.

Actually as children we were never much at the house in town, and as we grew older we seldom went upstairs at all. We knew Grandmama chiefly in the country, which with the years grew closer and closer to town, so that apart from an odd night now and then, Grandmama herself spent no more than a few weeks a year at "158." I mentioned this to Papa now and said, "Much of this is new to me, you know. When I was a kid I suppose I saw it, but I didn't see it with the eyes I have now. It's just there, dusky in the past. I suppose I would have known the room was beautiful, but I couldn't have said why. I've often wondered where she got her taste. Surely she wasn't educated? Women weren't, then." What I was saying was disconnected because I was wandering about *touching* things. "God, those poppies are marvelous. When you think what you can buy in Venice, in Murano, when all you have is money."

"I don't know how much she knew. I never did know. Partly of course it was the Galeries Charpentier and an instinct for the valuable. I don't think she ever bought even a new painter who didn't sometime make it. A kind of molec-

ular attraction, you could call it, to the supremely successful." I could tell Papa was pleased by being with me, and
proud of his phrasing. His eyes gleamed, and he went on.
"Most of it must have been herself. Sometimes I think I must
admire her taste just because it formed mine, you know?"

"I know. God knows I know. I get sick from knowing."
My thumb was working on the chiseled edge of a poppy
twisted from bronze into a drawer pull. "People don't
like this sort of thing now. Grace is going to hate those goddamned peacocks. White paint. Cheer. Chintz. That's
what I ought to be liking. Or, bringing the outdoors indoors.
Glass. Vacancy. Pre-Columbian sculpture. Masks. Oh, no.
Not for me. Give me" — I threw my arms wide. With
Papa I could do things like that — "Coromandel."

My tongue made love to the word because I was happy
too, and Papa heard the happiness because he said, "It sure
sounds good. You know about the pictures, don't you?"

"What about them?" There were no pictures on the wall
now at all.

"She changed them. What was hung was something
they were thinking of buying, and they liked to look and
look and look at it beforehand. Then when they'd decided,
the picture'd go to wherever they were buying it for."

"Do you think she knew about the 'No Exit' feature of the
joint?"

Papa laughed and said he didn't think so, that her mind
hadn't functioned in that way, that it hadn't been symbolic;
so I told him about thinking of the obelisk in the cemetery
which made him laugh even more. Then, I didn't really
know why, but I did later, he told me about having the
measles.

He'd been very sick with them, and not an inch of his body

had escaped. They had even infested his mouth and had climbed beneath his then flaming hair, "but were redder even than that." During the day he'd been allowed in his mother's room — this room — and had slept there dozing fitfully, feverishly on and off until he was transferred at night back to his bed. One day at the height of his infection, his mother was going to the opening of the opera, and Fisher, her maid, came in with the boxes of the big party jewelry that had come in from the bank. He asked to play with it, so Fisher put the boxes on the bed and went to tell Grandmama. They kept the room dark because of his eyes, but he could see the pieces well enough, and by the time Grandmama got there, his arms were heavy with the too-big bracelets, his fingers hooped with the too-big rings, and his neck ablaze with twisted diamonds and emeralds. He pinned the big elaborate brooches to his nightgown, whose flannelette was too light to hold their weight, and they pulled it forward on his skinny red neck, turning in on each other. Finally, on top of his eight-year-old curls, he set the diamond tiara that had been his mother's wedding present. "I thought I was King of the World, then, or Queen — I don't think I made any distinction. I held my neck high, the golden settings cool against its hotness" — oh my papa could talk, my papa could talk — "and I thought, If I had a whip, I'd whip my slaves."

When Grandmama came in, she sat on the foot of the bed, and he thought he remembered that her eyes began to glisten in the dark with tears. She took his hand which was really all rings, and he knew that what she said was "My poor little measle." Then she put the palm of her hand on his hot measled chest and said something about his being all uncovered. She tried to pull up his nightgown from the back, but the pins clattered together in a lump and just pulled it down again, so she had said, "Come on let's take them off. It can't be very comfortable."

"Oh no, Mama. I'm King of the World. Emperor of the Universe." Although Papa was in his late fifties when he told me the story, I could see the gesture, the sweep of the little-boy arm that half a century later was to become the arc, palm spread down, of the man's. I was fascinated by what he was telling me. You almost never know anything like this about anyone except yourself, and the thought that he should tell me it — here in that room of the caned and carved bed with the poppied damask — filled me with wonder. I knew, somehow, that it must be central to life — all life or just Papa's, I couldn't tell — to existence. Normally, even as he spoke, I would have been conscious of a gnawing curiosity, not for the outcome of the story but about how, when I came to write, I would use the details. There then that night, the details were using me, and what I can only explain as a kind of hush of spirit came over me. I listened and waited while Papa's voice washed over me telling me how he asked Grandmama for a looking glass and that at first she tried to dissuade him but finally had opened the dressing-room door's mirrored back. This wasn't enough, and reluctantly she brought him the hand glass. "I peered into it in the dark, but I suppose my eyes were really feeble. It was as if the glass were covered with silk, and I begged for light. Again she demurred, but I said 'Please, please.' It seems to me I remember the quietness with which she rose and stepped down and across the room to the windows. I know I can see her now with lace at the cuffs and throat. She raised her arm to pull back the pale blue-green poppied silk, and a shaft of November sunshine showed me the disease I had forgotten in my visions of splendor. I was — and I can laugh now — nothing but her poor little measle. Then, I wept. Salt tears on a measled face. Many things are hard to forgive Mama, but she always knew about boys — and men. I can feel her hands stripping the loose rings in kindliness from my limp, aching-sad fingers, slipping the clattery bracelets from my enervated arms, unpinning the heavy brooches, unwinding the scratchy diamonds from my neck, lifting the crown of the Emperor of the Universe from my head. All without a word. And the kiss without recoil on my measled mouth. You know, don't you, I think that's why you, Gordie, and Lee have never had the measles? I had them so bad that you were immune."

"But we weren't immune from wanting?"

"No, I guess there's no immunity from that."

Papa went out a few minutes afterwards to see about Benjie, give him a sedative, get us some of Fred's pajamas, and to say goodnight to the others. Papa always "wandered." This was Mama's word to describe how he'd walk around the house when everybody else was in bed. Everybody had to be down, the house his alone, before he'd begin. Then he'd go from room to room, at first turning off lights, but afterward just wandering in the dark, with his heart alive in the silence. As he left that night he said, "I'll leave the door open," and it was a help to see the big hall stretch out in its darkness, the Poop, halfway down the stairs, like a jewel box of crumpled, refracting glass alive with the reflected streetlights. The intimacy of the story flowed out, as it were. I knew that it would embarrass Papa, in the same fashion as ordinary mortals are supposed to be embarrassed at telling the facts of life to their sons, if he had been shut with me immediately afterward in that No Exit room. I stepped into the hall myself as if to break the spell, and breathed in the scent of the now wilting funeral flowers — "enpurpled roses, heavy-limp on closing stems" was a line I made up. I've never used it; it really isn't my poetic style, but if I do, it will be my standing there in the shadowed quiet of the hall. I think the poem would be faked, though, because in spite of the mortal hush of the last hours of Grandma Flora's house, I could literally feel my eardrums beat, throb. I knew what I was listening for was some last echo of four or so of the boys on a Sunday afternoon, brothers red and black, around the piano that Maud played with boarding-school trills as they sang "Far above Cayuga's Waters" — "Our best number because none of us ever went there." Sometimes—but only sometimes—Mama from the couch across the room would join in. Soft, clear, aching sweet she'd take a soprano obbligato to soar high above them.

I left the hall then and hurried through the room and the dressing room to turn on the bath. This is the sort of thing I meant when I said that in life as opposed to dreams reality always dilutes the moment. I wanted to be finished in the bathroom before Papa got back so that he wouldn't have to wait. Papa wasn't a good *waiter*. I could have told him. The poem I might have let have its way with me in the shadowed hall was gone, and the really fantastic postimpressionist scene that might have ballooned in the multiple harsh reflections of the dressing room never arose. The glasses held only my hairy, already faintly potbellied nakedness in their glaring surfaces. Of course I looked, but I didn't gaze as I might once have done. Narcissus was thirty-five. I did — and I suppose I have to tell this — lean over and parting the cheeks of my own now nearly assless ass saw for the only time its essential orifice. In the tub — there was no shower — I let the warm water take over and lay in lassitude, the tiredness of the day crowding in on me. Of course as I washed myself — slithery, slippery worm in soapy hands — I thought of Grandpapa in the same tub and how, really, it should be easy to do him, the kindly robber baron, and how nearly impossible it was to do Papa. Grandpapa had never told me the measle story. He was safely pinned, a specimen, in the past. There was the Zorn portrait in the director's room at the bank. The Duran over the fireplace in the hall. Line by line I could do the immobile, carefully painted face, and there were actual records of his financial manipulations. Grandpapa, Mr. Fredrick Harrison Scott, so identified in a group containing Sir Ernest Cassels and the Prince of Wales taken at a shooting party in front of Blenheim. Grandpapa in progress over Europe with his beautiful second wife and six or seven of his ten sons, tutors, valets, maids, taking whole floors of hotels incredibly uxorious, domestic — yet dying blind, syphilitic, before I was born, amid the ascertainable splendors of the house in the country. Grandpapa — yes even that I could do — in this tub, the worm tender-heavy with anticipation, the walk through the cave of mirrors, the begetting of Tom, who was only fourteen when I was born, in the caned and carved bed.

Grandpapa was easy, but it was Papa I knew I wanted to know. I smiled ruefully at the realization that it was his brother's, not Papa's begetting I had instinctively chosen. How simple life was for Tom Jones! Only the *person* of his father mattered. Yes I — we — were greedier now and what good did it do us? The obelisk was really stone, not flesh erect. Reflections did not linger in quick-silvered glass. The stare they returned was only the moment's gaze. Neither the brittle-blown nor the damasked poppies ever medicined a moment's pain, ever numbed a crowded mind to releasing sleep.

Papa — could it possibly make any difference whether he was begotten in prolonged love on the daised bed amid every splendid, carnal beauty or snatched quickly from time by a mechanical spasm in a wagon-lit of the Orient Express hurtling through the European night? I knew enough about my own life to know that the same woman is used — loved — at different times in different ways. Place, time, the events of the day, the sudden vision of the unpredictable blood were all part of the unfactorable equation, riddled by circumstance, explosive circumstance. The order of the universe? How was it difficult to impute this conception to accident? How believe in a divine concatenation of stars when the circumstance of your existence depended on so many variables? Had Papa delayed a psychic moment in the delivery of my seed, I might have been a girl: I might have been red, not black. Had Grandpapa swayed one more, one fewer time, on the careening Blue Train, Papa would not have been Papa. A gulp of water, one more turn of the leaden cap on the squeezed toothpaste and the history of the world is forever changed. Papa, the Emperor of the Universe, unique in diamonds on the pearwood bed, would never have been.

Time and again I had tried to do Papa, but while he was alive, I never could touch him. Oh I could write ordinary stories and brush him in. I think he's pretty good at the end of "To a Tenor Dying Old," but good in the way of a Sargent sketch — I'm thinking now of some croquet players, white-flanneled on a Newport lawn with wicker chairs. And this won't do because central to all my memories is the

memory of blood. And the blood isn't frightening at all.
It's sticky, it clings. Always it's there, but there's no horror
about it. It's not the Masque of the Red Death or anything
like that. I first saw it copious when I was four, maybe five.
I think of it as my earliest memory, and since Papa was
abroad with the A.E.F. during the first world war from 1918
to 1920, and the memory precedes this, I really could not
have been any older than four.

One day my mother stopped by the County Hospital
with Gordie and me to pick Papa up. I don't know why —
I suppose I must have begged — but I was allowed to go in
with her. We must have been in Grandmama's limousine because although my mother had an Electric and Papa a big
red Kissel "touring car," Gordie was left outside with a
chauffeur. I don't think we, ourselves, had a closed car apart
from the Electric until the mid-twenties.

The County Hospital was — is — an enormous building
built rather handsomely and certainly inconveniently in the
style of a Greek temple with a long flight of outside steps
leading to an immense porch of terra-cotta with Ionic pillars.
When I first had to learn the orders of Greek architecture,
Papa had said, "The bank's pillars are Doric. The hospital's
are Ionic, and Walter's porch has Corinthian. You can always
see them, so you'll always know."

Papa had a theory about eyes. "Look!" he would say,
"Take a snapshot, and there it will be whenever you want
it. There are five sepals, see?" We'd be walking the beach,
and he'd turn the wildflower one of us had picked in his
fingers. "But don't remember five. You can't remember
things like that and there's no use trying. See it again when
you want to and when you see it, count." He evidently
could control the return of these snapshots and when he'd

say, "Let me see," he meant precisely that. The process was visual, not meditative. Click. The slide would come into place before the inner eye, the sepals would be counted, and the information verified. He knew volumes of poetry, and with anyone else you would say it was "by heart," but with him, he was just looking at the double-column page he'd seen — twenty, forty years before in a schoolroom — and was reading it off. He had done this so often with things like "Lycidas" that he no longer had to "read" but could boom it as he got dressed, walked across the upstairs hall, down the stairs, across the downstairs hall, and into the dining room for breakfast. There Etter Mae, the cook we had for most of his life, would be sitting on his big leather chair to get it warm. He'd said to her years ago that it was too cold for him, and ever since she had come out of the kitchen and sat there until he appeared. Our mother never came down for breakfast, but my brothers and I were there and "Lycidas" would go on through "Blind mouths"— that as "Blind mouths that scarce themselves know how to feed" was often directed to us, roared with scorn, as a comment on our table manners — to "Look homeward, angel," truly melting with ruth as Papa took the chair Etter vacated. Nobody said, "Good morning" or anything. We just waited until he got to "mantel blue" when he'd "twitch" Etter's blue morning uniform, and after he had said "pastures new," he'd ask us how we wanted our eggs. This information he would pass on to Etter — although she had certainly heard it — and she would disappear into the kitchen she never left for the rest of the day. When we asked Papa about it — and I suppose we each must have in his turn said, "Why do you tell Etter about our eggs? She knows. She can hear" — he just said, "Because that's the way she likes it."

While we waited for the eggs, there might be a lecture on ovulation, or if there were kidneys or sweetbreads or brains — we all loved these things — Papa made sure we understood their function and position.

"If I were cutting you open — stand up — I'd make an incision here —" he'd trace the knife on your back — "and here. You understand? Look, so you'll know. I don't like people who don't know things."

"Henry Abbott doesn't know a thing. He thinks sweetbreads are balls."

"You shouldn't be talking to Henry about balls. His or your own. I'll have that goddamned woman calling me up again. But if balls were cooked they might taste like sweetbreads, so he has a point. But it *is* a vulgar error."

"Oh, Henry Abbott is very vulgar. He's always talking about you know and he lets off wind right in class."

"The word is *genitalia*, but that's not what a vulgar error is. It's more vulgar to say 'he lets off wind' than to say he 'farts,' as a matter of fact. *Vulgar error* means an error common to people who don't know. Cherished by them. I do not like vulgar errors."

"Is it all right to say 'fart,' then?"

"Oh for God's sake. This is a *philosophic* discussion. It hasn't anything to do with what's all right. No. You don't go saying 'fart' in front of ladies. But you don't say 'lets off wind' to your father, either. Look at it this way." *Look,* again, you see, and he really did mean look.

Inside the hospital, Mama asked for Papa, and a probationer of some kind who called Mama "Mrs. Doctor" was sent to take us to the Doctor's Room. In 1917 there was still a great deal of difference between the dress of even little boys, and while I was dressed in the only way I knew, I was all wrong for the halls and wards of the County Hospital. Mama herself must have been an apparition because a buzz followed us through those labyrinthian ways. I'd keep turning to look, and Mama'd keep pulling me by the arm.

"Don't stare, baby. It's rude. Now come along. Don't make me sorry I brought you."

"Don't make yourself conspicuous" was what we were always being told, yet everything was done to make us just that. Here I was in white piqué shorts that buttoned with mother-of-pearl buttons to a hand-tucked voile blouse which probably had an embroidered collar and embroidered, detachable cuffs — at least I remember these outfits — and I was being told not to be conspicuous in that Hogarthian hell. I don't know whether the woman who was leading us made a mistake or not, but instead of taking us to the Doctor's Room, she took us up in a great cage of an elevator. You could see the weights moving down as we moved slowly up and the pulleys unwinding and the other elevator coming down with a stretcher on a cart. We moved so slowly that you could look out, too, on the crowded, open acres of high beds all filled with people you didn't know or never would know, and you could see the nurses, the orderlies, the capped or shawled visitors moving about. The Mrs. Doctor woman took us all the way to the top and you could look down and see the other elevator at the bottom and the pulleys still trembling from their stop. The gate clanged open and there was lots of light because this was the top floor, and there were skylights, but the other floors had been dark because the elevator went up in the center far, far from the windows. The Mrs. Doctor woman, with whom Mama had been keeping up one of her endless social conversations about where she was from and did she like nursing and

how many more years did she have, said she'd find Papa for
us and left us in the hall. Then Mama turned on me and
said, "See, how do you like to be stared at? It really is most
rude. That elevator man just turned around and looked at
the two of us as if we were from Mars. Don't say you
didn't notice because you were quiet as a bug."

Just then the swinging double doors at the end of the hall
opened and out came Papa. He was covered with blood.
Great scarlet splotches on his gown, his duck trousers, his
sleeves; even the cap he wore was smeared. His brown eyes
were shining though, and I suppose he had no idea at all how
he looked any more than he could smell the great, bitter
clouds of ether that enveloped him. I had climbed on a
bench the better to see the marvels of the elevator through
the grillework, but Papa was splendor in blood and I
wanted to touch him. Mama was too quick for me — maybe
because she understood the fascination herself — and got
me by the hand.

"Oh no you don't, young man. Your father's a blood-
stained wretch."

"I guess I am, boy. I'll get cleaned up and be with you
right away. We had a real bleeder in there, but everything's
fine. They'll bring him out in a few minutes all clean, and
you can see for yourself."

Papa went away then, but I could still see the blood, and
I didn't turn back to the fascination of the open elevators.
Even when the orderlies brought the man, wrapped up like a
mummy, on a cart, it was Papa I kept thinking of. Looking
back, I know my mother was moved too — the warrior home
from the fields, the hunter from the chase — because she began telling me how wonderful Papa was. "He gives his
time here, you know, and he helps all these poor people."

Mama's family was Scottish and Presbyterian, and she put great store in good works and the good life. She looked on Papa's family as more than faintly pagan, and tried hard to bring us up in the ways of plain living and high thinking, but she — and we — were always being seduced by high living. We were sent to public schools — I think she would have liked us to deliver newspapers — and a great deal was said about self-reliance, but then Papa would be invited to give a series of lectures or a course in Europe — indubitably high thinking — and off we'd go, with Papa and Mama taking over our lessons. We never had a butler, for example. At least we were never allowed to call William one, although when he answered the phone he would say, "This is the butler speaking." If Mama heard him, she'd say, "So pretentious," and be annoyed, for we called him by his first, not his last name (*vide supra*), and she went to great pains to keep him in a white coat rather than in black for which he yearned. He never waited on the table or answered the door — except when one of the maids was off. Mama — I think she always knew this — really had the best of all possible worlds, for Papa provided good works and high thinking with the same lavish unconcern as he provided the high living. She had it both ways, which is always pleasant. But she worried about us.

Gordie was always more susceptible to the charms of high thinking and good works than I, and I — as the eldest son — was always "selling him my birthright" for the largest piece of candy or equivalent "mess of pottage" since I was quite firm in the conviction that I could "sell" it and at the same time retain it. Obscurely, I didn't want Mama to dilute Papa's bloodiness with good works for Gordie as she tried to do for me, so that night and in the days that followed, I tried to frighten him with tales about how Papa took baths in other people's blood at the hospital and how he had come out all covered with gore — "The blood dripping from his hands." This was done with horrid, satanic emphasis, and I was told to stop "torturing that poor child." Gordie doesn't remember it now, but I think it must have been the first of the elaborate teases, most of which he does remember, that I made up for him.

"Suddenly the door opened wide, wide open, and they brought in the dead man all wrapped up so he couldn't breathe, and after him came Papa all covered with his blood bleeding and Papa said, 'You must kiss the hem of my garment,' and Mama had to kneel and I had to kneel and kiss the hem of his garment. Mama had gloves on, so it really didn't count for her because she just threw the gloves down the elevator hole. That's why they have them open like that. So ladies can throw their gloves down them, I guess. But I didn't have any gloves on, so my hands got bloody and soaking with blood, and he took me into this room with all doctors and things and we washed our hands with water so hot you couldn't see it was water even."

I don't know whether it was before this or afterward that I heard the story of Papa and the cow. It was one of my favorite stories, though, and I heard it often from Mama, Papa himself, and even from Grandmama. I can see now that there were stylistic differences in the telling and that I really liked these differences, which is the reason I would beg first one and then the other to "tell" me. My version to Gordie was a combination of what I considered the best features of each and is, I suppose, my first remembered "composition," although I can't recall ever having written it out — as I very well might have in school or college as an assignment — until now. Papa was eight by his own account when this happened — the summer before or after the measles, I take it. Mama and Grandmama made him six. To Gordie I said, "Very, very little. Littler than me. Littler than you."

The family went to the country every summer. They really loved the country because there they were free — freer, if the truth were known, than Mama ever envisioned our being in town at the public school. Even when they were twelve, fourteen years old they never left the bridal-wreath hedge in town without a coachman or some male guard. There was a real fear of kidnapers, and at one time there was a regular detective. In the country there were tutors, but the boys could roam the woods and fields, and there was nearly a mile of perfect beach underneath the spectacular bluffs, cut by deep ravines overgrown with pine, cedar, oak. All of the boys knew the wild plants and flowers and could distinguish dozens of kinds of mushrooms. There was a cove for their sailboats with an elaborate boathouse, and there were great barns of farm animals. I used to envy Papa this paradise until one day he said, "But it wasn't perfect, you know. Things happened."

"What kind of things?"

"All sorts. We were very happy there — by and large — but life was there, too. You can't just with a mile-long wall shut it out. Nor should you. It was there, you know, I was baptized by blood."

What happened was that Papa, roaming the pine- and cedar-grown ravines had come upon a strayed cow. The cow had stumbled, and because the ground was steep, she had lost her footing entirely. When Papa came upon her,

her neck was wound with barbed wire and she dangled —
enormous, bellowing, bulge-eyed — somehow caught by the
neck between two twisted branches of an oak. Her hind legs
flailed above the sandy ground. Papa was very good —
better than Mama or Grandmama — when he told how he let
himself down the tangled ravine and cut his legs on the
thick oak bark in shinning up the tree. "And all the time
the bellowing, the roar of the mugient cow was less, because
it was dying, and I knew that if it died, the cow was lost and
never could be used." I loved the word "mugient" and every
time I'd ask what it meant so that Papa would puff out his
cheeks and shake his head with "Moo-cow mugient." "Luck-
ily I had my knife with me, my trusty knife." Papa could
make it sound like a labor of Hercules. Maybe because when
I first heard him tell it I had the eight-year-old legs to feel the
crumbling sand of that steep descent, the skinny arms to
know that will, not puny muscle alone, had to scale that
thick-trunked tree.

The actual death of the cow, Mama did better than Papa
who merely said, "I took out my knife and hacked at the vein,
and of course the cow bled to death instead of being hanged."
Mama, who hadn't seen it, who knew nothing about how a
cow *in extremis* could look but who had seen it in her mind's
eye with great exactness said, "He inched along the branch,
his Boy Scout knife between his teeth because he needed
his hands to keep his balance, until he got to the poor suffer-
ing cow. Then he had to balance himself with one hand
while he bent forward and sought the jugular vein with the
other. And all the time the cow was crying most piteously.
He could see the great pulse beating desperately" — Mama
was great on adverbs — "and he leaned down and pressed

the shiny point home." She also always said, "It was an
Act of Mercy," which seemed to me a fine and shining thing
for this to be.

Grandmama was best on the blood, for she had actually
seen with her own eyes the crumpled boy who had fallen
from the tree. The farmhand had carried him to her in the
rose garden. Afterwards I was to think how like Amy Lowell
in "Patterns," only it wasn't brocade she was wearing. I'm
perfectly certain of this because it was the first time I ever
heard the word "mull." Indeed it may be the only time I
have ever heard anyone pronounce the word. *Mull* and *mugient, mugient* and *mull* and *mercy* — these are the words
that somehow have to be in the tale if, like the child with the
bedtime story, I am to feel the incantation.

"I was just walking there in a dress of mull, mauve lilacs
on a cream ground." (I'm sure, too, about the progression
of "mull, mauve"; that it wasn't, could never be "mauve
mull.") "And then I saw Mackenzie with the boy in his arms.
I didn't know which of the brood it was, but whoever it was,
I knew he was dead, for he was covered with shining blood.
Mackenzie was blood, too, but the boy was nothing but
blood. I cried out, running toward them, not through the
paths, but across the beds, the thorns catching stalky on the
mull. Mackenzie called to me that there were no broken
bones, and I knew he wouldn't be talking about broken bones
if the boy were dead." Grandmama had a breathless way
of saying this so that it sounded frantic like a woman trying
to run in high heels. But then her voice would shift as she
went on, "By that time, I knew it was my Gordie." Grandmama always said, "Gordie" softening the "G" as it were with
special love, although all his brothers and my mother kept
the hard "G" as we do with my brother. "Mackenzie put

him on his feet, dripping blood. He stood there just grinning at me through the scarlet-smearing with the devil bright as rainbows in his eyes, his hair stiffened into two redder horns. Oh I was furious at having been so frightened, for letting my heart sink so, but it would never do for me to let the devil know that. We keep our weakness from the devil, you and I, don't we?"

"Oh yes, Grandmama." Grandmama was a great believer in audience participation, as indeed am I. Then she'd go on, "I told Mackenzie to put him in the fountain even though the children were forbidden to play in it. Well, Mackenzie couldn't get a hold of him, but he leaped into the fountain by himself, and the blood seeped from his clothes into the splashing water. He took off his shirt and let it float there and dropped his trousers and his pants." Grandmama always made the distinction. Pants were underwear; trousers were trousers. "There he stood naked as Adam, freckled beneath one of the *bouches,* the water washing away the blood, plastering dark his hair."

"And you in mull?"

"And I in mull. Mauve lilacs on a cream ground. Wine blood, not blood blood." Grandmama herself must have caught the mull-mauve progression. At first it would have been said accidentally, but I believe now that she was so immediately sensitive to even the peripheral responses of any — as Papa said — boy, man, that intuitively she pressed her advantage home. She always used her powers and believed in using them. That was what they were for. "It was very funny. The boy in the sunlight whom I loved so much for being alive that I could scarcely hear the tale Mackenzie was telling and that your father would interrupt. 'Oh Mama,' he said, 'I'm washed in the blood of the cow.' "

This was a joke we had together, and I'd repeat it antiphonally. "Washed in the blood, blood, blood of the cow." Grandmama's blond hands, so surprising with her black, black hair, would clap out, blazing with rings, the "blood, blood, blood of the cow."

But then her voice would darken, the hands would fall to her lap, the rings turned in, and she'd go on with, "The blood was hard and red and glistening on the gravel walk and wet and sticky on Mackenzie's hairy arms and his farmer's hands as he bent over to wash them in the fountain beside the pearly-naked boy. 'A brave lad, it was,' Mackenzie said as he told how the cow, when the knife found the throbbing vein, gave the tremendous, final lunge that cracked to the life the splintered branch. Crashing, flashing with leaves as they caught the sun, the branch fell heavy to the bottom of the ravine, but the cow, spurting the last of its life, was caught in the smashed cedar brush. There it died."

Mackenzie exists only for us in this moment. No one knows anything else about him except his name. Maybe Grandmama just gave him a name as I would have had to had the name not been there when I came to write. Someone had to be there for me as a child hearing the story. Someone had to speak with a Scot's burr, the Greek Chorus lines, "A brave lad, it was." I've wondered about the hairy arms and the pearly-naked boy. It isn't something you'd put into a story for a child, so they must have been real. Like Papa, Grandmama was visual, and for her, like Titian, the heavy boot of Mars was never far from Venus' rosy breast.

Afterwards the fountain in the rose garden was always called "Gordie's Fountain," and only Papa was ever allowed to go wading in it, a privilege which he and Grandmama extended to my brother Gordie in his day and which Gordie valued so highly that when the house was torn down, he paid fantastic freight charges to set the fountain, which really is nothing special, up in his garden in Florida, where it now stands. Where it now stands? That's silly, isn't it? Oh I see it there when I go down, but its moment is a moment of the mind, and when I see it waking — Papa blotched with summertime freckles, the glint of stone in the sun, the play of rosy waters, Grandmama in embroidered mull — it is very pretty. When I see it in dreams, it runs with blood.

There is nothing frightening about this blood, this memory of a memory I could not have had, nor is it ugly. Maybe it will be easier to understand when I tell you this. Papa always took care of members of his own family and often I have sat quiet when other doctors' children have explained how their fathers got someone else to operate on them, to deliver their children, because their own fathers were too "emotionally involved." Well, it was really because Papa was himself so "emotionally involved" that he had to, he was impelled to do the job himself. I don't suppose it ever occurred to him that anyone else in the world could do as well as he. His first important paper was written after he had delivered me. It was, indeed, the standard work on breech presentations for a generation or so until Caesarean sections became more common.

When my own children were born, it never occurred to me, in turn, that Papa himself should not deliver them. The night before Corey was born, Mary and I had been to my family's for dinner. I was already in the Navy, but was home for a few weeks, and it was my birthday. Of course there were presents for me, the flowers were freesias, which I particularly like, and everything we had to eat and drink was chosen because it was a favorite of mine. There was even a separate course of the first new asparagus with hollandaise sauce, and all of us, I think, took more when it was passed a second time. My mother had some tale about how many calls she had had to make to get such a mountain at the end of March but was enormously pleased that we liked it so much. We left about midnight, I, a little drunk, Mary enormously pregnant and reeling with the big, rich party food. We didn't expect the baby for another week, so we just laughed when, as we thought, the asparagus began coming through. At two-thirty or so in the morning, I decided on calling Papa if only to see if there was anything that could be done about the asparagus, and he told us to get to the hospital, that he would meet us there. Mary had been taken upstairs — the pains had not only begun on the trip in, they had become stronger and more frequent — when Papa came in and I met him in the empty, four-o'clock lobby.

"Asparagus, for Chrissake. Are you a man or a boy?"

"Well I didn't know."

"No. It's not your pain."

"Well, I didn't."

"Lets get up." He took me all the way up then and left me on the OB floor — the Constance Scott Memorial Floor — just outside the delivery rooms. There was a regular hospital room empty there, and the nurse came in and told me that it wouldn't be long, but that I might as well lie down on the bed. Everybody in hospitals was always enormously respectful of Papa and impressed by him; yet the nurse somehow wanted me to know the extent of the favor she was conferring on me and that it was in honor of Papa, not the Constance Scott Memorial. I don't think I could say I was worried, and I think I was amused when once or twice

I heard Mary cry out in enraged surprise at the strength of the pain. At any rate I remember thinking that so strong a voice could not proceed from anyone in real danger. I didn't lie down, though, but wandered about the room, looking out at the dirty early morning streets and the bluish-green tubular lights that still lit, turning back the dawn, the emergency entrance below. It was so quiet that I thought, If I were down there, I could hear the neon buzz of the lights, and I made out Papa's Lincoln and my Olds, toys side by side in the emptiness of the parking lot. I wasn't apprehensive, tender, torn, sad, reminiscent. I was just waiting there by the window watching the smogged-gray, big city dawn spread in the east when suddenly Papa was there in the doorway. Once more he was besplattered with blood, although this time the gown was faded green, not white and the blood seemed darker. In his sure, rubber hands was my child, my Corey, still unwashed, shiny wet, great clots of afterbirth darkly clinging.

"A girl," he said. "Look on thy works, ye Mighty, and despair!" The laughter of triumph was in his voice, and his brown eyes caught mine with wonderful pride before, in a second, he was gone. So swift was his appearance and disappearance that it seemed an apparition, but there were spots on the floor and pretty soon an orderly pushed a mop — Medusa's long, snake-coiled hair, for this was before plastic sponges on a stick — over the trail he had left from the delivery room.

These three scenes — Papa and Blood — exist for me always. Sometimes one is remembered more sharply, more exactly in focus than another, and there is a necessary, a reciprocal but by no means equal blurring of the other two. Some occult balance is at work; the images are interdependent,

and I cannot remember one incident unless each in turn is
relived.

When we were little there was an outdoor sign that
Gordie and I called "The Pretty Sign." It was only a few
blocks from where we lived, and we saw it often by day
and by night. It was three-dimensional and advertised
the "Terrace Gardens," a restaurant for dancing — we had
never heard of nightclubs then — in one of the hotels. The
tables, each with its own shaded candle, were arranged in
tiers around the dance floor where a half-dozen or so men
and women in evening dress were caught in different attitudes of the tango. By day these men and women had four,
even five or six legs of different colors and their flatness was
apparent even in the three-dimensional setting. At night
they were rounded and whole, and a system of flashing
floodlights — yellow, pink, rose, blue-white — set them in
motion. To our amazed eyes they dipped, swayed, tangoed
on the "Pretty Sign." Well, this is like that. I've told of the
three scenes, but there's no way of indicating — by day, by
words, by type — how each touches and moves with the
other. The waxy oak leaves flash in the sun as the bough
breaks and the blood leaps forth. The white gown, the green
gown are simultaneously besplattered, although they are
twenty years separated by sun, not psychic time.

That night with Papa in Grandmama's bedroom I was curiously open to all this, and when Papa told me that Maud had
had the bed hangings and draperies replaced that very year
from the last of the hundreds of yards that Grandmama had
had loomed a half century ago — knowing full well that silk
must rot when hung in the light of the sun — I understood
how committed we all were to an impossibly permanent
aesthetic dream. Ozymandias and the poet in the desert.

Bloody Papa there, my bloody daughter, bloody in his
bloody hands. The cage rising, the weights descending.
And now Papa standing in Fred's pajamas by the mul-
lioned, veritable casements, and opening them to the May
night, not on the foam of perilous seas in fairy lands forlorn,
but above the streaking lights and hypnotic hum of traffic on
the express lanes of the Drive.

So far I have been very just, very fair, and I have told you
only the events of the day, of what happened then or what
had happened before to give those events meaning for me. I
have, in a sense, been historical, as if it were the sun alone
that measured time into days, nights, weeks, months, years,
as if the thudding heart did not also mark the hours. Like
Grandmama with her hundreds of meters of silk, I have
made my obeisance to that sun; but when Papa climbed
into the bed that night, he brought with him not only remembrance of things past, but the pull of the springs, the
looming of this unaccustomed bulk in the poppied dark beside me, brought with it a sense of things to come. Remembering it now, knowing what has happened, I am incapable of being merely historic, of saying to myself as I write,
"No, I did not know that then; I cannot have been *aware*
of what was to come. It will do violence to memory itself if
I report more than I could have known. But memory is, I
have learned, a matter of the heart and follows the heart's
time more exactly than the tick of the clock.

There were no longer any clocks in Grandmama's room.
Actually she left the open ormolu clock that stood on her
desk to me. Its pendulum, its wheels, cogs, gears, even the
bells that still ring the hours, quarters, halves so sweetly,
softly in a shower of tune that you might think the passing
of time a benison, glint through the glass-paneled sides. I

wind it every Sunday night. I hear it as I write, if only I stop to listen. Yet when I stop to listen, what I hear is the ticking of the clock as I heard it that night in the pearwood room. For hear it I did even though it had been forty miles away in the room where now I write for fifteen years.

"Do you hear the clock?" I say to Papa beside me. He reaches over without answering and fumbles with my wrist. Although those washed and pinkish fingers have not been warm since his dying, I feel their pressure as they find my pulse, and I say, "What's the matter? Are you afraid I'm sick?" and he answers. "No. That's not it. It's habit. The ticking of the clock, the coursing of the blood." There's a silence then that crowds my ears as I close my eyes against the pale pink poppies, lustrous with the May brightness of the rain-washed moon.

"No," Papa says, "I'm not afraid of your heart. But somehow I wanted to say goodnight, to touch, and this seemed to be the way."

"Goodnight, Papa." My black-haired wrist lies lightly still in the palm of his hand, for his fingers have long loosened across the relaxed, cushioned flesh of his hand so that he will know, even though his fingers are limp and cannot close again. This is the way — at moments like this — that he is still beside me.

The vast tenderness I felt for Papa, that can possess me thus even though he is dead, is merely a measure of my love. What is far more important to me, what I would like to get down on paper, is not the sweet ache, the sensuous and sensual understanding that somehow I had arrived at by my mid-thirties, but the weight of love that came to me in a phrase Papa used often, only "in the fullness of time." I think now it came when I was ready for it, that it was given to me a little at a time despite the long habit I had of loving, and when he knew it was there in my breast, then Papa could die in peace. What I had, in the end, to understand was a mighty heart, no mere segment of worm.

Papa died the first week in October as the result — as far as we know — of a boating accident early in the summer. He was out at his brother Charley's place on the river, and Charley in bringing the boat in didn't see Papa jump from behind him onto the dock. The boat swung out, Papa lost his footing and fell in the water. As the boat came back, he was crushed between it and the pier. Both Papa and Charley knew everything there was to know about boats; they were used to them, as some people are used to horses, from childhood. No one could think it anything but an accident, and at first Papa himself thought it only a matter of a few cracked ribs, which he knew could be painful. A friend of his taped him up, some X-rays were taken and a few days later he called me and asked if I would drive for him until he could drive again himself. My mother was apprehensive, but then she always was, so there seemed no good reason why I shouldn't. Papa himself was excited when I picked him up that first morning, as if he were looking forward to having me to himself for the summer's day. As children we had often gone with him on house calls, fighting with each other while he was inside, listening to him talk as we drove from one house to another.

Papa always made house calls, and medicine was to him an art as much as a science. "For Christ Sake," I can hear him bellow over the phone to some younger doctor or student who was consulting him, "stop looking at the charts and begin by looking at the patient." He was never a specialist, for all his eminence, but took whatever case happened to interest him at the time. "There are two ways of limiting your practice. You can raise your fees, or you can do what seems to you important." He was a great believer, too, in the word "practice" to describe his activities. "It's all practice; it's all experiment. You never know what's going to happen, so you shouldn't act as if you did or, what's more important, you should never allow yourself to think that you do. God-damned IBM doctors. Prescribing over the phone. Science-Science is as bad as Christian Science." His patients — another word he liked because it was, he said, exact — were all over the city and there were a great many more poor than rich ones. When we were little we found the neighborhoods highly romantic, almost like stage sets, for by the time we got there, the kids were all in school, the men at work, and the women indoors. That Papa should be able to go into one of those houses seemed an inexplicable privilege of being grown up. A couple of times we had had to wait until an ambulance arrived and had followed it careening at top speed through the city streets to the hospital. If I could begin to do the joy and terror of this, the sirens screaming, the car swerving, everyone turning to look, the streetcars stopping, the trucks and wagons — for there were still wagons with enormous dray horses — pulling over to the side, you'd know right away about Papa and Mama. It was Mama who would have to come for us then, and sedately the ride would end with us bolt upright on the broadcloth seats of the flowers-in-the-vase Electric. We who had raced death itself pell-mell, tossed from side to side on the shiny, black tufted leather of the sporty red car. Mama, you see, had no chance.

This was before we went to school. Afterwards, we'd still go on Sundays or holidays and then the streets in front of the houses would be filled with people. People who didn't have on what we recognized as Sunday clothes but were sitting on their front steps in their undershirts just as if no one could see them, walking across the street to the saloon with bright tin pails for beer, coming back again, the foam thick on the top in the sun, stopping to talk to each other or to call out something to the factory daughters who were dressed up and teetered, high heeled, in pairs toward the streetcars on their way to the parks. We never could make out what they said. Sometimes indeed it was in German, Czech, Polish, but even with the kids who would cluster around the car and spoke to us in English, we had difficulty. "PRONOUNCE your words," we were always being told — even by Papa although his words were "stethoscope," "diphtheria," and "sphygmomanometer" — so when people didn't PRONOUNCE their words we had a hard time, "Whadchermane?" we got used to, and I suppose our carefully articulated answers sounded snotty, sissy; but of course we didn't mean them to be, and we really were hurt when the kids would mock us. Dirty, torn, patched, their eyes bright with a savage derision we weren't to understand for many years, they'd explode the "t's" of "Scott" with the resulting spittle, back at us, each in turn sticking his head over the car door. Sometimes a big boy would come along and push the others away.

I think the fascination was with the car, not us, for seldom in those days would any car apart from delivery trucks appear on such streets. I remember one time — it must have been Memorial Day or the Fourth of July — when an open vegetable truck drove up. It was the kind the vegetable man who came to our house had with a bright brass scale dangling from its roof. The scale was gone and the truck was decorated with red, white and blue bunting, flags, bunches of lilacs (it must have been Memorial Day) dying limp at the four corners of the open back which was filled with what we would have called ice-cream parlor chairs. "A. Fiduci Fruits and Vegs," it said on the side. A. Fiduci honked the horn, and in a little while a big boy in knickerbockers and high shoes came out with a baby carriage. The spokes of the wheels were wound with crepe paper. We stood up on our car seat to see the baby, but the carriage was filled with the Fiducis' lunch. Pretty soon a bunch more kids came from the house. The girls all had parasols of red, white, and blue bunting, and even the littlest boys had flags of the thin, stiff, starched, loosely woven stuff that I haven't seen in forty years and haven't thought of until now. Knife-edged, the flag was stapled to a softwood stick on which it would curl back, the colors running, the very stars blurred.

The girls sat expectant on the chairs, their parasols up. The boys waved the flags at us. Looking back I can see that aesthetically they should have left at once. A. Fiduci driving, the lilacs blowing, the parasols turning, the baby buggy bouncing, a Star-Spangled Banner joy overflowing as they left us behind. That's the way it would be in a musical. It didn't happen like that, though. There was a pause, a wait. At first A. Fiduci blew his horn long and angry and loud, and the kids became quiet, looking with wonder toward the house, the little girls turned on their chairs, the parasols drooping. The wait was prolonged, and every time the kids began to yell up a good time among themselves, A. Fiduci would blow the horn and they'd be frozen in the attitude which the first blast had arrested. Gordie and I thought we understood about horns because we were sternly forbidden ever to blow ours, but this man, this mere A. Fiduci, was blowing his horn, not once but a dozen times, at our father who was "inside." In a little while, A. Fiduci sent one of the girls into the house, but she came rushing out almost right away. She was crying and her parasol was broken. A softwood rib hung limp, grotesque, askew, and she tried to show it to her father, but he pushed her away. The big boy helped her up into the back of the truck and looked at the broken rib judiciously as if he thought he could fix it. The girl began to stifle her sobs, but the boy, in the very act of holding the parasol up, was assaulted by another blast of the horn and stood there transfixed. The girl, too, was caught by the blare.

"She hasn't un-sobbed her sob" was what Gordie said, and I still remember. I even remember letting him get by with it, although usually I would have hooted loudly at him, for I had begun to insist (say we were eight and nine years old) on his using an unimaginative language, which I somehow associated with "manliness," even in his talk with me. "Baby talk, baby talk, baby talk," I'd yell with real rage. Looking back, I can see that the rage came from the inhibition which I felt bound to place on myself because of my superior age and status and whose limitation I already found galling. I didn't stop him this time because I think we both felt, even from the distance, the electric quality of the quarrel that could so transform the holiday truck for all its bunting — a quarrel that its children could scarcely have understood any more than we.

It was this scene that I did for Papa that first day I drove him, and he was very pleased.

"Yes, I remember that. The woman died, you know. Not long afterward. It wasn't my fault, or hers, or Tony's."

"Oh don't you see, Papa. I *don't* know. All these things haunt me. The circumstances are all there to do the haunt-

ing. But I don't know. I have this goddamned scrapbook,
but its like a picture album with none of the pictures identified. What's it got to do with me?"

I was serious and worried, really. The happiness of being
with Papa that day wasn't enough somehow. I had to probe,
and I went on. "After the calls that day, we went out to the
country and Gordie and I stayed all night. The holiday
must have been Friday, and there was a weekend coming up. You know what it was out there. If one tiny lilac
withered before its time, or was stunted among the thousands of fat, perfect blooms, a gardener pruned it away
with a knife on the end of a bamboo pole, dropped it limp
to a bushel basket, and it was carted away." I hadn't thought
of this at all when I was in the act of telling the Fiduci story
to Papa, but now that I had spoken, the dreams of that long
ago, nine-year-old weekend came back.

Right after the first war, we spent the spring in Edinburgh.
Papa had something to do with the setting up of new hospitals, and that's why we were there. One of the things I saw
stayed with me — a funeral with an even then old-fashioned,
horse-drawn hearse. I'm sure I never saw one in this country, although they still survive in provincial French towns
and in the hills of Italy. Shiny wood sculptured into folds
of clothlike drapery, polished nickel lanterns, great sheets
of plate glass. This one had fluted vases filled with black
ostrich plumes at the four corners. The hearse was making its way down one of the steep, narrow hill streets behind
the Castle, and two men walking beside it held back the
straining horses' heads while the driver, a crepe rosette on
his silk hat, braked the carriage which groaned and creaked
hideously, tossing, jerking the will-less plumes to molting
frenzy. Shreds of feathers, black spiders, floated down to us

in the cleft of the narrow sidewalk beside the narrow, cob-
bled street of tall gray houses, and Mama said "Ugh" as her
tightly gloved fingers tried to free the clinging, threadlike
wisp of plume that clung to the raspberry wool of the suit
she was wearing. She had to take the glove off, though, in
order to get it with her fingernail. Then she began to rub
Gordie's back and my back with her bare white hand. When
we had seen the hearse coming, she had told us to take off
our hats — "They do that here, out of respect" — so my hat
was in my hand and I thought I felt a feather land in my
hair, weightless but springy like a spider on his legs. I was
glad my hair was black as the feather, so Mama wouldn't
see it, and even more glad when she said crossly, "Put on
your caps. There's no one in the hearse, and even if there
was, really it's barbarous." After that I thought I could
feel the feather under my cap, and I was planning to look
at it when we got home. I'd tell Gordie it was good luck or
bad luck or something. I'd know when the time came how
to use it, and I'd keep it black between my handkerchiefs, so
that even if Mama came upon it, she wouldn't know what it
was, but I would know and I'd see to it that Gordie did. I
never found the feather at all. It just floated away, melting
into the gray Scotch air of the gray street. There was no
coffin in the strange hearse lumbering, its reflecting glasses
smeared at the moment of passing by the brave raspberry
of Mama's suit; there was no curled wisp of plume when I
looked at home, yet here it is now. You can see what I mean,
though, when I talk about the details using me, rather than
my using the details?

The Edinburgh hearse came alive for me that weekend at
Grandmama's five, six years later when I dreamed, not of
the bronze-black hearse, but of the Fiducis' truck with its

limp, fading bunch of lilacs as plumes — a bruised, watery
blue — at the four corners of the open, faded-red Ford truck.
Papa was telling me now, forty or so years on in time, how
Tony, the husband, had been deeply ashamed that his wife
should need a doctor in her tenth pregnancy, but how the
woman had known that there was something very wrong
right from the beginning and had come to him. Fiduci,
bent on his day in the country, had nearly come to blows
with Papa on the street that day.

"But it wouldn't have made any difference, you know. Tony
was right. They might as well have had their picnic.
Maybe she'd have lived two weeks instead of ten days. So
what?" The quality of Papa's sadness when he said something like this, is difficult to come by. I suppose an actor
could do it with his face, gestures, tone of voice, but words
halt, stumble, crowd upon one another. "The wagon was full
of death that day" was what Papa said next, not really to me
or to himself, either. I think it must have been like this. Corinne always accused me of "not listening" and would say,
"Stop that goddamned *writing*. I'm talking to you." Now
Papa was not a writer. His letters were very poor. They had
no life in them at all. I haven't a single note he ever wrote
me. There was no reason to keep even one, although I can
remember his writing to my daughters when they were little.
What I liked and what they liked about the letters were the
cats made of circles with which he decorated the margins.
He was quite incapable of putting a characterizing or telling
phrase onto paper; yet the sentence "The wagon was full of
death that day" is essentially a *written,* not a spoken observation. I'm sure that only to me of all the world would he have
said it. It is not even something you might say to yourself.
What Papa said to himself were usually lines of poetry. He

relied on other people — poets particularly — to do his conscious writing for him, and he was so acutely aware of the quality of their minds that this was very successful. Unconsciously, subconsciously, of course, he wrote. But it never got onto paper and very seldom was it spoken.

One of Gordie's favorite stories about our mother is about the time the first of the houses in our neighborhood was torn down and an apartment building put up in its stead. Of course we were frantic with delight and used to climb ladders, jump sawhorses, and walk precariously around the foundations after the workmen had left for the day. This worried Mama considerably because she was afraid of our being hurt, but she couldn't absolutely forbid it — what with the self-reliance bit and all. One afternoon Gordie arrived home alone about five-thirty. Mama was cross because I wasn't with him, and he tried to explain that he hadn't been at the building, but that he supposed I was there. Mama went to her room to dress because she and Papa were going out. She came down the stairs in long white gloves and a gold lamé evening wrap across her shoulders just as Papa came in the front door.

"How pretty," Papa said, "I see I'll have to hurry." With that Mama burst into tears and rushed by him to Gordie who was sprawled on the living-room floor reading the Hardy Boys. She pulled him to his feet and said, "Come Gordie. We must find a lantern and go look for the body. Your father can get dressed." Mama was not without humor; indeed she still is a witty woman, but the point of this is not that she didn't see herself in gold lamé and white kid, but that she used the word *lantern*. There never had been a *lantern* in our house. Mama was a big-city girl. She had always lived in town. Lanterns simply did not exist for her or

for us, but here she was imploring Gordie to help her look
for one. She was writing. Writing *Ethan Frome* maybe,
or *Tess,* or *Great Expectations,* and the writing probably
began as she was dressing and was really worried about me.
Night was falling and I should have been home. She knew
me well, and knew that I might stay on there even if
there was no one left to play with. Loneliness, dark, and
danger would be irresistible, and I think they proved irresistible to Mama, too. She scooped the excavations even
deeper, and they became cavernous in her mind, even as
she worked on the absurd gloves, picked up the limp gold-
mesh bag with the cold sapphire clasp. What she could see,
glittering under the dressing-table lamps, and touch was
less real to her than the Stygian blackness a city block away
where by now I lay spread-eagled at the bottom of the pit
which had somehow become a New England quarry amid
black pines. When she heard Papa at the door, she had supposed him me and had hurried out to scold, which is the
point Gordie caught her glittering on the stairs. When Papa
spoke, the lamé became calico and she a crofter's wife in
search of a lantern to guide her across the moors.

Yes, Mama was a writer. The word Gordie caught even at
eight years old was *lantern,* and both of us have often teased
her with it since, for Mama at thirty-two was not Mama at
seventy-odd. There were forty more years of Papa in between. I asked her once after Papa's death why she had
never married any of the old friends of theirs who asked her
— and indeed there were many. She said, "It was too
great an effort of the imagination."

"You're getting old, Mama?"

"No. No. Not that I'm not old. Not that. But love with
Louis, Jim, Ronald would require imagination. You see

that surely?" I nodded amused. With Papa she had never needed to imagine. Not that Papa was easy to come by. He was strong meat, and I myself had had to approach him through my Uncle Tom, whom I loved early and long, and Edward Sciarrha who taught me that in the creative act — as opposed to the merely generative — love is freed from the prison of the self.

> Living man must speak to love
> And loving he must speak to live

is how I put it in a poem once.

Mama had the advantage, of course, because it was possible for her to know Papa as a lover; and in the full tide of love, for those few who give themselves to it, the imagination and reality are miraculously, even though momentarily, one. You are spared the rigors of writing, the absurdity of searching for lanterns in gold lamé that you alone of all the world can see as starchless flour sacking. I think I can say that Mama "wrote" so much, was so often the bereft mother simply because her imagination was never employed with wishing Papa any different from the man she married.

I thought of these things, in a sense I wrote them, those last summer days when I drove Papa on his calls. Only once, I think, did he use an antique word like *wagon* when *truck* would have been more just, but I was so entirely open to impression, trembling, as it were, on the edge of discovery, that I was able to catch it. Mostly it was not what Papa said, but his mere presence that made it possible for me to sit in the sunshine (for after the first day we had taken to using my convertible as nearer to the sporty red Kissel, I guess) while he went into the dark flat buildings with his black bag and was gone sometimes as much as an hour.

Science-Science had triumphed and while Papa had been enormously distinguished in his youth and middle age, as an old man he became once more a general practioner. He himself had stopped operating the moment he felt that others could do better. One of his great advantages as a surgeon had been the swiftness, the deftness with which he could move. He explained to me that this was no longer necessary or even desirable since anesthesia could be prolonged for however long the plodding surgeon required. "It's better to take time when time can be taken, you know. We never heard of four hours on the table, so I suppose we seem slap-dash to the young. We were. But we had to be. The urgency was greater. And will you understand if I say we had a keener sense of history? Always, even now, even in the simplest surgery, life hangs by a thread. The skein is unraveled and that's all it is, a thread. Embroidery cotton, do you remember that? In skeins, twisted. Green, pink, yellow. High colors. But you could unwind the twists way, way down so there was no color at all and it was just a piece of floss, lighter than air?" I said I did remember, but the colors were probably not so high for me, nor the floss so light, and Papa went on, "Well we took tonsils out in offices then, even in the city, and when I first began little was understood about the appendix. People died and died and died of 'locked bowels.' Fathers of families, you understand, mothers of children, children themselves. One time I poured kerosene and whiskey down a little boy's throat. Diphtheria. He was dying, choking to death right in my arms. You didn't have to be a doctor at all. The phlegm had to be dislodged. Whiskey, fingers didn't work, and I saw the kerosene. I used it. He gagged, shuddered, vomited, and lived." Papa, like old Walt Whitman, walked always with the thought of death as

holding one hand and the knowledge of death as holding the
other, I thought. But from what he said next, I knew this
was wrong. Death was not a companion; it was never
Komm, süsser Tod, and it never would be. Death was an
adversary. An honorable one, a worthy enemy like the lion,
dark-maned, red-mouthed, the forest roar deep in his lungs
at wounded rush. "Charged home," I think, is the phrase
African hunters use, and Papa once with Uncle Frank had
gone on a safari, but the phrase he used now was "Death
and I often fought it out swift on the scrubbed planks of a
kitchen table. With only a kerosene lamp, you have to be
able to see well and deep within the shadows."

Should I line that for you, or can you read it as it stands?
I didn't line it, although Papa spoke it lined, because it
wasn't in any sense written. Written as I had to write the
phrases on the lion to make articulate my own feeling toward Papa. Papa's articulation, these days, was the articulation of the heart and it was more real to me than the steady
decline of his other powers. At the end of the day, I'd deliver him into Mama's hands, and the two of us possessed
him in a way we never had before. He gave up reading and
would play endless games of solitaire at night, Mama told me,
and he even went to bed very early, in the nine o'clock summer dusk. He no longer wandered, ranged the house before he slept, but climbed into bed, the windows open to
July and then August while children still played at hide-and-
seek, sweetly shrill among the fireflies of the shadowed
yards. Mary and I would look in on him before we went
home if we had been out to dinner, but usually he'd be upstairs and it was Mama who would open the door or would
be sitting on the porch when we drove up. One night, one
night only, she was in tears, and although we were not a

demonstrative family, I put my arm around her and tried to kiss them away. She shook me off.

"Oh don't be silly. I'll just weep more and they aren't sad tears, really. Just silly-soft ones. I suppose I have great tears to weep, but I've never had to, you know. Never had to at all. And I thought, that's wrong." The tears were still in her voice, but she stopped crying. "I've never lost a child. You're none of you disappointments to me. I've always had Gordie to say 'That's not so bad now, was it?' We've all had him to say that."

"The shift of tense, Mama? Was that Freudian?"

She smiled when I spoke and said, "Freud. We didn't have *him*. I'm not so sure I have him now. But we knew what he knew, really. Deep down, we knew. Or I knew. Because of the man who's up there now." She turned then to Mary and there was a muted defiance in her voice as she clipped out, "With whom I still sleep." She gave a little clap of her hands. "Or this one, whom I have never envied you, whatever classically you are supposed to think. One such is enough for anyone and this one" — she turned her eyes back to me and there was a kind of forgiveness in them although at first I didn't understand what there was to forgive — "loves me only because I love his father." She grabbed my hand then and pulled me to kiss her cheek. The tug she gave my arm, even though I now towered head and shoulders over her, was the same impatient pull she had given it that day in the County Hospital when she had said, "Now don't make me sorry I brought you."

As we turned to go into the house — for all this had been said on the porch, in the dark, away from the fullness of eyes — she asked me to change the sprinkler on the lawn and then to be sure to turn it off before we left. There was always

some such task now that they were alone except for Etter
Mae and what shifting girls came in by the day. It was sad,
really; these two old people who through no fault of their
own had been waited on all their lives to the extent that I
don't think Papa, at any rate, had ever even turned down his
own bed. Etter was now old, too, and had wanted to retire
for years, but she thought herself stronger than they and
stayed on. I've read all my life of faithful servants but I
never met one like Etter. She, my mother, my father were by
no means friends. Mama never sat with her of an evening or
talked with her long during the day, but I think they imagined one another, and that became the bond. Mama not only
recognized Etter's avarice — her wages were so fantastic
that Mama held that at one time she had paid all the maids
and Etter herself less than she paid Etter alone now — she
allowed it her, understood the insecurity from which it had
originally sprung, and actually took pleasure in writing out
her whopping check at the end of the month. Etter herself,
who in her palmy days would no more have peeled a po-
tato which it was her job to cook or have rinsed off a plate
which had come back from the dining room, became, like
Papa, a general practioner because she understood how
dearly both Mama and Papa depended on having the beds
made and turned down, the bells answered, even the sauces
and rolls handed ceremoniously to them at the table and
not just put down for them to help themselves. "Culture
lag" was the way Lee described it, but Mama and Papa both
had been taught from earliest childhood not merely that
there were right ways and wrong ways of doing things,
but they had been brought up to have the highest regard
for their own and, happily by extension, all human comfort.
I can remember two of Mama's sisters, my aunts, saying at

the end of a visit, "I hope you've nothing planned for us today because we intend to devote the entire time to considering whether we'll be more comfortable in two bedrooms or
one drawing room on the way home" — a distance of
three hundred and eighty train miles. This was facetious, of
course, but it represented how they truly felt.

When the screen door gave its summertime thump after
Mary and Mama, I stood in the yard watching the sprinkler
for a moment, deciding where to move it next. There was a
man for the yard, but he wasn't supposed to water during the day, and he wasn't there at night. The sprinkler was
one of those on a long, seven-foot stem and stood high with
three thin, bent arms sending scattered drops — bright now
in the dazzling August light of a new-risen moon — through
a tremendous swift arc. For some reason I didn't turn off the
water at the house right away, but bent down and kinked
the hose with my hands as I had so often done as a kid.
The swaying arms came slowly to a dribbled stop before
gradually I'd release the twist of hose and let them jerk into
a frantic short-lived whir. Short-lived because with the hose
between my palms, I could flail the arms off and on at will.
I played with the sprinkler like that for a while, only once letting the full arc reach out — buzzing, clicking at the base
— swishing free into the moonlight, hitting the dripping un-
derleaves of the low-growing maples, chestnuts, oaks, wetting black the trunks of arching elms. It was a kid stunt,
and I remembered now, burning trash in the dusk or the just-
new night, I'd spread a whole, single sheet of newspaper
over the top of the wire burning basket. I'd watch the paper
suck up the rush of fire and then rise itself, a kite of flame,
high, high above the fans of elm, dissolving to black and
brittle ash in the liberating, consuming air. I put this once

in a poem, "Assorted Ornaments," and I wondered whether
the memory wasn't somehow less pure for me, less *mine*, less
immediately available as emotion because it had already
been set to words. Fire, water, earth, air. Well, I still had
water, and my slippery palms — shreds of grass cuttings
clinging, compulsively pushed the hose tight. Too fast. I
could see the tall sprinkler rise from the earth on its trident
feet, pulling up pieces of the soaked sod by its claws. I let
the hose fall, and the water rushed forward. It was too late;
the long pipe ungainly keeled and fell. Two of the arms,
caught on the lawn, hissed madly, their mouths — would
Grandmama have said *bouches?* — crazy with restriction.
The mouth of the third arm was still free and arched a
spout high and far into the moonlight. Papa must have
heard it because he came to the window and shouted with
the full-timbered voice of his youth.

"Stop playing with that goddamned thing. And get the
hell up here. Right away. You hear?"

"Yes, sir." It was always "Yes, Papa" now; but at one
time it had been "Yes, sir." I guess it was always "Yes, sir"
when he was mad. Reflexively, my shoulders hunched forward, the habit of a boy expecting a blow, and then I
laughed and deliberately pulled them down, thumbing my
nose — double-thumbing my nose at the now vacant window. Papa would have laughed, had he seen me, but even
so, even at fifty, I had to be pretty sure he couldn't see. I did
do one thing I would not have dared to do at twelve; I kept
him waiting. Deliberately, I disconnected the hose as it was
attached to the sprinkler and leaned down to drink. Those
who know only plastic hoses, pretty with the bubbles running swiftly green in the sun, will never know the summer
thirsts that water warmed in rubber dark, then gushing cool,

but aromatic still, could once allay. I squatted to taste it, and as it ran over my lips and nose wetting the soggy ground at my feet, I felt the shock of glee we'd known as kids when on a hot day we'd been allowed to play in our bathing suits — "Put them on in the garage and get dressed there" — under the sharp, cold sting of the sprinklers playing. It was this part that I told Papa when I went up, and after I'd turned out the light, the sprinklers still humming bright outside across the lawn, he said slowly, "Yes. Glee. Glee. Glee." His voice was deep. Deeper, I think, than I ever heard it, as if the string of some enormous double bass had been plucked and its reverberations, dying away, bore with them the final memories of kinesthetic happiness.

I think that was the first time I knew Papa wasn't going to get well. It's hard to say because the next morning Corinne got back from Colorado where she usually spent August with her father, my Uncle Frank. She hadn't seen Papa as we had from day to day, and she realized how far he had failed. She was particularly angry with me.

"For God's sake get him to a hospital. There are things that can be done, you know. People don't just die like that anymore. They find out what's wrong with them. I just can't understand you. I can't understand you at all" — and then her voice broke. I tried to comfort her, but she threw me off with, "You should have had me come back. And Gordie should be home. It's soon. Soon. It's near. Near."

Even so it was two or three days before we could convince Papa, and Corinne had to get George Thompson, the doctor he trusted most in the world, to say "Physician, heal thyself." I took him to the hospital in the late afternoon, but even so he had seen thirty-five patients that day before he gave up.

"The Science-Science boys'll have their chance now. I'll become charts, graphs, readings. Smeared, I'll smear their glass slides." It was very strange. Both Papa and Mama were as afraid of hospitals as any European peasant, as A Fiduci in the flag-draped wagon. Yet they lived with and by hospitals all their lives, and Papa would be attended by the most distinguished men in a profession he loved. They couldn't do anything for him, though. He had every test known, some of them hideously painful because he was violently allergic to all opium derivatives, as if psychically he was impelled to know the pain he had for so many years witnessed. They never found out; we never knew what really killed him. There was a postmortem and he left his body to the medical school of the University, where he had taught. No one could say. They couldn't even say that it was a general deterioration of the faculties. At the end, of course, it was the heart — one of Papa's jokes was always to say, when asked of what a man died, "His heart stopped beating" — and yet in that moment the sun's time ceases and the heart's time goes forward alone. But there was no reason, no medical reason ticked to a cardiogram, why the heart should have gone as it did in the few days that remained to him after we'd brought him home from the hospital. The heart's time was true and constant — physically as well as metaphorically — until then. We hadn't even planned to have nurses. Miss Archer, the office nurse, came in in the morning and again at eight to make him comfortable, but during the day Mama took care of him and slept beside him, as she always had, at night. There was a constant parade of doctors, mostly because of friendship, who'd come in, listen to his chest, take his pulse and pass — as the phrase goes — the time of day. The charts told nothing, and the doctor friends would cheer Mama up as she walked them slowly down the stairs to the front hall.

But Gordie, when he came, Mama, Corinne, Lee, and I felt all the time the presence of death, and all of us were staying in our old rooms in the house. I don't think anyone asked us, or that we even discussed it. We just stayed. Oh, we'd say things like "When he gets a little more strength, they ought to go right to Florida. There's no sense waiting until after Christmas," but no one would continue such a conversation. The remark would just fall and lie there. When we went down to breakfast, Etter'd be sitting in Papa's chair, and we'd say, "He seems a little better this morning. Mama says he had a good night," but she'd never say, "That's good," or act as if she believed us at all. She'd just ask us how we wanted our eggs, and after a while Corinne would go in and get them from her because there was no one to wait on the table. No one ever said, "Why don't you just scramble them all and we can pick them up in the kitchen on the way down," and I think I know why. Papa's sense of ritual, which he shared more nearly with Etter than his own flesh and blood, clung to us now. "Because that's the way she likes it," he had said when we were little, and now we were middle-aged we knew what it meant.

A Catholic, outside of the church for twenty, thirty years, will genuflect when he enters for a wedding, a funeral, not out of belief long outworn, but because of an almost reflexive sense of propriety. As a Protestant, I may bend my knee because of mere manners, a make-believe bending; a convert might do so with awe; but with the apostate the ligaments are pulled, the muscles ripple, the head is dropped by a residual spiritual necessity, for even should he refuse upon reflection to bow, it would require a concomitant effort of will to deny the ligaments, to still the rippling muscles, to hold the head in pride. For Etter, busy as she was, merely to have scrambled all the eggs, would have been to deny the necessity of Papa's having told her for all those years how they were to be prepared. She herself understood this, I'm sure, because when she had heard us speak, she'd go over it all again — "Two scrambled, one boiled, two poached, two fried?" — as if she were incapable of seizing the idea without the intercession of Papa's repetition. We might be the sons of God, but Etter's communion was with Papa himself. It was a ready, easy, and — for the two of them — natural condition. That there was a theology behind it, I have tried to indicate. I was, and have been, so conscious in my efforts to arrive at an understanding of Papa that the unconscious lost the miraculous urgency that made him immediately real to Etter. I approached him through others — my Uncle Tom, Grandmama, my mother, Edward, even through myself in obedience to the old saw, "if you want to draw a picture of your father, draw a picture of yourself." Maybe this works sometimes, but here I don't think it will. Papa was — is — the larger entity, and while he knew more of me than I knew of myself, I have never had the feeling until he died that the reverse was true — that I knew more of him than he himself knew. Emotionally I am so essentially Protestant that the intercession of others is little help, and the ritualism which succored, fed the love of Etter no longer held the magic that it had for me that night in Grandmama's room when I had drawn the wiry hairs on the back of my wrist to silk across his loosened palm.

The afternoon before Papa died, Corinne took Mama out. They were to have their hair done — "cranked out of Arden's" — was the phrase Corinne used, and we all thought it a good idea. Gordie had gone to his mother-in-law's where his wife was staying, and Lee was with his children at the Zoo. Grace had brought them in to see their grandfather and they had stood around for a few minutes, more intent on the improbable giraffes they had been promised than the new green dollar bills Papa handed them ceremoniously for yellow balloons, pink cotton candy, and crinkled peanuts. Papa enumerated these things as if he wanted to see the colors, feel the textures. When he got to the fourth boy, little Tom, his arm drooped, and the stiff bill slipped from his white fingers to the bedclothes. Little Tom just stood there, but Papa said, "Pick it up, Tom. It's yours. It was your turn, you know. I just didn't know what to say."

"Rides on the pones, Papa? Rides on the ponies?"

"Rides on the ponies'll be fine, Tom. Just fine. Dappled ponies. But that's Hopkins' word, not mine."

When Lee, Grace, and the kids left, Etter went with them. They were to drop her off at the store, and she was to walk back. I didn't go back upstairs right away because I thought Papa would sleep for a while, but I didn't sit down to read or anything, I just "wandered" the downstairs rooms. It was different wandering in the afternoon bright with October from wandering at night. In a way the shadows of the night were more real — they peopled, as it were, the emptiness — than the vacancy of the sunlit day. In the darkness the odor of the roses would overtake you — at times to the point where the throat would close in ache at their sweetness — but by day, the roses seen — these were the last of the summer's flowering and had been picked in anticipation of a sudden, deeper frost — had no scent at all. Buds, some of which would droop before they opened, half-flowers that had developed in a final, grudged surge after their regular feeding was stopped, and even two or three full-blown blooms that Indian summer had globed to the perfection of June filled the bowl on the piano. If you looked, though, the leaves had shrunk from the veinings and were ribbed hard, faintly purple, crabbed with fall. Mama had them in the biggish, fluted bowl she called "Mrs. Winchester's bowl" after the woman who had given it to them for a wedding present. Limoges, "hand-painted" with wild blackberries, its once gilt edges were smudged in places to white with use because the bowl had appeared ordinarily throughout our lives for everyday desserts. Lee, years ago, had discovered a way of helping himself to the puddings it held so that their jellied shapes gave forth an almost human and what Mama called "an utterly disgusting sound. Poor Mrs. W." It was some trick of twisting the spoon, and none of the rest of us ever managed it.

I don't think I ever saw "poor Mrs. W." or knew anything about her except that she hand-painted china and was the aunt of Louise, Corinne's mother, my Uncle Frank's one-time wife. I never saw much of Louise, for that matter, but she'd drift in and out of our lives. "Corinne's going to Louise for a week," "Tom ran into Louise at Cannes," "Louise is in from California," we'd be told, and although at one time she was a source of embarrassment to Corinne, Corinne said now, "That was just kid stuff. I should have realized she was an artifact and not to be judged in high human terms." With this, Mama agreed and had often said that had Louise been born even five years earlier or later, she never would have been noticed at all. By one of those miracles of fashion, her flat chest, her straight black hair fitted to her head like a bathing cap, her birdlike chipper, her stick legs had, in the twenties after ten years of marriage, been found irresistible. The rather dowdy matron suddenly knew herself capable of the highest chic. Mrs. Friar Scott — for so she was called upon her divorce — became quite a figure, boyish figure, and we envied Corinne the pictures of her very own mother dancing with the Aga Khan, lunching with Ramon Navarro, astride Ben Bolt in the first jodhpurs seen on a woman in this country, above all, using Pond's Cold Cream in the shiniest magazines.

"Tell! Tell! Tell!" we'd greet Corinne when we got her alone after one of her visits to Louise, and there'd be tales of the rose chiffon nightgown with bands of American Beauty velvet under the lace and an accordion-pleated train. I don't think the impracticality of this shocked us so much — at that date even our souls had no intimations of wash-and-wear to come — as the fact that Corinne had managed to find out that it cost seven hundred dollars. Then there was the maid who appeared one morning with two black eyes never explained or even mentioned. The next trip there was a burglar who neglected a dressing table strewn with diamonds to take only a hundred and twenty pairs of high-heeled shoes, size three B. Corinne is six years older than I, eight years older than Gordie, and too soon — far too soon — she began censoring the more sinister details of life in Santa Barbara or Cannes, but we did hear of the famous comic — a great friend of ours from the Saturday matinées of the time — the patsy, pasty-faced, who appeared beside a swimming pool in nothing but an emerald-green négligée trimmed with electric-blue coq feathers. "Oh, Corinne," we'd cry exalted, but most of all I think we really envied her her grandparents — the Friars — who had gone down on the Nearer-my-God-to-thee *Titanic.* Cleopatra, you know, worries about being "boyed" in Rome. Well, night after night

Gordie and I boyed forth the Friars' water death from our *Titanic* bed, hymning brave until the last realistic gurgle from under the pillow hugged tight to the face.

While Papa was in the hospital, Louise would often creep into the conversation, and I learned things about her that I didn't know at the one time I had to study her as an adult. She came to Corinne's wedding, which took place at Grandmama's house in the country. Grandmama had been dead nine or ten years and the house had stood empty — although it was still half furnished — for all that time. Opening it up meant an army of cleaners had to be brought in, carpets relaid, pictures called back from the galleries where they were on loan, and it all seemed very silly to me. The wedding was to be small — if any gathering of my family could be called small — and our house would easily have held it. Corinne was thirty-four — maybe thirty-five — when she finally married Bob Patterson. He had been her beau when she first came out but had refused to wait for her when she decided she wanted to study the piano in Paris for a year after she graduated from Smith. I won't tell all her story here, but when she returned, Bob was married to Marge Lawson, and Corinne left our house and went to live in the gardener's cottage in the country. It was a handsome house, really, and had been built as part of the scheme of general grandeur the center of which was the big house. It just happened that the head gardener lived there at one time. Grandmama gave the house and three acres to Corinne, and that's where she lived during the long years of her affair with Bob. I never knew when this began, but shortly after Bob and Marge's son was born, Marge was discovered to have multiple sclerosis. Whether or not Bob and Marge would have divorced but for this, I don't suppose anyone will ever know, but I do know that Corinne preferred to live with Bob rather than to marry anyone else and that even after Marge's death, they waited the statutory year. Mama, of course, found this only decent as, I am sure, did the Pattersons and the Lawsons. The marriage would be held to be a matter of proper public interest and record; the affair would have been considered nobody's business.

"Panaches, pure panaches" was what Corinne said to me when I asked her why the elaborate wedding plans. "I want to be married at Grandmama's, and I can't help it. Not white, not even eggshell. Nattier blue. The lace made into a petticoat, not a veil. And everyone there" — Corinne didn't have to finish this for me because once Gordie, asked what kind of a party he'd been to, said, "Everyone there had on clean underwear," which we made into a chanting rhyme.

Corinne and I have a running argument. It begins with her telling me that I can't in point of years remember the twenties. " 'Follow the Swallow back Home,' 'Look for the Silver Lining,' Marilyn Miller — there's *your* twenties, Frederick Lewis Allen." I in turn accuse her of not having lived the thirties, of having sat them out in the country. When I get really vicious, I compare her learning — really learning — to play the piano in those years with her aunt's china painting, and she will retort that for all my excited involvement with the then good causes, I was careful to keep on working in the Seventeenth Century Drama. "We were pretty peripheral. It's only Uncle Doc who day in day out was able to work at the physical center of life. The war, I guess, did that for us finally. Maybe it was his war that did it for him. Remember the stories of twenty amputations in a day? Have you considered the detachment he had to will himself — twenty-eight years old — for that?" Maybe it is a matter of detachment. I've never really been able to do the thirties. I was too involved. On the other hand I'm better at the twenties than Corinne who lived them.

The Louise who came to Corinne's strange wedding was a wraith right out of "Hit the Deck," even though she wore the clothes of 1940. Joan Crawford had long succeeded Gloria Swanson as the clotheshorse of the world, and her big frame was nothing like Louise's tininess. Louise, who was getting on toward sixty, looked as if she were a wizened infant dressed in her mother's clothes. A big, elaborate hat of silk roses, an incredible length of quivering silver foxes, and a floor-length afternoon dress of shocking pink, its shoulders padded like a football player's, completely defeated her. She clung somehow to Lorelei Lee's diamond bracelets and these clattered around her embroidered gloves, but strangest of all was her mouth, made over from the careful cupid's bow of her prime into what Gordie called "the two hunks of raw liver" that gashed the faces of the beauties of that heavily lipsticked later day.

Louise was staying with Corinne, and we picked her up there when we dropped off Frank, who was staying at our house and who was to come with Corinne just before the wedding. We were early because Mama had to see everything was going as planned and was to receive the guests. Louise was watching for us and came out of Corinne's just as we drove up. Frank was at her side right away and met her at the foot of the steps, his silk hat glinting in the sun as he tipped it and took her hand. Corinne always called him Richard Cory, and he was indeed imperially slim and glittered as he walked the teetering travesty Louise had become back to our car. There was a slant to his body as he leaned toward her that had the antique grace of a young courtier attendant on an aging queen. Louise must have felt something of this because as she ruffled herself in between Papa and Mama on the back seat, she said, "Fancy Pants. Still old Fancy Pants."

"Oh come, Louise. It's twenty years. More than twenty," Mama said, pushing aside Louise's foxes which actually seemed to be nibbling at her.

"You talk as if that made any difference." Louise was still twitching from side to side, the foxes springy with life, and I remembered Corinne's once saying, "She's pure Vo-do-di-oh-do. Not Boop-boop-a-doop. Vo-do-di-oh-do."

Papa entered in with, "But Louise, of course it does," and she looked toward him sharply but with a kind of shuddering contempt in her eyes that I couldn't at the time place but that was to haunt me, that was going to be relived the summer of Papa's dying. I had never seen anyone even for a moment look at Papa like that, and the idea that anyone could was new to me.

Ordinarily Corinne and I would run into one another while Papa was in the hospital being reduced to charts, for we tried to spend the afternoons with him, and just as he had told us years ago the long continued bedtime story of a magical dog named Bow-wow, he kept up a fragmented kind of family history, highly anecdotal; often very funny. When he mentioned Frank and Louise, though, the anecdotes vanished. There was never the telling incident, the memorable phrase. It was as if even at the end of his life he had not come to terms with them, was unable to memorialize them. There was something there that neither Corinne nor I recognized.

Frank — Franklin Lee — was my grandfather's seventh son, the oldest of my own grandmother's children. Grand-

mama was not quite twenty when he was born, and my grandfather, delighted that he had produced yet another boy of
another woman, gave her a collar of diamonds and emeralds.
By the time my cousins and I came along such pieces were
out of fashion, and I never saw her with it on, although of
course it is the necklace that Papa wore in the measled dark.
I remember Grandmama showing it to us sometimes, holding it up in the sun so that its glitter was splendid indeed.

Arthur, the next older brother, was five when Frank was
born but Papa followed Frank in little more than sixteen
months (a bracelet to match the collar) and Papa and Frank
were very close. "Frank," Papa would say, "is the first human
being I ever loved. I remember how I knew what the word
meant, although of course I must have loved him all along.
He had diphtheria and they put him in one of the bedrooms
way away from me, and I mourned, really mourned. Then I
got it too, and they carried me back to him. You know, sick
as I was, I was happy? I said 'I love Frank' as I lay there, and
I knew what it meant." From the tales we heard of their life
as boys, there was every reason to love Frank. He had a gen-
erous, sunny disposition, and in the pictures that have sur-
vived, even the dresslike suits and the Fauntleroy curls of
the time cannot conceal the fact that he would be enormously handsome as a man. A watercolor was done of Papa
and him when they were ten and twelve. Moranzoni is
the name of the artist, but I've never been able to find
out anything about him in the halfhearted way I've looked.
He was a Florentine, and although there is no background,
the picture was done there. The two boys are sitting on
straight gilt chairs whose spindle legs have been deliberately elongated so that the boys sit high, back to back, their
faces turned full front. Their sailor hats, white with long,

sky-blue ribbons — the same sky blue as was to flutter for me at fifteen across the proud-eyed, powdered breasts of the girls at the Folies Bergères — hang on pegs behind them. Papa — red — is to the left; Frank — taller, black — is right. They both have on white sailor suits, and at that age mercifully their hair has been cut. Papa's feet don't quite reach the floor, his body is faintly twisted in chubby discomfort, his curly hair bandolined — there was a hair guck called Bandoline in my day — to momentary stiffness, and his heavy brown eyes are alive with a wittily observed frustration. About Frank there is an almost sinister elegance. His patent leather pumps rest easily on the floor, every springy curl of his jet hair lies naturally in its parted place, and his sailor suit is arranged by shadow and fold so that you sense the fleshing slimness of the long body beneath. This is a boy who is never to have a pimple, whose every attitude is one of natural grace; yet there is a savage bewilderment in the great blond eyes and the lids fall faintly full so that he does not look wide-eyed as Papa does. Later in life he achieved a vacant candor in his gaze, while Papa's eyes, not Frank's, were apt to be withdrawn the moment the exaction of good manners — "You must look people straight in the eyes," we were always being told — was satisfied. Louise said to me of the later eyes, "They devour you. Quite devour. But they give nothing of themselves, and afterwards they are as empty as before. That blue china vacancy. Porcelain. Quite Porcelain." The eyes of the picture though, are crowded — it was Papa who said this — with hurt.

By all the rules Grandmama should have been enormously proud of Frank, her oldest son, but even when he was little there was an antagonism that can only be explained in terms of Papa's "She had a molecular attraction to the supremely successful," which implies of course an equally instinctive revulsion from failure. From Grandmama's point of view Frank was a failure as a boy. He never broke a bone; he never fell from a tree; if the clouds lowered, he brought in his boat expertly enough before the storm broke, and they never had to stand, pelted with sudden hail, peering from the darkened beach while he rode the churning breakers home. Grandmama liked her boys bloody. To Papa as a boy it always seemed that Frank was successful. All the things they were supposed to admire, he was — neat, clean, obedient, accomplished. But except by tutors, he was never held up as a model, so that none of the boys had to hate him. He himself fell so naturally, like the curls on his head, into what his mother and father classically should have expected of him that there were never the teary scenes of intransigence, never the opposition of mighty wills for which Grandfather and Grandmama were so singularly trained from birth to expect of life and from which it was their happiness to emerge victorious. Victorious but, in the case of their own sons, tender, forgiving, magnanimous. Frank, Papa told us during the hospital days, denied them these pleasures, and they never forgave him. They could not love him.

"All this is after the fact, you understand. At the time we were just boys. I didn't know that anything was happening, and although I'm sure Frank felt it, he didn't know what it was. Who would?" Papa looked from me to Corinne, but his eyes could only hold Corinne's for a moment, and then he had to look down. At first I thought it was from a weary sadness, an oppressive woe that came over him as he reconstructed Frank's terrible need for love and was new-haunted by the memory of the little, day-by-day destruction of his beautiful brother when that love was irrationally, unjustly, perversely withheld. I still think in a way that that's what it was, but Corinne saw it differently, for as we walked the long hospital corridors, toward the elevator, she said, "You know, don't you, oh Sigmund Freud, what he's doing? He's myth-making for me. I'm supposed to see my dad more sinned against than sinning."

"Is that so bad?"

"No." Her voice was crisp. "I didn't say it was bad. But that's what he's doing. He knows I haven't got Bob any-more" — Bob had drowned in the Coral Seas, "such a nice-sounding place to die," she'd once said — "and that there's not much left of my Uncle Doc." She put out her finger to touch the bell for the elevator, so she wasn't looking at me as she went on, "It's dangerous for me to have as much of you as I do have — at least that's what Uncle Doc thinks and God knows he's a trained observer. Oh yes, oh yes" — this was very swift. Breathless so that I wouldn't take it in — "He's myth-making for me all right. That's what the old boy is doing. He wants to give me back my father. Gift-wrapped. He wants me to have something." She was pre-tending to look at the indicator that told the progress of the elevator, but she turned to me full to say, "He knows I'm a real wanter and that he's always been able to" — there was a little snort — "dilute you for me."

Two orderlies came then pushing a stretcher cart, and we separated, one to each side of the elevator doors. Even though the cart, like the Edinburgh hearse, was empty, I suppose you could say we did this "out of respect," and the two of us like awed, polite mourners, stood gazing at the taut whiteness of the thick muslin sheets drawn hard. The electric doors sighed open, pulling apart its rubber lips, and we followed the suddenly larger stretcher into the enameled, sealed — not open — cage.

We had to walk all the way across the shadeless parking lot that still shimmered with the retained heat of that high September afternoon before Corinne spoke again, her hand raised to shield her vision from the sudden glare of the sun.

"You can't see hurt in watercolor eyes. In oils maybe. Not in watercolor. I looked at that picture just last night. It's graceful. Beautiful. *Composed* as all get-out. But hurt — no. Just eyes. Just eyes."

"But if you know the hurt is there. If someone tells you, then you can see it, can't you?"

"I'll have to look again now. But even so, it's something I'm bringing to the picture not that the picture has."

"Oh Corinne, you always bring something to a picture, don't you? You take your emotional lunch along. It's all right to say you don't, to say you oughtn't to, but you do, you know. If they weren't our fathers, if we just saw it in a gallery someplace and were really looking, wouldn't we see something more than we allow ourselves to see just because we know whose particular flesh is painted? Pictures have always been Rorschach to us."

"Maybe. It's a long habit I have of not thinking about Dad or my mother. Of not imagining them. It was safer that way. Always safer. Even when I was little. I'd come back, and you'd say, 'Tell, tell, tell' because it was glamorous to you, and even though I wanted to be glamorous in your eyes, the words wouldn't come out of my throat." Her hand fell from shading her eyes to her neck, and her fingers began to twist her pearls. "The sun is utterly blinding."

There was a business then of Corinne's getting into her

car, and she decided to put the top up against the sun. I stood outside while the engine hummed it into place and the heavy chrome clasps rattled loose until she leaned forward, twisting her body with the peculiar quick grace she still had in all such movements, to snap them closed and tight as the pronged top settled into the two slots.

"Male and female, created He them" — she had a little trouble with the one farthest from the driver's seat, and this was what she said as she fiddled with it. She didn't mutter, though, as if she were talking to herself, but said it distinctly in the way we had of mocking "PRONOUNCE your words." When she leaned back, my head outside was above the roof of the car, and I couldn't see her face until I leaned over. There was a little grimace — amused, but more shame-faced than *amused* — on her mouth, and she went on.

"It's flattering really at my age. To have him myth-making for me as if I were fifteen. Do you suppose he sees us that way? Young and beautiful. And experimental? In need still of something to cling to. Something physical." She turned the key. "Okay. Okay. I'll love old Fancy Pants. Largely hung." The motor raced, and she was off.

I remembered all of this the day before Papa died as I stood alone by the scentless roses in "Poor Mrs. W's" bowl so surprisingly capable of disgusting noises. I suppose *remember* is not the right word for an emotion so recent that it was still quick, alive, that still shadowed the conscious mind and was not yet a matter of recall. I flicked the edge of the bowl with my fingernail as you do to test the quality of the china, and was surprised at the resonance in spite of the water and the metal frog that held the flowers. "Daedalus." I spoke aloud and remembered a phrase of a poet friend of mine,

"Architect of zig and zag." Well, it was one thing to be the architect of zig and zag, and another to be the inheritor of a labyrinth. Little-boy Icarus, wax-winged, unfit for the heats of the sun. Was that what he thought? A soft ache spread in my heart as if the last months had held only sadness. I put out my hand to still the reverberating bowl and as I did so I spoke again the words of the dream, the words the minister had spoken in the flickered movie beneath the bellowing marquee, "In my Father's house."

I went up the stairs then, my hand on the wide, polished banister. At one time in knickerbockers I could do four in a single stride. I have lived twenty-odd years in my own house, but these were the stairs my legs would remember until they died, and if I had to make my way in the dark as Grandfather did at the last, these would be the steps which by instinct my muscles would expect. Gordie and I used to close our eyes going up, and sometimes we could take an extra step or miss one. It was a game we played, but after a while no darkness, no stopping a third, a half the way up could fool us. We'd give up then for a while and try again weeks later, but finally it was like playing the piano where the bones of your fingers, not your mind at all, will remember after years the notes they had once ached in practice to find. When that happened, and it happened long ago, we never tried anymore, nor had to.

"Nor had to" — this has something to do with what I tell you now. When I looked in on Papa, I knew his breathing had changed and my hand went out to his forehead, which wasn't hot.

"There's probably no fever. I wouldn't expect it particularly. It isn't a case of infection, you know," he said.

"Well that's good, isn't it?"

"Yes. It's good. Infection would complicate. Would complicate what we're doing. Beating the horse."

"Beating the horse?"

"The heart. Digitalis. It's like a horse. Only you beat it with drugs. That's all I meant." He closed his eyes. He had opened them when I had put my hand on his forehead. "It was good your mother got out with Corinne." His lips began to tremble, and I could see the wetness of unwept tears gather in his fair lashes. "Don't mind me. It's just such a beautiful day. That's all."

I knew the tears well, not that I had ever seen Papa weep, but the day was utterly bridal, and Papa could see the big golden maple against the lingering, lessened blue of the October sky beyond the open window. The combination of such full beauty and physical weakness was something I remembered. I was very sick one time, my gut bleeding in the hospital, and the nurse came in with some white tulips, enormously fleshy cups of bloom on arched stems of spring-pale green. The sort of thing certainly that can be had for money, and that's what these were. They weren't from any-one I was fond of — just some people we sent flowers to and so they sent them to us — but when the nurse put them down and left, warm, salt tears — the tears themselves, not just the feeling of tears at heart — filled my eyes, and I wept. I don't think I put my finger on the source of the sensation at the time, but as I looked away from Papa to the sky, paled through the thin, coin-bright leaves, I knew right away with-out Papa's saying — as he did — not in his sickbed voice but in his old deep, poetry voice, "To thy high requiem become a sod."

I knew Papa was speaking for both of us even though most

terribly it was for himself. I couldn't trust myself to turn to him. I just stood there in the autumn quiet looking out. Soon his breathing took on again the harsh rasping sound that dismayed me when I first came up, and I realized it had quieted as we spoke together. I was gone now to Papa, I suppose, and with the closing of his eyes and new sleep, he surrendered himself to the sickness alive in his frame. My hand went out to the back of Mama's big chair, and I let myself sink into its down, putting my calves out on the softness of the stool. I may have slept — my own even breathing against Papa's laboring rise and fall — but I was conscious of Etter's coming in from her errand and a little later of the yardman's swishing on the high sprinklers. The light had failed some; the leaves were a darker gold but still held the intensely reflected sun more closely than the paling sky when Papa spoke.

"I'll want the bed pan."

"Sure."

"But bring a flask. Out of the bottom drawer. I'm going to take a look. A leak and a look." I rummaged in the bathroom dresser and found one to take to him. He looked very white and his breathing had not returned this time from the breathing of sleep. He was lying on his back, his eyes fixed on the tree. I pulled back the covers and waited for him to take the flask but he said, "You'll have to hold it. This isn't going well at all." I stood there stupidly because he almost barked, "Go on. Go on. Put it in. There's nothing there anymore. Nothing" — a great breath filled his body — "nothing for you to be afraid of." It was very little. A little boy's except for the still red hairs and the thick-skinned moisting warmth. My wondering fingers put it inside the flask, but I looked away, my heart not daring to think. The hand holding the flask began to feel the dribbled heat that seemed wetness although I knew the smooth glass was silk between. Papa gave a sigh. The breath he had taken expired.

"That was good. So very good. Hold it up. I want to see." I held the flask to the light for him and he looked. The urine was a heavy amber, but that evidently meant nothing, for he went on, "The old light and sink test. Light and sink. Nobody can look anymore. They send it to the lab."

When I had emptied the flask, I washed my hands thinking, An act of prayer, boys, an act of prayer, and when I came back into the room, Papa was breathing better and wanted to talk.

"I think I'll tell you something. Maybe it's just funny. Goddamned funny. But maybe its funniness is more. Sit down. Sit down." Mama's chair was too low for me to see him from, so I turned around the armchair from the desk and sat beside the bed.

"Connie? You don't know about that?"

"Just what we've always been told."

"Such a waste of beauty, youth, love. But she fell in swift, sudden, remorseless" — there was an angry beat behind the assumed matter-of-factness of Papa's voice — "sixteen-year-old love with Frank. None of us, least of all Frank, knew how much it was. But it was, and it was much. I've thought since then, she must have been a wanter. My papa knew. Blind, he knew, but instead of getting Frank off for London, or Connie out of the way, he felt sorry for her and gave her the snowflake. A piece of jewelry instead of love. His own granddaughter. But it's not as bad as it sounds." Papa's voice was not so firm on "But it's not as bad as it sounds." I suppose he really knew in his heart that it sounded very bad indeed, but that he couldn't fully admit that it was. "I don't suppose Frederick Harrison Scott could have remembered being sixteen." He used his father's newspaper name with an ironic forgiveness, not at all as I should have. "I hope even now I still do." He turned to me sharply, and asked, "Do you?" I nodded "Yes." I did. I do. A girl named Virginia. Nothing happened. Looking back, it had always seemed just being sixteen. A kiss different from a kissing-game kiss, but not so different either. Still hard lipped. It wasn't Connie's sixteen, surely, but Connie's seemed possible, so I nodded again, and Papa went on —

"Women — and men, a tutor once — were always falling in love with Frank. He just was beautiful. If he could have been an actor, it would have been all right. He'd be *using* his face, you know. But he couldn't, and Frank — Frank couldn't help but go along. He always did go along." Papa was saying these things about Frank with love, you could tell. He was worried about loving him, but he still did. He thought that somehow he shouldn't, and he was torn. "There was never any final act with Connie," he assured me, as if it would have made a difference if Frank had seduced her. "But he'd give her little seat what could pass for an avuncular pat. He could easily let his arm linger a moment longer around her waist. He could even say to himself, I suppose, that it was good for the kid. Twice, only twice, did he kiss her, and after the second time, he laughed and called her Nita Naldi right in front of everyone." Papa knew well the cruelty of this. He had himself washed the blood from the snowflake. The strange part was that temperamentally he could see Frank's guilt as far more absolute than I. He didn't for a moment believe the excuses he made for him; they were in a way tailored to what he thought were my tolerances because he wanted to excuse the love he still had for his brother. Yet his fundamental tenderness wouldn't allow him to destroy Connie. To see her as the wild girl, the temptress, even if in so doing he could love his brother the more. I was for Frank, but I knew Papa so well that I was afraid that his next step would be to take on himself some part of Frank's guilt, and although I wanted to say, "Oh Papa, it's all right. It's all right for you — for anyone — to love the guilty. That doesn't make the lover guilty." I couldn't let him know I had followed him so well. It was wrong that I couldn't. I can see that now, but all I said then was, "Oh Papa, maybe you oughtn't to talk."

He looked at me. Not really, but toward me rather, as if he knew that if he met my eyes he'd have to say, "Guilty? Innocent? It makes no difference. I love Frank," and that that would be all right with me. Papa wasn't ready for that from me or even from life. What he didn't understand, what I don't know that I understood at the time, was that while I might have to be given reasons for loving Frank, those reasons would never operate for Papa who had loved him always with the confusions of the heart. These confusions were heavy then in his sickness, for he went on —

"Talking? I'm not talking. Or if I weren't, I'd be thinking anyway. When you have to speak, you can't think so much." He fiddled with the bedclothes. "No, it's not hurting me. Just the breathing to talk is easier." The great rasping had indeed subsided, and his lungs filled almost naturally as if with the sweet fall air for what he said next. "You know, I know what was done to Frank. I saw it happen. I was always watching Mama and Papa, and while I don't mean to say that I knew at the time, I knew afterwards when it meant more and more and more and then, even more sadly, less and less and less. The woe of that less and less." His voice trailed away and he looked toward the maple, not toward me. I knew he felt my presence because he said with a strange, stiff formality, "It would be most sad to me, sadder than I think you can know, if now it had become so meaningless I could not bother to find words, words I can speak to you." My heart was stabbed with my own, Living man must speak to love / and loving he must speak to live. It came to life in me again as if I were writing it for a new time.

Papa still didn't turn but his voice lost its faltering and became even, calm. "I watched Mama and Papa. I can't remember the time I didn't. Even when I didn't have much to watch with, I was looking. Papa caught Frank and Bert Jorgenson in the boathouse. Nothing terrible. I guess just nakedness. Bert Jorgenson was our tutor the summer Frank was sixteen. He was probably twenty. A Minnesota Swede. Nice. Very nice. We both loved him and he taught us a lot of things. Nice things. I'm not just talking about Frank. But I think now I was jealous without knowing of what. Otherwise" — here he turned his eyes full toward me — "Otherwise I wouldn't smell the boathouse?" His voice made the question.

I couldn't refuse his eyes, but if he didn't know the answer himself, how could I? Was he asking forgiveness of me? Had I become the father, he the son? Of course I could write up the boathouse scene, but I don't see why I should. I'm glad at the moment I'm not an omniscient observer. My heart was made sore with the thought that fathers should not burden their sons thus. It was unbecoming. He became less. Looking back, I realize that I was cruel in my insistence that he play a role he had played so well and so long, and I know the bravery of his imploring glance, the courage it took to have been ready to accept the instinctive recoil which he might have met in my eyes. Papa would know, would know certainly that it wasn't because of the mere doubt of his own feeling, but because cruelly I held him responsible for not having resolved those doubts in a lifetime. One of the penalties, the flaws, of adoration such as mine was that I became impatient, I raged even, at any sign of weakness. Papa, I think, forgave me because he became my father again and said calmly —

"I'm going on because of what the robber baron did. I just want to tell you, that's all. Of course Bert Jorgenson disappeared — but that isn't what seemed worse and worse as I got older and then less. I don't suppose I ever questioned the justice of it until this moment. You got caught and that was that. It's the way things were in the world. But Frank — at least from his point of view — got rewarded. Papa got one of the tellers at the bank — an aspiring teller, that's the part I couldn't have known at the time — to take Frank to the Everleigh Sisters." He gave a little swagger to his shoulders. "Fanciest house in the world, they used to brag. A hundred dollars. Every once in a while there's something in the Sunday supplements. Of course Frank couldn't keep it from me — although he was supposed to — and maybe it was a good idea of Papa's?" Again his voice made the question, and he gave me what he imagined to be his man-of-the-world glance, but although Papa now was role-playing, my own imagination had picked up the story — not just the narrative to which Papa's tone confined it — and I was peopling it with the characters I knew were involved.

I spoke sharply, "Don't be silly. It couldn't have been a good idea. A monstrous cliché. At sixteen. A house like that? Papa! Papa!"

"There are different sixteens. You were young for sixteen."

I'd gone away to college then, so I hadn't known that this was what he thought. "But Frank was young, too. I was fourteen, but you know what I said?" — I shook my head — " 'Why didn't Papa take you himself?' I don't think that was a young remark. I think it was an old remark. If you are going to do it, that was the way to do it, wasn't it?"

It was not at all like Papa to talk like this. It was *goofy*, I said to myself, and he wasn't a *goofy* man.

"I'd have to think. You'd sure have embarrassed me."

He laughed, but the laugh ended in a kind of sigh and I knew he was going to trust me again. "I did think for a long time. I was much more moved than ever Frank. He — you know, he had a good time. I never went. I never would have gone. There'd have been nothing of me to go with. 'You just put it in, Gordie; that's all,' that's what he said. Not me. Not me. Not ever me." He shook his head from side to side. The denial was absolute.

"Weren't you ever sorry, Papa? Just curious-sorry, that's all I ask?"

He told me I had chosen a good time to ask, but it wasn't that he was trying to take any credit for it. "I always thought that somehow mechanically I couldn't, that there would have to be love, and so, and so" — you could tell he already had the phrase, that he'd had it a long time but now that he came to utter it to me he became shy — "I had the habit always of building myself palaces. Mansions of the mind. Will that do?"

I knew he was imploring me to understand, and in a way I could. I was quite a little mansion builder myself but it had always seemed to me that Papa's superiority, his moral grandeur — I don't think the phrase is too strong — arose from his habit of basing judgments on reality, not fantasy, what Corinne meant when she said, "It's only Uncle Doc who day in and day out is able to work at the physical center of life." Now there were these mansions of the mind. Was that where he really dwelt? Where he'd been living all along? Away from us all? Even Mama? There was a peculiar tearing break to my heart, even though I sensed we were talking at cross purposes. Talking? I had hardly spoken at all, and that day beneath the monument "In my Father's house" had been spoken of Fred quite literally — a sad, wry jest. If ever I was to speak, I knew it had to be now, that I couldn't be afraid of my little-boy voice even if that were all that came.

"Papa, Papa. We were real. All of us were real. Now you're telling me we were imagined, peopling the mansions of your mind. Couldn't you let me *become*? Let me *be*? Is that what's wrong with me and always has been wrong? Oh, I knew you had this image of us. And I tried. Really I tried. We'd come home from school with good grades, and Mama'd say, 'Papa will be so pleased.' But beyond this was always your reality, your flesh and —" I could feel the quaver — "blood. That's what I thought counted." I struggled, how I struggled for words. It wasn't at all like the struggle of writing because the words had to be fast or I knew I would never get through. "With me, you know what? You want to know how it was with me? It wasn't the way it was with you, Papa. But you were there. You were there. What I thought was you. So odd. So odd. Don't ask me to make it out now. It was a Boston-Irish girl. Chippies, we called them. Not a real whore. Red hair — if you want that. She lived with a grandmother she said was deaf. A Bleeding Heart on the wall. A real Bleeding Heart not just a stage prop. Should I have built a mansion, Papa? When the couch was pulled down there was no room in the room for anything except the bed it became. You even had to move the chairs back against the wall." I was trying to see, but the slide would not click into place. What I remembered most was afterwards in the bathroom where I stood looking up at the ceiling-high flush box of the old-fashioned toilet, the chain wound round with dried Palm Sunday palms. "You know what I said then, to you Papa? Aloud there in that bathroom I said, 'She was nice to me, Papa. Nice to me.' I thought, you see, that that would make you glad." Then, because otherwise my voice would have blurred had it not taken on the edge of scorn, I said, "I washed myself. Tender-sore, I washed myself *thoroughly* because that's what you'd always said."

Papa didn't look as if I had struck him or that he was hurt by what I said. His mouth was a little open, that's all, and in a minute I heard the concern in his voice.

"I don't know how you can have expected that somehow I wouldn't have been there. I don't think you had to tell me! —"

"I never have until now — "

"But I liked your telling me. It was very wonderful. There's nothing wrong with you. 'Mansions of the mind' — that was just a phrase I used. That's the trouble with phrases" — Papa was apologetic — retreating, but I didn't want him to go yet. I wanted the two of us there for the first time still looking, and what I said was perverse, unconsciously designed to stir him, to draw him even closer to me. In this sense of course it was dishonest but I didn't think so then.

"Yes. There's a lot wrong with me, oh Mansion-builder. Or you think there is. I don't do that to you. I see you as you

are and were. 'Bloody Saturn bloody eating bloody sons,' I
didn't know that was you when I wrote it. It was just a
painted ceiling somewhere in Italy. Venice. Venice. Grandmama's town."

His voice came back calm, a father's voice. "With love.
With love. She could build palaces, too. She just couldn't
build one for Frank. Your're not Frank. That's not what I'm
saying. Anybody who'd say 'You just put it in, Gordie.' Because that's all he ever did, you know. Louise was right.
She — and this is what began all this — she'd come to '158'
that summer I was in town for my State Boards. She'd make
excuses and come in for the day to — to shop. Corinne was
two, maybe three. The Constance business was a little later,
but they weren't happy. Women threw themselves at Frank.
He looked as if he knew everything there was. And Louise
was young and dowdy, really, so there wasn't anybody
much but me."

"What did he marry her for if she was so dowdy?"

"Part of the other business. As soon as he could, Papa
wanted Frank married. Louise was around and she was an
orphan. Papa liked that part of it, too. Oh Papa lived
through the Oscar Wilde trial and a lot of tolerance depends
on what you've lived through yourself. What you allow
yourself to remember. 'Beastliness' — that was his word.
Beastliness. You know, the funny thing is that with me
that's what it would have been. A palace of beastliness.
But with Frank, it wasn't at all. There never was any danger — if that's the word — but he could leave Yale and
have Louise and a house in town, his own servants, be
grown up, and Papa perfectly willing. Even proud again.
I can see how it happened all right. Anyway it did, but when

Corinne came, there wasn't any *wonder*. A godfather, I thought, Humanity in my arms."

I wanted very much to say what I wanted to say. To reach Papa with myself. But it was he who was reaching out to me now.

"When I was born, Papa, was there any wonder? You know what I mean by wonder? Here was something, flesh and blood. Not imagined before. Or since?"

Papa stiffened visibly and there was a tiny rattle in his breath. "Yes. Oh God, I can't talk that out. Not at all —" He looked to me with present wonder. "I pulled you ass-backwards from the very" — his voice faded — "torn, shaven temple of my delight. Tender, I was harsh. Harsh, I became tender. Bloody-Saturn me will you? I could have cut you to little ribbons. I've done it when I've had to. I would again. No one would have said a word. No one would have known, even. 'We couldn't save the baby' — that's all that would have been said. I couldn't have loved you yet, you know. And I did love your mother. A fierce professional pride. That's what I taunted myself with afterwards. In my deepest heart. Deeper even than love." His head drooped to one side, and he closed his eyes. I wanted to touch him, but something held me back. Something in my own past; I didn't know what. Since then I've identified it, and I know I was right. Instead, I spoke.

"Not deeper than love. I don't think that. You wouldn't have spoken now had that been it." He gave me a wonderful smile, opening his eyes so they smiled too. I don't suppose I knew when I spoke how deeply Papa would be moved, that I would somewhat loudly sweep the string and that my assurance would mean so much. But instead of being made glad, my heart plunged to a bitter blackness of its own, and although my eyes held the smile for as long as they could, the smile was a lie — or I would think it a lie when — inheritor of zig and zag — I tried to believe it.

Yet a world without love was a horror, a terror to me. Oh I had loved. I loved Papa now. All my life I had loved. Like God. I sometimes felt I was nothing but love. But what good did love ever do? A moment's content? An hour's? I? I had had weeks, months, seasons. I was a true lover and loved long. Yet I always did this to myself. The sorrow would well up, and the tenderest moments I would deny. It wasn't a question of the heats of love, my not being able to come to terms with hotness. These, this I well understood, but with trembling, sooty finger always I would smutch the whitest flower.

For all my talk of love, didn't I distrust it? Or rather didn't I distrust myself? See myself as incapable? Papa had said that "fierce professional pride" rather than love was the reason I sat in the desk chair now. He had tortured himself thus for fifty years. It was nicer to think that it was love, and so I told him it had been love, not pride. I could see it that way. That made *me* the kindly one. The one who loved less and was safe. But it was real love that came to his eyes, when he heard me, and it was indeed love that informed my tongue. I could feel it within me. I uttered it deep in my being, from my being. Love passed from me to him, from him to me. We became alive in the passing. We lived. Not in some mansion of the mind, but then and there in October. And to that living each of us brought the whole of his maleness, his nature, the memory of his limbs. The towering mansions crumbled.

I write this now. It is remembered; but the moment of

creation belongs back there in time where the emotion had its being. In that time, coincident with it, I could not find the metaphor. My hands clawed after the powdery mansion's bricks to build me a hovel where I could doubt. It takes a kind of courage even now for me to write as I have, for who is there to believe me? The writing is baroque, and we distrust the baroque. But the sentiment, the moment itself, is so essentially grand that a meaner rhetoric is profane.

After the smile, Papa seemed unaware of the ambivalence that trapped me, and my long ago birth slipped away from him. He hadn't been old enough to deliver Corinne, and he often wondered whether or not that had made a difference. "I owed her a debt of tenderness I had paid you, Gordie, Lee at birth. But I suppose what it was was that Frank was no longer Frank, and I didn't know yet that this always happened. You, you yourself were no longer you for a time when you first were married. You know that?"

"Oh but Papa there was a war. We were away. I was away."

He looked up quizzically. "Well, when you came back, you and Mary were playing house, and I understood that all right, but you stopped writing and I don't think you had any sense — that you knew in your own mind as I'm pretty sure you know this afternoon — that Corey and Amy were" — Papa swallowed, distrusting the Van Dyke billow of satin shadows, the Titian pomp of what he was going to say, but he was not one to intimidate himself — "gold, frankincense and myrrh to me. No, you didn't know that or how much — without you — I needed them."

"I'm sure I didn't, Papa. My own continuity seemed to be what mattered." One of the things that happened to me during the war was that when it was over, what I wanted was to go to Colorado, some mountain fastness, and with a gun protect only Mary and my girls. I wanted no one else ever again. I'd make up scenes about our life there and in my loneliness the fantasy of another loneliness would grip me so completely that I could *bark* orders with savage precision while all the tenderness of my heart was far, far away in hills that never had been home.

"You know when you came back to me?" In speaking again Papa startled me, and as the icy waves washed the plated deck of a pitching destroyer, I was back at "158" and knew that that's where he was too.

"The night in Grandmama's room. Yes, I know. But I don't think I knew I'd been away."

"Far, far away. Far away. I don't say this to hurt you." The concern in those brown eyes —

"I know —"

"It's to tell you, to explain that I didn't know this about life when Frank left me. He was gone, and I had watched him grow. You know how that's different from you and Gordie, don't you? He's the one who watched you. You must understand that there's a difference." He looked at me intently. "Even though I was the younger, I was the watcher. I knew the blight, but from him had come Corinne. There was wonder. There was hope. Now, I thought, everything will be all right." He looked at the palms of his hands. "It wasn't, of course, and I knew even before Louise began to hang around '158' that summer."

What happened — Papa did it very well but it was in snatches, for he was visibly weaker and I felt guilty in letting him speak at all — was that even from the first he knew why she came and it wasn't anywhere nearly so simple as saying that she had fallen in love with him. "She loved me,

I still think, because she thought I loved Frank and through me was the way to him." Of course at the time, he pretended he was innocent and that it was merely natural that his brother's wife should look in on him that monastic summer. He was very much in love with Mama, was actually still a virgin, and was to be married in the fall. He could weave no fantasy around Louise and he might have succeeded in turning her away without any actual cruelty — the word was his — had it not been that Louise herself by instinct had arrived at the one fantasy against which he had no defense. She came to him as a doctor for advice. Papa wasn't a doctor yet and said so, but she was too embarrassed, she said, to go to Dr. Small. It was all childish and dirty, and I don't suppose anyone will believe it now, but Papa did at twenty. I do at fifty.

"She was wearing a beige linen summer dress with a thousand tiny buttons down the back. I undid the top ones for her, my fumbling fingers ice, and then she went upstairs to my room. I waited, my heart thumping, beside the stairs looking up. By that time I knew what would happen, that it could happen, that it had to happen. I said to myself, 'You'll have to go into that room, and there she'll be,' and I wondered whether I'd keep up the doctor pretense. It's the kind of thing you think at twenty has to be decided. I hadn't decided even though my hand was trembling on the newel post when I heard the front door. It was Mama. The only day she'd come into town all summer. Pure, pure accident."

Since then I've thought that maybe it wasn't, that Grandmama was checking up, but of course that part makes no difference. She was there, and Louise never reappeared. She could not have heard Grandmama from Papa's bedroom in

that house, and Grandmama's plan was for Papa to drive her
back to the country. Guilty, he could not bring himself to
say that Louise had gone up to lie down, and the moment
for the simple lie vanished. Guilty, he tried to get upstairs
by saying he had to pick up his goggles and duster — it was
in the days of goggles, dusters, and motoring — but Grandmama had produced them from the hall closet. Guilty, relieved that Grandmama herself had no intention of going up,
he dared no further excuse. They'd driven off, leaving Louise
in the vastly empty house.

Papa was less coherent in what followed. I can put it together because I knew the man, his habit of reference, but
to set it down as spoken would result in a kind of private
poem — oblique, skewed, the wings of death flapping,
thrashing grotesquely to the suddenly loud swish of the
sprinkler moving beneath the maple, no longer lingering
gold but bulking into shadow outside the window. Swish.
Papa knew the cruelty of having left her there all the dusty
road he had to drive to the country. Swish. He imagined
then and for many years — swish — her trip down the
broad stairs — swish — to the unexplained, unexplaining
emptiness. Swish. He even struggled with her over the
thousand buttons — swish — and stood with her dazed,
waiting, unbelieving — swish — on the leaded, distorting
Poop looking out. He knew then, he still knew that the young
Louise he left in the empty house was not the Vo-do-di-oh-do
she became, and unsaid for me what he said to her the day
of Corinne's wedding about the number of years making a
difference.

His voice was gone toward the end and a deathly weariness weighted the silence that separated him from me. After
a while I became conscious in the quietness of the yardman

moving among the bushes close to the house, the sprinkler dribbling to a beaded stop and the hose slithering through the wetted grass as his slippery hands drew its lengths to coil beside the outlet. My old guilts flared up in me as Papa's had in him, for there could be no doubt that he held himself responsible all these years for letting his own father act when he knew himself wiser, kindlier, more humane. He had thought there was no choice when at each juncture there had been. Even Connie might have been saved had he spoken. Were the guilts burned away now in speaking, in dying, like the long ago newspaper spread across the trash basket, flaming in the twilight sky and then descending, brittle ash to earth?

"The expense of spirit," I heard Papa say, and I was drawn forward from the straight-backed desk chair, bending over far until I put my half-open mouth on the veined back of Papa's hand. For a moment or so, he didn't move. I couldn't tell whether my being there meant anything to him or not, but then he drew his hand from beneath my mouth to cap my bristled chin in his palm, his fingers stroking the black and daily stubbling of my cheek.

Mama and Corinne came in right afterwards. I heard them in the drive, and I moved around turning on the lamps as their chatter floated up. They'd been away from death for the afternoon, and their own vitality had reestablished itself. Mama kissed Papa conscience-stricken and said with her old flirtatious voice, "You missed us, I hope?"

"I should think so. But you look so beautiful and you smell so expensive."

"Oh we had the works. Even our toenails. Hidden Dawn. And then Corinne and I both got dresses. Marked down. We saved you hundreds of dollars." Corinne was much richer than Papa — indeed he had never paid for her clothes — but Mama always maintained the fiction that he did, just as she had for the past few days pretended that we were all living in the house not just staying, waiting. There was a rustle of tissue paper, the smell of newness, as she shook out the dress to show it to us.

"Blue. You always liked me to have blue?" Mama looked to Papa as she did about clothes to see if he liked them. "It's a summer dress. Of course that's why it was marked down." You could see her figure in her own mind again if it had been marked down enough. "But I can wear it for a little while now, and it'll be perfect to go into next summer with."

"Why don't you put it on?"

"Oh don't be ridiculous. There are only us for dinner. Gordie and Lee won't be back."

"I'd like to see it. Isn't that enough?" It was the game Mama and Papa had played all their lives, and for which even now he was not too tired.

"It's a very expensive dress. Even marked down." Mama patted it over her arm with real affection, and went into the dressing room to change. Papa shook his head at me, amused. During the terrible night that followed, Papa called out once in a voice of terror, "Othello's occupation's gone." Mama heard it too, because afterwards she mentioned it, thinking he must have referred to himself, but I could see her crumpled unlovely on the bed beside him, her just-done hair awry, her flesh crepy with age, her mouth slack, her eyes hurt by his pain. I knew he was speaking of her. She was the one to be left with no one to act out the scene he had played with her that afternoon for the last of many tender times.

While Mama was gone, it seemed to me that I began to smell the sickbed odors again. I had closed the window when I heard their voices first — that was probably it, and the clouds of perfume Corinne and Mama still moved in — but it seemed to me peculiarly sharp until Mama reappeared and Corinne zipped up her back.

"Nice. Very nice," Papa said, but there was no luster to his glance, and Mama went to him to sit on the bed.

Corinne began to pick up the tissue paper and the boxes, and Mama said, "See all those little covered buttons down the back? You were so cross when we were first married? And I had to get the maid to help me? You wouldn't, you know. And every one of those buttons had to be buttoned then." Papa's hand was on her waist. But I don't think he heard or knew. "Now there's a zipper underneath and the buttons are just show."

I followed Corinne into the hall, and we went down together. I wasn't paying much attention to her at first, haunted as I was by Louise's buttons and then remembering my outburst in the cemetery the day of Fred's funeral. Corinne, I think, mistook my silence. At any rate, she said, "He's much worse, isn't he?"

"Yes. But actually he was better when you came in than he was most of the afternoon."

"I could sense it though. Did you talk?"

"Yes. It didn't come out very well. Snatches, Threads. You know when you speak with the heart how it is." I was lying to Corinne. I couldn't bear to share even a fragment of the time with her.

"It's going to be very bad for you, isn't it?"

"Not having him? You know I tell myself and tell myself that I need to have him die? That that's the only way there is. Mama, Mama has a right to him. I have to live out a big part of my life still. I'm not him. From what we said this afternoon, I never have been." I had never told myself that. I had never even thought it. I was closing Corinne out. Why I was doing it, I couldn't have said.

"A reasonable facsimile. A reasonable facsimile, surely." Corinne spoke as if there were no argument.

When Grandmama died, the boys had discovered some of the sketches Sargent did for the big, full-length portrait he painted of her. These were framed — each of the boys had some — and one of them hung on the stairs. On our way down I stopped Corinne and called her attention to it, partly, I suppose, to distract her from thinking about what had gone on while she had been away. There was a line of shoulder in one corner, a disconnected right hand, the ringed fingers cupped, and an utterly wonderful length of naked arm. In the picture itself, Grandmama is wearing long gloves and her right hand holds a closed fan.

"Oyster satin, diamonds, emeralds, pearls, rosy flesh. It's all put together in the picture. Nothing like this. Nothing like this at all. These are scattered all over. Bits and pieces. Wanton scribbles, some of them. How'd he get them back together?"

"I don't think that should bother you." Corinne supposed I was talking about the problem of reassembling the snatches of the afternoon's talk. Actually, I suppose, I had begun to write and it was the larger problem of reassembling an image. "We've got these. We kept these. The oyster satin we gave to the University where not one person in a hundred knows the naked flesh" — her finger tapped the glass covered arm — "or can even sense it. Come on, let's get a drink."

We'd just got to the bottom of the stairs when Miss Archer came to the front door, and we invited her to have a drink with us before she went up to Papa. A tray — the Ashenbrenners' tray, Mama would have said — was set out in the living room, and we stood there talking for a few moments when Mama called down in her lilting social voice, "Was that Miss Archer? Papa'd like her to come up." Miss Archer was apologetic and downed the double shot I had poured preparatory to making her martini, without batting an eye. "Her Master's Voice" was what she said before she scooted up the stairs — ugly feet in ugly shoes but competence and personality.

Mama came down then, slowly as she always had to now, her hand on the banister. When she got to the living room, she said, "That woman doesn't like me, you know. I wanted to stay, and Papa really did need her." She looked stunned. "But she shoved me out."

How could you tell her? Tell her Miss Archer had no reason to like her in that absurd, fashionable dress, every hair in place, her veined old hand, whose only real use had been to delight Papa, roseate with Hidden Dawn, brave with the rings he had given her? Ah Miss Archer, Miss Archer, all Miss Archers, I knew you well in the thirties. You put ambitious gangling boys through graduate schools. If they married you, you never knew about the mansions of the mind, and so you were divorced or went to the suburbs and the League of Women Voters. If they didn't marry you, either the musk of truer houri glances or the yapping of the Hound of Heaven would defeat you. Is all you see of Mama oyster satin? A double slug of gin, neat, the ugly shoes at nearly sixty — would it be kind if this were all I saw of you?

Miss Archer had not come down by the time we went in to dinner. Mama was worried — as indeed were Corinne and I — but when I suggested going up, she said we shouldn't keep Etter waiting. We had sat down when Miss Archer came into the dining room. Of course I got up — although in the thirties I wouldn't have — and a kind of conversational pavane was set into motion. The awkward honesty of Miss Archer against Mama's graceful courage.

"I've been putting on rubber sheets. They will be needed."

"Won't you sit down? Please let us give you some dinner?"

"And I called Dr. Thompson. He will be here as soon as they have finished eating. I intend to stay the night." Etter began to set a place.

"In that case you must eat. It is so very kind of you."

"I could have called the registry, but I preferred to remain myself."

"I quite understand. It is most kind. Do you think one of us should go up?"

"If I thought so, I wouldn't have left." There was a pause, and then she added a faintly tremulous "Would I?" to the bald statement.

"I'm sure you wouldn't. It was thoughtless of me to ask. Quite thoughtless. But I have been much concerned, as indeed I know you have."

Miss Archer drew herself up. The thirties could have taught her such bravery. "Mrs. Scott, I love your husband."

"Then surely you know he would want you to have dinner?"

"I would do anything for him I could."

"It's very simple at the moment because here is Etter with the chops, and they won't improve if they wait."

Defeated, Miss Archer slipped into the chair I held for her.

Gruesome, starched, she stared at the platter Etter offered her. As her voice changed from the honest, rude concern of her exchange with Mama to the cackle she imagined proper for the occasion, she protested that the platter be passed to Mama first.

"But Miss Archer, you're our guest. Please do believe me. And I think you'll find the sauce" — the chops were arranged about the silver sauceboat — "most delicious. Still our own mint from our own yard." Mama spoke as if this were achievement equal to having raised, butchered, skinned, quartered, hung the lamb, and I noticed that the implacable softness had gone from the voice with which she had shoved Miss Archer into the chair as surely as Miss Archer had physically shoved her from the room a short time before. I was willing to share a conspiratorial glance about growing our own mint with Miss Archer, but her hands, enormous and red, had become as detached from her body as they might have on a sheet of sketch paper. Lumbering, they pursued the lamb chop with the serving fork and spoon. I remembered one of the thirties' hygienic, safe Miss Archers whom I had taken to a consolatory dinner just after she had lost her boy, a friend of mine, and I felt vaguely guilty. The dinner was in the cafeteria of International House — she'd chosen the place — and all she took was a round sauce dish of teary, rubber spinach — steam-table green — and a cow-flap of a cookie. Seventeen cents. Twelve and five. So low a rate. Ah Miss Archer, all Miss Archers, what is it like at nearly sixty to have refused the eighty-five cent special at strident, diaphragmed twenty-seven?

If I was sensitive to Mama's manner, she was sensitive to mine, and she must have caught me staring at the disembodied hands because she directed my attention to Corinne.

"I wanted Corinne to have a rinse. She's too young to have let herself get gray." Miss Archer's hair was black as Shinola, so it wasn't the happiest distraction she could have hit upon, and her voice trailed away with an abashed "Don't you think." I picked it up though — I didn't want to tease her — and the three of us, Corinne, Mama, and I kept up the chatter that Miss Archer could and would despise for the rest of her life. "The man lay dying you understand" — I can hear her — "they knew he was dying. A great man, really. You don't know anything about medicine, Dora, but I assure you his *contribution*" — she'd use the word with the same emphasis she'd have given it when she was talking about ambulances for Spain — "cannot be overlooked. And all they talked about were clothes, hair, the presents" — no, *gifts* was Miss Archer's word — "at the Poulson's wedding. Things. Just things. That's all they ever think about. Do you know those Poulsons got *two* VW's from *two* different people for gifts?" I have known Miss Archers who would have been capable of "You never can have too many VW's," but not this one.

When we left the table, Mama and Miss Archer went upstairs together. Either Miss Archer had been hypnotized by the ritual — the precise ordering of the plates, the liturgical exchange of politely meaningless gossip — or somehow she had sensed Mama's love as something as worthwhile as her own. This I would not put beyond Miss Archer. Mama, well, Mama would recognize Miss Archer's love as fine, stalwart, sterling — all words I have heard her use — but I don't think she could love Miss Archer in return. She didn't know, she had never had to imagine the urgency of heart behind the statement, "Mrs. Scott, I love your husband." Had Mama taken the words literally, she would have reacted in the same manner. That's what manners were for — to get you through such moments — but in her heart she'd have begun writing a tale of passion totally unsuited to Miss Archer. The spiked iron fence, however, lined with bridal wreath, held Mama captive.

Soon after they'd gone up, Dr. Thompson came in and was upstairs for a good while. He must have done some calling, because two other doctors arrived shortly afterwards, stayed awhile and then left. Gordie and Lee returned, and Gordie and I took the dog out for a walk. When we got back, Dr. Thompson and Mama were in the living room. Mama had changed her dress and was in a robe, but she told us what I guess we knew.

"George says it can't be long now. He's called Mack" — Mack was the young doctor who was in the office with Papa — "and Mack's already upstairs. He'll spend the night here. Papa doesn't know anything about the pain he's in, so that part's all right. Is there anything else, George?"

"No. Except get your mother to bed. And the rest of you get there too. Miss Archer will call you if there's any need. But he's a strong man still, and I don't look for any change until morning." He swallowed a couple of times and bent down towards Mama who kissed his cheek. "We do what we can, you know and then —"

"Oh George don't be silly. After all these years, we musn't tremble now." Mama was crying, not aloud, but tears were in her eyes, and Lee put his arm around her.

"You boys have always been good to him. And you, too, Corinne. Much more than 'And you, too.'" He began shaking hands and when he'd shaken them all, he picked up his black bag and left.

Papa didn't die until noon the next day. I was the last one up that night and Miss Archer met me in the hall which was loud with Papa's breathing.

"She won't leave. She's on the bed. Curled up there."

"Maybe it's all right."

"It can't do him any *good*. Or her."

"I don't know. Does it do Papa any harm?"

"No. Not really. I couldn't say that it did. But it's silly for the two of us."

"Well? Do you want me to try to get her into another room?"

"Oh Mr. Scott, I don't know. It's one of the things I learned from your father. 'Why not,' he'd always say." The Shinola hair. The not-pretty eyes. She had learned love late. Maybe today was the first time.

"It's a sad comfort for her. But I think it will help her to be brave." Papa's breath was very loud.

"All right. I'll just go lie down on top of the covers. Is here all right?" She pointed to the little room we only had used as a guest room, and I nodded the "Yes." She wanted to be sure I understood, so she put her big, rubberish hand on my coat sleeve. "What I had to think was, was that what I would want to do?"

"That — that you could learn from Papa." I said this from my heart and she knew that I did, but her real dignity dissolved — I don't know why although, of course, this was her tragedy — and mock-girlish she said, "Oh my, yes."

I didn't go in to Mama right after that, but I went to my own room and got undressed. I didn't in any sense relive the past. The present crowded too near my heart. I sat naked for a long time on the edge of my boyhood bed just staring. I couldn't have stood anyone to comfort me, and I was glad that Mary wasn't there. I didn't get up to turn off the light. My legs were heavy with dread, and I couldn't reach sideways to pick up the pajamas folded there, so I just sat in sadness without trying to make anything out of it. No tears came, and I didn't think of tears. I didn't think of Papa even or Mama or anyone I loved or had loved. Time simply stopped. It must have been a long while because the night was balmy, October-warm, but even so I began to feel chill before I could bring myself to put my anguished arm the few inches to the left where my pajamas lay. When I felt the cloth my fingers closed in a paroxysm and twisted it cruelly into the bedclothes. I could feel the muscles contract all up my arm, across my shoulder blades, my back. Tense, so hard, so stern in agony I could not lift the weightless cloth until of themselves the fingers relaxed and in awful weakness became capable of drawing the coat across my legs. I sat even so for a while, my breathing heavy, but I was now aware of Papa's rattled gasps from the next room, and slowly time began again with the soft glide of the cotton murmurous over my skin.

In the hall, the bedroom doors all closed around me, Papa's breathing was louder, and as I stood, my hand on the knob, I thought, I shouldn't have left Mama there with that, but I lifted the door, as I knew you had to to avoid a squeak, and the sound clamored around me. Real. My papa's breath hard, hard taken. Blow. Blow. Blow upon the heart, and I eased the door closed behind me. Mama looked up. I've described how she lay curled there far, far on her own side of the bed but her left hand stretched out and covered by Papa's. With her free hand she motioned me quiet, and I nodded that I understood. The big, big cage of his chest would drag itself full somehow, rising lumpy beneath the white sheets, and then twist in wild gasps of fall as tortured as the ascent. Before the rise, before the fall, a long moment of black silence would prolong itself in the room and hang will-less for what at first seemed an ended time, but then the flight from death would flutter into agony again.

I slipped into the desk chair I had drawn over in the afternoon and which the doctors must have each used in turn, and Mama nodded in the darkness a slow, understanding "Yes" to me. She nodded twice as if she wanted me to understand that, "Yes," this was the right thing to do. After a pause, her head bowed again with the deliberated affirmation of the heart. This was the way it should be, one of us at each hand — I took Papa's, damp with the dews of death, in mine — even if he didn't know, even if the struggle were lost. I didn't at the time think of Mama in terms of Molly Bloom's "Yes," but I have since, and I think I knew for the first time that night in the raucous dark that love — even the very act of love — must always and always have its full existence beyond the knowing, beyond the knowledge of the loved. Papa struggling became a mirror for Mama and me. It was our flesh that labored — Mama's through knowing, mine through being — and for me to look away or refuse to see would have been to shatter the glass he became through the gift of himself, through love.

Mama and I sat the night with him. Twice I called Miss Archer to change the sheets and, blinking in the sudden switching on of the ceiling light, marveled at the tender ease with which she handled his laboring heaviness. The second time, near morning, she called Dr. Mack, which surprised me because I could detect no difference in his struggle. Even the unmeasured unmeasurable waits at the top and the bottom of his breathing achieved a kind of crazed order, but Mack gave him a shot of some kind without explaining, and he and Miss Archer went out, switching off the light. A few years ago the wiring in Mama's and Papa's bedroom had been changed, and this was one of the then new switches without a click. Papa had complained about it at the time. "Let there be light; let there be darkness," he had said showing it to us, "but I like the click. It's punctuation." We laughed with him, but now tonight I too wanted the click.

I don't know whether I dozed after that or not, but Mama surely did for with the light of morning, Papa's hand which had been passive turned, drew itself together and crushed the unprepared limpness of my hand with real strength. The same thing happened to Mama because, she whimpered, "Oh Gordon, Gordon" — strange to my ears, not "Gordie" — and drew herself awkwardly up to kiss his cheek and rest her head for a moment on his shoulder. It was only a moment though, because she moved then from the bed into their bathroom. Papa's clutching on my hand became stronger, but I didn't try to free myself until he flung it aside, and with a tremendous effort he threw his legs, tossing the sheets in a wild scissor's kick apart. Then arching his back, he drew his knees together and flung his legs full length to the bottom of the bed. It was a grotesque parody of an exercise he taught us when we were very little. He'd line us up on my bed after our baths and naked with giggles we'd throw our legs through the bouncing scissor's kicks. It was supposed to strengthen the muscles in our groins against hernia.

"You're boys. It's good for you," and then with the little-finger edge of his hands, he'd mark the "V" on one of us and the others would clamor to look.

"If we were girls what would we have to do, Papa?" This was probably Gordie. I'd be too ashamed not to know.

"I don't know, boy. I don't know. I never had any."

"But you know about girls, Papa. All there is to know because you're a doctor for girls too."

"I guess so. Knee-chest, it would be. Knee-chest. Turn over. I'll show you." We turned over then, our knees under our chins, our trusting, sightless, one-eyed behinds raised to him, and he gave each of us a slap — "Bong. Bong. Bong" — and left us to get into our pajamas by ourselves.

"Papa don't go! Papa don't go!" This would be Lee, the littlest, really frightened, so Papa'd come back, put Lee high on his shoulders where he'd thumb his nose at Gordie and me as he rode in triumph to his own room.

I didn't relive this scene consciously at the time. There was the horror of the ruin of the bed; there was Papa spent and ashen, besmeared, but the tears, the first I had wept, came hot to my eyes and I must have remembered, and remembering imputed to Papa's limbs that same memory. I got Miss Archer right away, and when she saw the bed she called to Mama, "Why don't you freshen up, Mrs. Scott? I'll be busy with the Doctor's bath for a while, so there's nothing you can do." Mama herself could have done no better.

"That was very kind of you," I said. "Is there anything I can do?"

"Yes. You can help me a minute with the sheets, and you can get some fresh ones. We've used all that were laid out." I helped her untwist Papa, and then went for clean sheets. She sent me into Mama's bathroom for a pan, soap, and water.

Mama was sitting at the table in their dressing room trying to do something with her hair, screwing on her ear-rings, putting on and off the rings she wore every day. Her hands moved like a migrant bird I'd seen once with wings broken after a storm. Although I turned my head from hers, she saw the tears because she said, "Don't worry. I think it would be good to cry. But not like that. I'm deliberately not remembering anything. It's just now for me." Her eyes were staring at the ring Papa had given her when I was born.

I did the things Miss Archer had for me to do, and carried the mountain of sheets to the basement tubs. I stood there, letting the cold water run, thinking how different things had always been for us, and wondering if I would have thought of the sheets at all had Miss Archer not mentioned them to me with silent irony, "Rich Boy, pick 'em up. Rich Boy, pick 'em up," and then warned me against throwing them down the chute and told me about using *cold* water.

Downstairs, morning had begun, and Gordie was on the telephone in the butler's pantry calling Tom and the others. Etter was already setting the table, so I hurried to get dressed. The life of the house took over. Dr. Thompson came back, and one by one the other doctors returned, flowers were delivered. My Uncle Tom came, and soon afterwards Uncle Charley and the others. Corinne emerged from a talk with Etter and walked straight into my arms in the study. I hadn't been able to go upstairs at all after breakfast although Mama had stayed there. Corinne trem-bled, shuddered compulsively, and I tried to calm her.

"It's awful. It's horrible. There are fifteen people in the living room. Jackals. Jackals. Can't they leave us alone?"

"Oh Corinne, they think they have a right. They mean to

be kind." She was standing at the window looking out at the street.

"It's obscene. Just obscene. The drive, the street. Everything is Cadillacs. The house'll sink. Look at them. Oh God, Benjie!"

Benjie was indeed waddling up the walk. Lee was answering the door and keeping people downstairs while Gordie was trying to talk to them in the living room. The house phone and the office phone rang constantly because if people couldn't get us on one line, they used the other. Even the newspapers called. Mama, I suppose, could have dealt with it all, but she didn't leave Papa's room, and the four of us were totally inadequate. I've wondered about it since, for a great ache began in my heart and grew there like some enormous succulent filling itself on the saps of my flesh. There's a cactus I've seen, growing many-branched, and trunked as a tree. Touch but one of the stiff, tiny spines at the thickest base and the movement is repeated, echoed in the farthest mad reaches of its ungainly growing. This was like that. The hushed, polite noises from the other rooms, the ringing of bells, the continual movement to and from the front door, up and down the stairs, quivered over me, but in me too. Even Corinne was no help and I began to long for Mary. Mary could hear these things for me and leave me to ache my ache alone. The ache was nothing like my feeling during the night, for then Papa himself had seemed to take within his frame the sense of my own loss and to labor with it along with his own pain. Even though Miss Archer assured us he knew nothing of present pain, it began to haunt me that he was no longer able to bear even a fragment of mine and with the scissor's kick — tremendous, adult — he had relinquished memory to me.

I had never wanted to be a doctor. Mama and Papa had
both been highly scrupulous about ever even suggesting it.
It was there for me, yes, but they never spoke a word, never
even a "Papa would be so proud." I knew what was coming
now, but I couldn't stop it. I'd been through it before. This
time, though, there was an almost cataleptic terror. Papa
hadn't wanted me to be a doctor! It was something he
couldn't share! He was too afraid I'd fail! That final trust,
he couldn't have. He was unwilling to give. "Give" shrieked
like a swooping gull in my inner ear. My hand hurt sharply,
but even when I looked down and saw it had grasped with
all its power the bronze Ulysses-Prospero, I couldn't stop.
I pushed my palm home against the chiseled edges and as
the pain spread through me, the polite murmur of the other
rooms rose to mute the faraway cries of gulls. I looked at
my hand. There was no blood.

A few minutes later I saw Grace and Mary walking up the
street. I had known that Mary was to pick up Grace but to
see them together, high-heeled in their best black suits and
furs at ten o'clock in the morning, seemed obscene — Corinne's word — but I knew that my rage would not be like
hers. I wanted Mary to myself. I needed her for my arms.
Desperately I needed her, and there she ambled in the October sunshine with goddamned Grace. The two of them
stopped and laughed while Grace, one-legged like a heron,
picked a maple leaf from the spike of her heel. Grace was
ten years younger and the arch of her body was pretty there
beneath the trees, but I could remember Mary much pret-
tier and much younger. My momentary rage flooded into
unspeakable love. Beautiful, beautiful, she had been and
there was nothing I did not know of her. These days,
these October days, her girdle left welts about what had

once been a waist so dear that my hands knew a kind of awe in stroking. My breath would catch and I thought I must weep. Now, now — I looked to the fingertips that knew those welts in sweetest habitude. Old Girl! Old Girl! Today it would be the best girdle, the newest, the stiffest, and you'd have to wear it for hours and hours because there was to be a death in the family. Come in from the wallow of Cadillacs gleaming by the curb. Come golden beneath the shadowing maples. This tenderness I cannot bear alone. You must weep my tears for me lest mugient I bellow. And blood burst my lungs. The oak bough broken, the leaves waxy with fullest summer falling to the blood drenched sand.

She was there then, by the library door, and when she saw me the tears came to her eyes, the tears I would have her weep for me.

"Oh darling, I'm sorry. I'm sorry. I love him, but I love you." Her softness, fat with years, was in my arms, and her face, her cheek were against the firmness of my chest. As I held her, I breathed deep, and strength and purpose flowed from the odor of her hair into me. She, not I, became the willing less, for it was I who spoke miraculous comfort to her. I had found my father's voice.

Soon afterwards, the minister came in — Gordie had probably called him — and all of us went upstairs with him. Papa was high on his pillows, his eyes unseeing, and his breathing still the rattling climb and fall of the night. Dr. Thompson, Dr. Mack, and Miss Archer stood around the bed, Mama sat doll-like, fully dressed, on her soft, low chair. The doctors parted when we came in, and Mama rose to offer her hand and murmur politeness. I followed the doctors back into the hall while this was going on and asked the "How much longer" that was in my mind. They

both told me they had never seen such a prolonged fight.
"Measured. Deliberate, you would say, except that it must be
reflexive." We stopped talking then because we heard the
beginning of some kind of prayer. I couldn't bow my head
and neither did they. Miss Archer, who had stayed by the
bed, her hand on Papa's pulse, must have dropped to her
knees because I could see only the ungainly white feet up-
side-down through the door. Mama and the others just stood.
I was amazed at myself because I felt no flicker of the old
rage rise within me, not even when the minister began the
Twenty-third Psalm in some flat Revised version and I knew
how Papa loved to tongue the older cadence. I had become
capable of politeness even to God, my eyes riveted to the detached white feet until they dragged themselves along the
carpet out of sight when the prayers were over. There was
some more murmuring then, and Dr. Thompson said to me,
"If this guy's worth anything, he should be able to get rid
of some of those people downstairs. It's your mother we'll
have to think of now, and she shouldn't have to see them
right away." He turned as if to go, but then put his arm
around my shoulders and went on. "Wonderful man, your
Dad. Wonderful man. My best friend. And you know I say
that without any sorrow even when I can't say at the same
time that I was *his* best friend?" He released his grip on
my upper arm. "I think we'll go down the back stairs and
get some coffee in the kitchen. Come on, Mack."

Soon afterwards I was back in the room and we heard the
cars pulling away. Mama crawled back beside Papa, and
although Miss Archer began to say something, she decided
against it, and left herself. From time to time Papa would
say distinctly, clearly, some tag lines of poetry, but it was impossible to know why they had come to him. Toward the

end, his breathing became shallower. There were no longer the great falls but only tight gasps at the top of his lungs, and he called out in terror for Frank. When I took his hand, he thought I was Frank and would say, "Don't Frank. Don't. It hurts. It hurts. Oh Frank, please, please don't," but I think these were memories of childish cruelties, the arm twisted behind the back, the thumbs relentless pressed to the base of the neck.

We were all there when it happened. He had been quiet for only a few minutes, and then there was nothing. My eyes looked to the silent light switch on the wall. It was like that. No sound. No click. Neither darkness nor light. You just knew that he was dead. Mama raised herself and kissed him, but then she turned on the bed, her back to him, and rested a moment. Corinne and Dr. Thompson went to her and she said, "Thank you, George dear. I'll go to Corinne's room for a time." Gordie kneeled at her angling legs to put on her slippers, and the little group moved from the room.

Lee and Grace stood for a moment and then they, too, left with Miss Archer. Mary and I stood there until Dr. Mack said, "There are some things I have to do. They aren't terrible, but they aren't pleasant. It would be better for you to go."

I shook my head. I wanted to stay.

"It's all right, all that matters is how you feel." He began then. Little things. I don't remember them all. Turning back the eyelids, things like that. It was the beginning of the busy-ness of death, and I watched. When he finished, he said, "I'll call for you. Who will you want?" and I said not in a little boy's voice at all,

"Willie. Silly Willy."

"That would be Piperson's?"

"Yes. Piperson's."

He closed the door behind him. He didn't know about its squeak.

I put my dark hand to each side of Papa's white cheek, but I didn't bend over to kiss him. I've wondered since why, but I haven't been sorry. I took his hand in mine and sat on the desk chair. There was no chair for Mary, so she stood above me, a hand on my shoulder like the bride in a country photograph. It wasn't long before I knew the nerveless hand was cold, and I let it fall. I pulled back the sheet and felt his legs. They too were chill. His thighs were still warm, but I put my hand on his nippled heart. Mary's hand came forward then and rested flat beside mine and together we felt the warmth decline. I remember these things not with sorrow, sadness, wonder, awe. They are a part of the memory of my flesh.

"Flesh and blood," though, is the phrase, and as I write the words, my eyes become Papa's eyes and follow beyond the mere triumph and pride that were all I saw that day on the Constance Scott Memorial Floor when he appeared to me, my still glistening child firm in his hands. My eyes now were a match for his and saw unafraid the high happiness of life. They saw, as they had not before, deep into the shadows. I knew that the self from which I had been alienated for so many years of a life was not the passport self whose gut could bleed, whose eyes took fright at the gleam of the marble obelisk at the end of a street new-marked "One Way," the self intensely aware of Venus' rosy breast and the blood-caked boot of Mars. This self I had pampered. The circumstances of my life made it possible for me to do so; to see the Palm Sunday fronds entwined upon the toilet chain, to hold the peachblow porcelain in my hands. To lip importunate the bluest veins of a classroom's Egypt, reincarnate

before a chalk-smeared board. To hear once more the rever-
berate voice of Shadow beyond the shade. These in turn pampered me with assurances of permanence. Together we grew
fat and in unholy marriage began the fishwife quarrels of
terrible involution which I have tried to describe. But always in everything that I have set down there is a flickering
awareness of another self, long hungry and unfed, that waits
humbly on the truth, endures its alienation quietly and
alone, and loves in an unpeopled emptiness beyond the passport's dream of sweet satiety.

> Full fathom five, thy father lies,
>   Of his bones are coral made:
> Those are pearls that were his eyes:
>   Nothing of him that doth fade,
> But doth suffer sea-change
> Into something rich and strange.
> Sea-nymphs hourly ring his knell.
> Ding-dong. Ding-dong, bell.

So Ariel sings, but sings only of the fading, inevitably ship-
wrecked self. My hand on the stilled heart I knew could love
of itself until it too was cold. The cutaneous memory is
clear, sharp, real. I need never have written a word. But
there is another memory, another self, and of this I had to
speak. All men are aware of it: drunken Trinculo, Stephano,
even bestial Caliban, for Ariel says they

> lifted up their noses
> As they smelt music

to follow the insubstantial tabor's song. I am no Ariel, having
fed long on lamb chops around a silver sauceboat of mint
from my own yard, so I have struggled the zig-zag ways of
gossip, remembrance, dream to say that the fathering of
sons is the lifelong business of man and to rebeget in all
kindred love the father who so fathered me.